DRAGON'S BLOOD

A DYSTOPIAN FANTASY

ANN GIMPEL

CONTENTS

Dragon's Blood   1
Book Description, Dragon's Blood   3
Books in the Dragon Heir Series   5
Author's Note   7
1. Chapter One, Rowan   9
2. Chapter Two, Bjorn   25
3. Chapter Three, Rowan   39
4. Chapter Four, Bjorn   55
5. Chapter Five, Rowan   71
6. Chapter Six, Bjorn   85
7. Chapter Seven, Rowan   101
8. Chapter Eight, Bjorn   115
9. Chapter Nine, Rowan   131
10. Chapter Ten, Bjorn   147
11. Chapter Eleven, Rowan   161
12. Chapter Twelve, Bjorn   175
13. Chapter Thirteen, Rowan   189
14. Chapter Fourteen, Zelli   205
15. Chapter Fifteen, Bjorn   209
16. Chapter Sixteen, Rowan   227
17. Chapter Seventeen, Bjorn   241
18. Chapter Eighteen, Rowan   257
19. Chapter Nineteen, Bjorn   275
20. Chapter Twenty, Rowan   293
Book Description, Dragon's Heir   307
Dragon's Heir, Chapter One, Rowan   309

About the Author   325
Also by Ann Gimpel   327

A Dystopian Fantasy

By
Ann Gimpel

Tumble off reality's edge into myth, magic, and dragons

Copyright Page

BOOK DESCRIPTION, DRAGON'S BLOOD

After discovering she's half dragon, Rowan figures it can't be any worse than being related to the Celts. That's the thing about assumptions, though. They come round and bite you in the ass.

The second book in a magic-laced, fast-paced, fantasy trilogy. With dragons.

I'd rather fight than study, but I'm stuck poring over dusty scrolls. I promised I'd learn about the dragon part of my magic, but I'm having a hell of a hard time believing there's some concealed strain of power just waiting for me to kindle it. Meanwhile, my friends the witches are playing fast and loose with remaining hidden.

My Celtic kin won't bother them anymore—at least I

don't think they will. But far worse things rove Earth than the Celtic gods. The Breaking has developed an energy all its own. The longer it runs wild, the harder it will be to contain.

Soon, very soon, no magic in the Nine Worlds will be enough to counteract it. Once that happens, the few remaining mortals will go first, but the rest of us won't be far behind them.

BOOKS IN THE DRAGON HEIR SERIES

Dragon's Call, Book One
Dragon's Blood, Book Two
Dragon's Heir, Book Three

If I seem to be on a dragon kick here, it began long ago. My first runaway bestselling trilogy, Earth Reclaimed, had dragons in it. So did my almost-as-successful Dragon Lore series. Dragons have made cameo appearances in other books as well.

Well, maybe slightly more than cameos in the Ice Dragon series.

Beyond dragons, I've had a lifelong love affair with both the Celtic and Norse pantheons. While writing one long-ago book, I swore no Celtic gods. Nope. Nary a one. Well, along about Chapter Five, who should come strolling out of the wasteland but Fionn MacCumhaill, Celtic god of creation, protection, knowledge, and divination.

I gave up to my muse thereafter. She hasn't led me astray yet.

Welcome to another series that blends the Celtic and

Norse pantheons. In my imagination, the deities all know one another. It was a pretty intimate circle filled with petty—and not so petty—squabbling. Add enough acts of unbelievable valor to keep things on an even keel, and the foundations of a story magically appear.

CHAPTER ONE, ROWAN

Fire painted the sky and the ground, so much fire I saw red even through my closed lids. Keeping my eyes shut was a very bad idea, though. Dragons surrounded me. Maybe not more than a dozen, but they were so freaking big, it felt like more. They were ostensibly teaching me how to fight, except I already possessed that particular talent. In between salvos, they chittered merrily among themselves like a pack of oversized crows. Occasionally, I picked up bits and pieces of their mind speech.

Coming out victorious in a good scrap has always been high on my list. I haven't had a hell of a lot of choice in the matter. Mostly, it was fight or be vanquished. It's not possible to kill me, but there are many, many punishments that would make me long for my own death.

Anyway, it surprised and annoyed the crap out of me when a red dragon who hadn't introduced himself—herself?

—announced that today we'd shore up my battle talents. If he'd asked what I wanted, I'd have replied, "No thank you."

I'm at the bottom of their pecking order, though. Probably less than the bottom. No one ever asks me jack crap.

A cloud of ash and smoke billowed around me, followed by trumpeting. Clearly, one of my tormentors—er, teachers—had discovered my attention was wandering. Wracked by coughing from all the smoke, I resorted to telepathy.

"Stop!"

Ysien, one of the blue dragons, hooted laughter. "Aye. And the enemy will surely cease if ye but tell them ye've had enough."

No one made fun of me. No one.

Trapped between embarrassment and fury, I made a grab for Bjorn's power. He had to be out there somewhere beyond the impenetrable blanket of smoke. We were amazing fighting together, but today for whatever reason, the dragons had apparently told him to sit this one out. He's not the type to take orders, so they must have forced him to remain off the field.

Blech. Dragons.

When Nidhogg, the chief Norse dragon who was also conveniently absent today, told me I had to learn about the dragon half of my blood, I'd reluctantly agreed. I'd had zero idea about the non-Celtic sector of my parentage until a scant handful of days ago. Anyway, at the time Nidhogg floated the idea about tutors for me, he'd intimated a single dragon would show up each day.

I had no fucking idea why I merited the attentions of so

many. Were they bored? Had they come to examine the one and only Dragon Heir ever, who was a mix of Celtic and dragon bloodlines?

Was one of them my father?

So far, everyone had been closemouthed about that little tidbit. So secretive, I wasn't expecting a dragon to burst out of the ether and scoop me up in his scaled forelegs, greeting me as fathers did in my imagination. The dragons had known about me since my birth, and no one bothered to show up with flowers and a pile of excuses about why they'd left me in Ceridwen's care. Or non-care, which was closer to the way things played out.

My thoughts may have taken off at Mach 10, but I can think and fight. My current mission was lobbing jolts of defensive magic to clear a circle around me. My bid to locate Bjorn had failed, so the dragons' barrier between us must cut both ways. If he could have reached me, he would have.

Bjorn Nighthorse is another mystery, but I didn't have time to pick it apart right now. With his ice-blond hair and eyes like a storm-tossed ocean, he's so striking it's sometimes tough for me to look at him. Feels like I've fallen off a cliff into a dangerous no-man's land. One where the only way out is to wrap my body around his and never, never let him go.

My defensive perimeter had expanded to a ring a meter wide. Within its boundaries, the smoke had almost cleared. Being able to get a full breath into my lungs helped.

I resorted to the same strategy I've always used. Nothing fancy about it. When I'm surrounded, I pick 'em off one at a time. I live in a body that looks human, but most of the bastards I fight are bigger than me, or they have thick hides or horns or scales or other impediments—like poison—that make it tough to do anything straightforward. Like reaching inside them to stop their hearts. Hell, some of them, like trolls, don't even have hearts. Goddess only knows what keeps them upright.

From somewhere far away, I heard Bjorn shouting. He sounded furious and worried. The tone of his curses suggested he'd been trying to break through to me from his end of things, exactly as I'd suspected.

I focused my attention on a single dragon. And I sort of cheated because I picked the smallest one, small being relative. This one was green and stood a bit over two meters tall. I'd never vanquish it in straight-on combat, so I teleported onto its back where it couldn't reach me with fire. Breathing shallowly, I tried to bring some of my protective bubble along.

Didn't work very well. Teleport spells are picky like that. I didn't want to take the time to resurrect my shielding. Besides, the smoke had only been bad next to me—before I'd gone into full attack mode. The dragon I'd selected was bellowing and wrapping power-imbued strips around itself to either shake me off or press me into its thorny hide so hard its scales would cut into my flesh.

Couldn't let that happen. My blood would give it power over me. Enough to immobilize my efforts. I unleashed my instincts, pulled the dirk I always carry from its sheath banded to my thigh, and used scales for purchase to crawl up its neck.

Sticking the point of my dagger in the one place beneath its jaws not coated by horny plates, I shrieked, "Surrender."

Everything around me went quiet. No more bellows, trumpets, or bugles. For the moment, no more fire.

Ysien lumbered close. "Well done, Dragon Heir."

"No lack of guts." The dragon beneath me shook itself again, but I had a good hold on it. Its praise pleased me, but words were cheap.

I wasn't in a hurry to cede my advantage, so I left the knife in place. Dragons are immortal. I couldn't do much damage, but I wanted to hang onto the illusion of having the upper hand.

"Runa!" Ysien's tone had developed an edge. "Stand down."

"Don't call me that." I couldn't risk taking my attention from the hand that held my blade.

"'Tis your name, and high time ye claimed it."

"We are done for today," I announced.

"I told you to sheathe your weapon. Dragons do not raise their talons against their own."

"So, it's only acceptable if you're attacking me?" I clung to my almost nonexistent advantage and repeated, "We are done for today. Once you agree, I will jump down."

A sheet of fire roared past me. Roared was an understatement. It sounded like a giant blowtorch and felt as if someone had opened a gateway into Hell. Sweat sheened my body; I curled my damp fingers tighter around the hilt of my knife.

"Agreed," Ysien snarled.

Blade still in hand, I climbed down Greenie's neck, jumped lightly to the ground, and tucked my weapon away. Ysien furled his wings, but I shot in front of him and said,

"Hold up a moment." I tacked, "please," on as an afterthought.

He didn't fold his wings, but he didn't flap them, either. The dragon stared at me with his whirling gaze. Maybe because of my dragon blood, I can look directly at them without becoming snared in whatever spell they choose to weave. I've only tested that theory recently, mind you. Before that, I hadn't come across any dragons to practice on.

I settled my hands on my hips. "I have claimed my name. I'm not using it because true names offer power over the bearer."

Smoke puffed from his nostrils. "But we all know your name. We've known it since your birth."

Awk. There it was again. Proof of one more set of relatives who could give a fuck less about me. At least the Celts hadn't made a secret over not giving a crap. Discovering a second batch who'd considered me irrelevant should be like water slipping off a dolphin's back. Except it wasn't. Their indifference stung.

I cursed myself for a chump.

"The length of time you've known my name is irrelevant. If it's rolling around in your minds, anyone with magic could discover it. I've been Rowan since my birth, and Rowan I shall remain until I tell you different."

Before he could protest or tell me it wasn't my choice—which it goddamn well was—I went on. "When Nidhogg told me I'd have assistance learning the dragon portion of my magic, he said one dragon would show up each day. One." I flapped my hands for emphasis before resettling them on my hips.

"What the fuck?" I went on. I was on a roll, and not in the mood to shut up. "Why are all of you here? Don't you have anything more interesting to occupy your time?"

No one answered, but twelve sets of whirling eyes bored into me. Unpleasant doesn't come close to describing how creepy that felt. I forged ahead anyhow. What choice did I have? When you clue bullies in that they're getting to you, you're screwed. I shoved my shoulders straighter and said, "I thought part of my training was to push the boundaries of how my magic slots with Bjorn's, but you blocked us from each other. Why?"

Ysien did answer that question. "To see how ye did on your own. Why else?"

"Pfft. I've been 'on my own' practically since I was born." I would have stamped my foot, except it felt juvenile. "I'm starting to feel like some kind of circus attraction. Does Nidhogg know all of you are milling in circles practically salivating over the anomaly you've known about but ignored for centuries?"

A red dragon took a step toward me. "We had our reasons."

"And they were?"

"Ye shall know at the proper time," Ysien told me. He's always had a patronizing way about him that grates on my nerves.

Breath swooshed from my lungs. I wanted to punch him, but he wouldn't even have noticed, no matter how much force I put behind the blow. "You're as bad as Ceridwen," I growled. "At least she was honest about how much she hated me."

"Apologize." Ysien hooded his eyes and bent his neck so his head was more on a level with mine. "I am nothing like your Celtic whore of a mother."

My temper has always been a stumbling block, and I reined mine in. Still, I wasn't about to grovel. I settled for saying, "Insofar as I know, no dragon has lied to me directly." I stopped before launching into how lies of omission weren't any better.

"Dragons do not lie." He snapped his jaws with their double rows of teeth shut. The *clack* sounded like a small cannon exploding.

Yeah, but you're masters at twisting the truth.

I cleared my thoughts fast. Among their other talents, dragons are exceptional mind readers. I'd been excited to discover I had a brand new extended family, but the novelty had faded fast. My commitment to learn about how to maximize my dragon-linked magic was waffling too.

I wanted to return to Midgard—Earth—and the witches who'd offered me home and hearth and family after I'd walked out on the Celtic pantheon. The witches were worth my time and my magic.

Instead, I was in Vanaheim standing in a substantial clearing not far from Bjorn's cottage. Made of cunningly interlocking stones with very little mortar between them, the cottage looked as if it had been here for hundreds of years. Who knows? Perhaps it had. Unlike Earth, where most didn't wield magic, everyone I'd met in Vanaheim had at least some.

Bjorn possessed far more than "some." He's the master

sorcerer in all the Nine Worlds, and his power defied description.

"We shall leave you to your *student*," the red dragon told Ysien. From the beast's voice tones, I was fairly certain it was female. Her emphasis on student made it sound like what she meant was, "good luck corralling that headstrong monster you were stupid enough to invite into our midst." But perhaps I was overreacting.

"Ye will leave when I dismiss you." Ysien stopped staring at me and glared at her.

I fully expected the Red to tell him to piss up a rope. Instead she bowed her head ever so briefly. The only indication she wanted to strangle him was the smoke wafting from her nostrils and around her jammed-shut jaws.

"We have one final task today while many of us are here," Ysien announced.

Crappity crap. There was that tone again. The one that screamed he ran the universe. Why the others put up with it for a second was beyond me. He scanned the dragons and crooked a talon at a copper-colored one. Dragon talons are blood-red, maybe ten centimeters long, and razor sharp. They're beautiful if you can get past how deadly they are.

The coppery dragon ambled forward. Not built as heavily as some, it was tall with a graceful set to its long neck. Ysien said, "Zelli, meet Runa."

I nodded at the dragon and managed, "Pleased to meet you." It wasn't as if I could shake hands. The name, Zelli, argued the beast was female, and unlike Ysien, she hadn't done anything to alienate me.

Not yet.

She puffed steam my way, a good sign from a dragon. "Pleased to meet you as well, *Rowan*." She stressed my proper—as opposed to my true—name, and I loved her for it. Maybe she and I were destined to get along.

Ysien glared at her. She glared right back and said, "'Tis a small enough thing. I say we accommodate where we can."

Before Ysien could correct her or order her to call me Runa, I smiled brightly and said, "What is this one last thing we have to do? Whatever it is, could we hurry it along? Bjorn and I were heading back to Earth in a little bit."

"Why?" Ysien bit off the word.

"Now you look here." I craned my neck back to attempt to look him in the eyes. "I don't answer to you. My life and my *home*"—I stressed the word home—"are there. I do not require your permission to return home. Besides, I want to experiment to see if I can move some of the lore materials from world to world."

"Mmph. Does Nidhogg know?"

"I don't answer to him, either," I replied tartly.

Zelli pushed between us. "How would ye feel about riding me? 'Tisn't something dragons normally offer, and 'twas the death knell of our relationship with the Celtic gods. They would have used us for steeds." She turned her head, and the steam turned to a rain of ashy smoke.

My eyes widened. I'm sure my mouth fell open, but I shut it fast. Of all the things she might have said, her invitation to jump on her back was the last one I'd have anticipated. I'd ridden in the occasional airplane back before the Breaking, but this was different.

"Rowan?" Zelli prodded.

"Uh, sure. I guess it would be interesting," I stammered. I'm not usually at a loss for words. "Why would I be doing this?"

"None of us are certain what ye'll be capable of. Ye may find your own dragon form. In the meantime, ye must needs practice aerial warcraft. For that, ye require a companion who can fly." After a hesitation, she added, "I volunteered."

I had a feeling she hadn't had any competition. More than once, I'd thought how convenient wings would be. For one thing, flight offered a superior view of the battlefield. For another, wings would move me out of harm's way from some predators.

Her jaws lolled in an approximation of a smile.

Magic jumped to my summons, and I vaulted onto her back. "What about Bjorn?" I asked. "We're a team. We fight together."

"I haven't forgotten," Ysien said sourly and jerked his head to one side.

The smoke had finally cleared sufficiently for me to make out Bjorn astride a black dragon who'd just leapt skyward. I reached for him with mind speech, not expecting much, but I broke through. *"Hey there."*

"We'll talk later," he said. I knew him well enough to hear controlled fury beneath his words. He hadn't liked it at all when the dragons had erected a barrier between us.

"Ready?" Zelli spread her great wings. When I glanced over a shoulder, I was awestruck by how big they were close-up.

"I think so. Anything I need to know?"

She bugled laughter. "Doona fall off."

I settled myself farther forward until I could wrap my arms around her neck. A pair of horns sprouted from the juncture where her neck attached to her back. They looked like a better bet balance-wise, so I gripped them instead.

She edged away from the group and sprang into the air. The transition felt effortless. One moment her hind legs were planted on the ground, the next, we were flying. *"Just a little bit here to get you used to things,"* she spoke into my mind.

I must have been more nervous than I thought because I had those horns in a death grip, and my eyes were shut. I pried them open as we banked left and right and flew in a figure-eight. Next, she climbed steeply, and I pressed my legs into her hide. She was warm. Might come in handy on a cold day. We hit some kind of zenith because she dove toward the ground, pulling up at the last moment. A heady exhilaration ran through me, and I whooped for the sheer joy of moving through the skies.

"How are ye doing?" she asked.

"I love this!" It wasn't an exaggeration. Riding Zelli was a lot like when Bjorn and I had first joined our magic. Destiny had speared me that day, making it abundantly clear our power was created to work together. Riding the dragon had a familiar feel to it, as if I'd done it in another lifetime.

"Ready to fight?"

"Yes!" I gathered defensive magic, while warding myself. Should I ward her too?

She must have been in my mind because she said, *"Worry about yourself, Dragon Heir. I will be fine."*

I scanned the ground. While we'd been experimenting,

Ysien—or someone—had been busy. Targets lined the far side of the clearing. Bjorn and the black dragon were heading right for them. Power burst from Bjorn, and the two targets on the end disintegrated.

We waited for them to clear the area before we did our own strafing run. This was easy. Too easy. While I recognized that no enemy would just stand there and wait for me to mow them down, my aerial perch added a whole new dimension to my offensive strategies.

Fighting aside, riding the dragon sang to something deep inside me. It held a rightness that filled me with giddy joy. I'd have whooped again, but it wasn't dignified. Beneath us, dragons replaced the spent targets, infusing smaller ones with magic to make them harder to hit.

"Once more," I shouted, too excited to hide my enthusiasm. I felt like a kid who'd just been handed the best toy ever. A glance at Bjorn told me he was as caught up in the whole dragon-riding gig as me. His usually stern face had relaxed into a smile. Power crackled around him, enhancing his unearthly beauty.

And then it was our turn again. Zelli added her power to mine, and we annihilated the entire rest of the row. I did whoop then, and she bugled. Maybe my crude shrieks were buried by her victory cries. I hoped so.

I wanted to fly and fly and fly, but we thumped onto the ground, and she folded her wings. Turning her head, she puffed steam around me. "Thank you," I said. "That was unbelievable."

"Doona tell anyone," she whispered into my mind, *"but I enjoyed our flight."*

"*It will be our secret.*" I hesitated before adding, "*Until next time?*" I held my breath. There had to be a next time. This had been too brilliant not to have a repeat.

I tossed a leg over her side and jumped down, disappointed she hadn't confirmed there would be a next time. I was almost across the clearing to where Bjorn stood when she said, "*Until next time, Dragon Heir.*"

I spun to face her and raised a hand in farewell. My throat was thick with emotion, and I didn't want her to leave. She puffed smoke my way, spread her wings, and circled to gain altitude. One by one, the other dragons departed as well. While I might be sorry to see Zelli go, I was grateful to avoid another confrontation with Ysien. I was a disappointment to him. I read those signs well enough. Mother had been a master at teaching them to me.

Bjorn covered the remaining distance between us and draped an arm around my shoulders. "Flying was unexpected. And delightful."

I leaned my head against him for a moment. It had been all those things, and a whole lot more. I didn't want to muck about describing what had felt surreal. Words might ruin it, so I asked, "What's next?" It was past midday from the angle of the sun.

"Ysien reminded me I need to commission several magical blades. He and Nidhogg worked on a list with me before we battled the griffon. Since then—"

"We haven't had any time," I cut in. "Yeah, I'm well aware of that." I looked away from his direct gaze. It wasn't as if we were mated or anything. We could—no, should—do things separately. "How about this?"

I wriggled out from beneath his arm. Leaving his side was harder than getting off Zelli had been, and both those things worried me. I'd gotten by being strong, needing no one.

"How about what?" Warmth and caring streamed from him. I could lose myself in his blue eyes, fall into their beauty and never surface.

Alarm bells rang deep in my mind. "I'll go inside and finish the section I was working on in that one scroll. If you're not back by the time I finish, I'll teleport to Earth and look in on the witches."

His smile faded a notch. "Sure, Rowan. Will you meet me back here, or—"

"Either way," I said. "I'll be at one of the two coven strongholds. When I'm done there, I'll head back this way. Might be a couple of days, though. Is it still all right for me to try to take one of the lore books with me?"

He nodded. "It will let you know quick enough if it doesn't want to leave." Before he was even done speaking, power flickered around him as he built a teleport spell.

I wanted to grab his arm, tell him I'd go with him, that we'd do everything together, but I kept my mouth clamped shut and hopefully concealed my stupid, ridiculous neediness. We had a job to do. A world to save. Once we'd pulled Earth out of the gutter, we could focus on each other.

I nodded a farewell and sprinted for the house not trusting myself to stick around. I'd bought us a little space from one another. May as well make good use of it. I was certain I'd done the right thing, but desolation battered me.

I didn't get it. Before, being on my own had always been not only acceptable, but preferable to hanging around with others. I shook myself from stem to stern. I had to locate that solo headspace again, and pronto. Bjorn's cottage was not the place to accomplish it. The second I got near the place, his scent reached for me. The sea mingled with sunbaked clay tugged at my heart. My soul.

Resolute, I trotted to the place I'd been working and picked up the scroll. I'd promised, given my word I'd work through this one scroll. When I finished it, though, I'd be gone.

CHAPTER TWO, BJORN

I didn't want to leave Rowan. Major understatement. It damn near killed me to leave her, but I'd finally freed up a spot of time to see about commissioning magical blades. From the looks of things, Rowan was steeped in conflicts, the ones where she was determined not to need me or anyone. So maybe giving her some space wasn't a bad idea.

The smith with the best reputation was located several leagues from my cottage in Vanaheim. I could have walked, but I teleported to save time. I wasn't sure what I expected, probably something more modern. His forge stood in an ancient stone structure with mortar chipping out from between the rocks.

A spring bubbled into a rock-lined pool just outside his falling-off-its-hinges front door. The mostly open door made it easy to knock and walk inside. It took a while before he looked up from the molten metal he was shaping.

After I gave him the list of what I needed, he turned and scanned a row of lethal-looking blades, clucking before he handed me one. I hefted the broadsword and swung it. The damn thing nearly unbalanced me, but I recovered. Kind of.

Hagar, the smith, bellowed laughter.

Once he got himself under control, he asked, "Mayhap something a wee bit lighter, Master Sorcerer?" Build like an ox, he was beefy and broad. A leather apron spanned his waist and covered stained leather breeks. His upper body was naked, and sweat glistened on his deeply tanned chest and shoulders. Black hair streaked with white was gathered into a single braid that fell to midback. He regarded me out of shrewd dark eyes tucked under bushy black brows.

I was certain a giant had to be somewhere in his family line.

Before I had a chance to respond, he plucked my list from a raised table where he'd dropped it atop an array of metal-working tools. The forge put out an ungodly amount of heat, given it was two meters away from us.

Annoyed by my lackluster performance, I picked up the blade once more and added my magic to the mix. This time, I swung it handily. When I set it back in its spot in the row of gleaming weapons, I said, "Not necessarily lighter."

Hagar peered at the list. "When do you want all these items?" he growled. "And who is paying for them? I require half up front."

"Nidhogg will reimburse you, and I must be present when you pour the blades."

"Nidhogg, as in the Norse dragon?" Hagar's eyebrows crawled up his broad, flat forehead.

"The same." I nodded affably.

"Pfft. Never known a dragon to pay for anything. Gold goes into their hoards, but it never leaves. Assuming I'm wrong, why do you have to be here when I pour the blades?"

We'd covered that ground right after I arrived. Not about Nidhogg, but about me needing to be here. I resisted the temptation to tell him his brawn had robbed him of brains. No worries about him reading my mind. He didn't have the magic to light a candle.

"I must add enchantment to the casting, so the blades will be specific for different types of evil. If magic is part of their makeup, the blades will be simpler to control."

Hagar nodded slowly. "Aye. You did say that. I'd forgotten." He exhaled noisily and mopped his forehead with the back of one ham-sized hand. "Fine. Bjorn Nighthorse. You have Nidhogg stop in here and pay me a hundred guilders. Once that's done, I'll set up time to make your blades and send a runner to let you know."

"I'm not always here." I did my best to maintain an even expression. I'd never commissioned a custom blade before, but a hundred guilders was an immense amount, and it was only half the total.

He shrugged. "If you aren't, I'll set the project to one side until you are. Of course, then you'll have to wait until a slot opens in my schedule."

"I understand. Thanks for seeing me on short notice."

"Actually, it was no notice, but people stop by here all the time."

I seriously doubted it. Hagar was so far off the beaten path, no one was likely to drop in, but his reputation as a craftsman was well-known. It was why I'd selected him over other smiths.

I extended my hand. He clasped it hard enough to break bones, but then backed off. "See you soon. Or not." He laughed uproariously, clearly convinced he'd seen the last of me because the dragon would rather immolate himself than part with any of his precious treasure.

I strode away, determined to walk a while before I teleported back to my cottage. The fucking place had turned into a three-ring circus, complete with dragons, since Rowan and I returned from Midgard. She was picky about her name, and I was proud of how she'd stood up to Ysien earlier when he'd insisted on calling her Runa.

I understood. Names offered power. If an enemy didn't have her true name, it gave her a slight advantage. Goddess knew, we needed all the help we could get. After an hour or so, I summoned magic and rode it to my cottage, hoping I'd return in time to catch Rowan before she teleported back to Earth. She might be conflicted about me, but I didn't share her ambivalence. She was the only woman for me, and I'd wait lifetimes for her if need be.

I planned things so I emerged about two hundred paces from my cottage.

Dragons were there. A bunch of them. What the unholy hell? They'd already been here today. And left. I'd assumed they'd remain gone, but assumptions were like assholes. Everyone had at least one. Back to the dragons. They were so big, it made counting them difficult. If there were two or three of a particular color—and one moved—I wasn't sure if I'd counted him or another one. Or neither.

Regardless, a whole lot of dragons bugled and trumpeted and flew about and landed, with Rowan in the middle of them. She wasn't aware I'd returned, and it offered me a quiet moment to drink her in. Gods, she's lovely with her masses of red-gold hair and golden eyes. Tall and well-built, she looks every inch her Celtic heritage. Or she would if she wore fancy garments. Patched clothes hung from her hips and shoulders. A long, black skirt, colorful tunic, and lace-up leather boots covered her body, but an inner light shone through so brilliantly she could have been garbed in sackcloth and ashes.

With Rowan, no one ever noticed her clothes.

The distinctive feel of her magic zapped me, followed by the scents of vanilla, mint, and amber. "Bjorn!" Her musical voice crossed the clearing to where I lurked on its edge. At least she was welcoming me as an ally. When I'd left a couple of hours before, she'd been relieved to see me go.

Judging from her voice, she was clutching the end of a dangerously frayed rope. It didn't surprise me. Things hadn't gone all that well between her and Ysien, one of the dragon leaders, earlier today. I could only imagine her annoyance when the flight showed back up.

I hurried forward and got swept into another combat exercise. They're not my favorite. I'm far from a warrior, never mind Nidhogg's campaign to turn me into one. I have gotten better at ducking and weaving and warding myself while I chuck magic about.

Better, not excellent.

We'd already had one practice session today. Damn dragons. They're born fighters. Guess they couldn't wait to return for round two. I have to admit I enjoyed the fuck out of flying. If we could have more training sessions that included me on top of a dragon, I'd feel differently about them.

Rowan's magic slammed into me. It was always a shock how well-matched our power was. I've never experienced its like. It was like putting two and two together and getting fifty. Or a hundred. Or a thousand. The experience of being joined with her that way held a rough intimacy all its own. One that inflamed my senses and brought out the warrior side I was certain I didn't possess.

She and I fought and parried against dragons who took turns pretending to attack us from the ground and the air. "Flying isn't fair," I shouted at a green fellow painting the ground with fire.

"War isn't fair," he yelled back in between gouts of flame.

"Yeah, neither is life," I muttered. I'm sure he heard me, but he was too busy threading fire close enough to keep me nimble, but not so near as to damage me—unless I was really stupid.

Smoke billowed around me. I coughed, but it didn't help. My eyes stung. My mouth and throat were raw from dragonfire, smoke, ash, and all the rest of the crap dragons spew. A low, keening whistle was all the warning I got before I stumbled—or was pushed—against a boulder that wasn't stone after all. It sucked me into darkness.

Searing pain cut through me, but it was more psychic than physical. A quick check told me Rowan and I weren't joined any longer. Was she all right? Had she been yanked in some other direction? Sucked into a different alternate universe? Nothing I could do to help her until I got myself out of my current predicament.

I made a grab for my magic, intent on kindling a mage light, but nothing happened. All right. If light wasn't on the menu, how about short-circuiting the strange magic that had kicked me out of Vanaheim? I'd figured out that much passing through the stone's illusion. I was still within the Nine Worlds, but someone had expelled me from the field near the humble cottage I called home.

And from all the rest of Vanaheim too. It's not as if I'd been jettisoned onto a familiar moor or next to one of the many lakes in my world.

I reconstructed what had happened just before my impromptu trip into oblivion. We'd been sparring, Rowan's magic linked with mine. She hadn't said much, but she must miss her privacy too. We can scarcely turn around without stumbling over dragons. And I know she misses the witches. It was past time for us to return to Midgard, and we were headed there right after today's practice session. Or she was, anyway. Without me, if I wasn't back from the smith's in time. But I would have followed her.

I punched the darkness with a closed fist. That had to be it. The blasted dragonstone Nidhogg had given me, the one that shackled me to him twenty-four/seven, must have alerted him to our plans.

Or else Ysien had told him.

The stone hummed from the recesses of my pocket. Its equivalent of sticking out its tongue at me. I didn't give it the satisfaction of telling it to shut up. Wouldn't have made any difference. The stone is an extension of the dragon who shoved it down my throat.

Rowan was perfectly capable of leaving Vanaheim without me, but perhaps Nidhogg thought it less likely. Ha! He didn't know her at all. Loki's balls, that woman has magic to burn. Especially now that she'd owned her dragon side. I always thought I was a powerhouse. Well, she's got me beat in that department.

I'd never actually admit it out loud to anyone, mind you. We men have our pride. I'm the master sorcerer in the Nine Worlds, a post I didn't exactly earn, but I've warmed to it over the years since Odin dropped it into my lap. Aye, I'm a wizard, and I need to remember my trade.

I was sick of turning end over end in warm, fluffy blackness, so I barked a power word. One that would take me to Yggdrasil. The One Tree's roots extend throughout the Nine Worlds. Once I located it, I could go anywhere. And where I intended to go was right back to my cottage.

Blasted dragons. They had no right to dick with me.

The velvet black ceded to a grayish mist, and the damp, earthy scent of the One Tree surrounded me before I saw it. Impossibly large, it welcomed me, branches soughing and creaking despite there being no wind. I was near the treetop, which meant the nearest world was Asgard.

If I was canny about things, I could sneak past its boundaries, jump onto Bifrost, the bridge that connects the worlds, and be gone all in a matter of a few minutes. I hadn't seen Odin since our ill-fated meeting with the Celtic gods. It hadn't been anyone's finest hour, mostly because of Rowan's mother. The Celtic bitch goddess had broken Midgard on a lark, killing over half the mortals and opening channels for evil to run unhindered. At least she was out of the way for a while. The dragons had barricaded her into Fire Mountain. A good deed that wiped the slate clean and gave them license to take up residence in my courtyard if they wanted to.

It was nearly time for the Celts to show up in Asgard—if they weren't there already—and I didn't want to be apprehended sneaking through like a thief in the night. No, I wanted to make an entrance garbed in my wizard's robes with Rowan by my side.

The meeting was slated to last a few days. I'd assumed we'd show up once the deities had a chance to stop circling one another like packs of wolves sizing up their rivals.

I laid my palms flat against the tree, soaking in its ancient power. As I thought back on things, neither Ro nor I had exactly been invited to the Norse-Celtic powwow. Should we go anyway? Seemed like a question for Nidhogg. Or not. The Norse dragon would be there, along with several of his kinsmen.

Working on the belief it was better to ask forgiveness than permission, I decided Rowan and I would simply show up. If the gods wanted to toss us out, of course we'd have to leave.

And then I thought again. Rowan was her own person. She might not want to go. No love lost between her and the Celts. Ceridwen had treated her abysmally; the other Celts had followed Ceridwen's lead and ignored Rowan. I'd have to ask her what she wanted to do. Not an easy task here of late. In the few days since we've been in Vanaheim, we've scarcely spoken about anything personal.

Rowan's buried herself in dragon lore from the scrolls in my library, only surfacing to ask the occasional question or two. When she wasn't studying, dragons were instructing her. Not sure what I'd hoped for... Eh, that's a boldfaced lie. I knew exactly what I wanted.

Her. Naked. Beneath me. Or on top. I'm not especially picky in that regard. We'd almost, almost made love. And I wanted more of her lush body. Not exactly a possibility since dragons banged their heads against my single window, bugling if we were inside when they arrived.

Not a shred of privacy.

Hell, we hadn't had a single conversation that didn't revolve around dragon history. I was still leaning against Yggdrasil. Something about its energy was soothing, calming, and energizing all mixed up together. More than just the roots of the Nine Worlds, the One Tree was also the source of our magic. No wonder it felt like coming home.

I'd been incensed over the dragons keeping me away from Rowan when they challenged her ingenuity and ability to think on her feet. More than incensed, I'd been as spun out as if the beasts had robbed me of a prized possession, one I was willing to put my life on the line and fight for.

I shook my head hard to clear my thoughts. My expectations around Rowan were unrealistic. And unreasonable. She had plenty to occupy her mind without me adding demands to the mix. I loved her, but I'd keep my distance. Let her find her own way.

She'd accepted comfort from me, but then she'd pulled

away. When I'd shown up after my visit with Hagar, she'd welcomed me, but as a comrade in arms. Someone to stand by her side and cleave through all the dragon craziness. I smiled to myself, certain she'd been furious she hadn't left when the getting was good.

I'd never have guessed the dragons would return so soon, and I'm certain neither did she. The tree was crooning to me, singing a wordless song. It dragged me out of my mental wanderings. Past time for me to leave. If I remained, I'd end up sucked into Yggdrasil's roots and turn into memories for the One Tree to pore over. The mighty ash was sentient. If it could speak, it would have told me it owned the Nine Worlds and everything in them.

Including me.

I tugged my hands from its gnarled bark and visualized a portal. It was slow to form, flickering into nothingness time and again. The tree liked me. It upped the ante on its song, and something about the melody eroded my magic and gave me a filtered view into the tree's heart. It was sad about Midgard, fighting the damage but losing the battle. It needed help.

It needed me.

Its plea seared my soul. How could I refuse Yggdrasil? But if I gave in to its plea, Rowan would be alone.

The next time the edges of a gateway formed, I jumped through.

No matter where I came out, it was better than ending up fodder for Yggdrasil. The One Tree would suck me dry, and I'd wander among its twisted roots forever. Midgard was a problem, but one I was better equipped to face in my current form.

I held an image of Bifrost, urging it to show itself so I could get the hell out of there. The darkness around me ceded to gray and then to the golden streets of Asgard. Alrighty, not the bridge, but at least I could reach it from here. I built a hasty ward and fled down the nearest alley. Buildings towered above me, and it took me a moment to figure out where I was.

Far from the palace.

Thank the gods for small favors. And for escaping Yggdrasil. I'd been an idiot and remained far too long. The One Tree had taken my measure and liked me enough to make a bid to absorb me. It was quite an honor on one level, but I wasn't ready to devote my life to maintaining the Nine Worlds. Not yet. And not that way.

Asgard is different from the other segments of the Nine Worlds in that there's a single entrance to Bifrost. I calculated how I could make a run for it and stay mostly out of sight. I did a smattering of work on my ward to strengthen it, but not a lot. No point. If I ran into one of the gods, they'd see straight through it.

And then I'd tell them the truth about how I ended up here, bid them a good day, and continue onward. So long as they didn't decide to ship me off on a quest. They were famous for shit like that. And I'd have to go; no one told Thor or Loki or Odin thanks, but no thanks.

Scuttling from one shadowed alley to another, I was almost to the bridge. Magic arced as I checked the pathway between me and my goal. So far, so good. I was within a hairsbreadth of being gone, but "nearly" didn't make the cut.

I froze.

Celts were arriving. Why they were anywhere near the bridge was anyone's guess, but they were. I hunkered down, intent on waiting things out. Meanwhile, I absorbed scents and energy. Gwydion, Arawn, Bran, Arianrhod, Andraste, Poseidon, and each of the four winds passed into Asgard. Dewi arrived a few minutes later in all her blood-red glory.

Odin, Thor, and Loki's booming greetings were audible from my hiding spot. An hour dribbled past with them exchanging jibes and pleasantries. Finally, the group started slowly up the gold-paved streets of Asgard toward Valhalla.

I wanted to leave. My legs were cramping, but I gave it another quarter hour to make certain no one would bother me. When I stood, pins and needles shot up both legs. I shook them out and marched in place until I was certain they'd hold me. Magic fixes a lot of things, but leg cramps aren't one of them.

I checked the area, checked it once more, and made a run for the bridge, jumping through its shining gateway and congratulating myself for having made a clean getaway. I still had no idea how I'd ended up falling through the boulder that spit me out in limbo, and I needed to sort that out before it happened again. Worry soured my stomach. Was Rowan all right? Had the dragons pushed me out of the way for some agenda of their own?

Not the dragons. The explanation didn't fit. They wouldn't be paying for blades for me or having me ride them, if they had plans for Ro that didn't include me. Other possibilities were far more insidious. For one thing, whatever had grabbed me had escaped the notice of all those dragons.

I fisted both hands and watched markers fly by. Vanaheim couldn't arrive quickly enough.

I might not be a warrior, but I'd kill anything or anyone who stood between me and Rowan. Her maybe not wanting me in the same way I longed for her made no difference at all. I'm a patient man. Meanwhile, I'll find whoever sent me on that one-way journey and make them sorry they were ever born.

CHAPTER THREE, ROWAN

"*B*jorn's gone," I shrieked. The moment his magic ripped away from mine burned like a knife in my guts. I shucked playing strategy games with the dragons and bolted to the last place he'd stood. Nothing jumped out at me, so I sent a seeking spell whirling outward.

Zelli lumbered close. "Are ye certain he isn't trying a new stealth maneuver?"

I wasn't in an answering mood. I was still gathering what information I could. Wherever he was, he wasn't close enough to raise with telepathy. I'd have to sense his magic to be able to talk with him. The boulder near where he'd stood fairly sizzled with an eerie power all its own.

"That." I pointed at the rock, but didn't touch it. "Something's wrong with it." Even as the words left my lips, the air around the pillar folded in on itself. It's tough to describe, but I was certain whatever entity had taken over the stone had just departed.

Goddess damn it all to fuck. Bjorn had been yanked through some kind of gateway, but it had slammed shut behind him. Finding him would be a trick-and-a-half—unless the dragons commanded far subtler power than I thought they did.

I viewed them as the slash-and-crash and-burn type. Figuring out what happened to Bjorn would be like threading a teensy needle with slippery thread.

Zelli aimed her whirling gaze at the boulder. It stood nearly as tall as she was, and its northern side sported a thick coating of gray-green moss. A glistening spray of dragon essence surrounded it. Zelli was thorough. I'll hand her that much. Her probing circled the stone from top to bottom and back again, checking every side.

The smell of clay baked beneath a smothering sun rose around us. It figured the dragons' characteristic scent would remind me of a desert. I'd clenched both hands into fists so hard my nails were cutting into my palms. With a great deal of effort, I relaxed my fingers, uncurling them one hand at a time.

I wanted to claw at Zelli, demand she hurry things up, but she might be my only friend in the flight of dragons, all of whom had gathered around us. If it weren't for the witches, I'd not have had clue one how friends treated each other. Thanks to them, I understood pressing her to speak before she was ready would be inconsiderate.

"We're wasting time. Back to it," a red dragon who seemed to be standing in for Ysien ordered.

I was willing to extend plenty of slack to Zelli, but my generosity didn't encompass Red No-Name. I spun to face him. "No. I'm not doing anything except my level best to locate Bjorn."

A blizzard of smoky ash settled around me. Coughing, I batted the bigger chunks aside and said, "Stop that. It's rude."

"Why ye upstart—" Red began.

"She is one of us." Zelli's voice sounded from behind me, full of venom and warning.

"The rest of *us*"—Red huffed after emphasizing the inclusive pronoun—"do what I say."

"Only if we concur with you," a blue dragon piped up.

I clamped down hard on a harsh grin that wanted out. Apparently, dragons dealt with the occasional insurrection too, when disagreements surfaced.

Fire roared out of Zelli. Luckily, I was short and it flowed over my head. The displacement of air made my neck prickle. The dragons, who'd been chatting among themselves, fell silent.

"We have a problem," Zelli announced once she had everyone's attention. "While we were merrily lobbing magic at each other, and having a gay old time, something wicked scuttled into our midst. Whatever it was turned the stone into a portal and made off with Bjorn."

Red rolled his whirling eyes. The effect was decidedly off-putting. "And ye picked this up from gazing at yon pillar? I think not."

Zelli sashayed around me and plodded until she stood snout to snout with Red. "I think so, Ceirrot. Test the stone for yourself. The villain would have stymied us, but bits of wickedness yet cling to the moss."

Grumbling and spitting ash, Ceirrot shambled to where Zelli had stood. His assessment went far quicker than hers had, but he was slow to turn back toward us. I'd moved off to one side. I still didn't trust the beasts not to step on me.

Smoke puffed from Ceirrot before he grudgingly admitted, "Aye, traces of insidious magic remain embedded in the moss, but they could have been there for months, years." He shook himself until his scales rattled ominously. "I say Bjorn was called away to investigate a problem, likely on another world. He is the chief sorcerer, so that type of thing must be common."

I ground my jaws in frustration. I'd had it up to here with dragon discussions, dragons acting like they knew everything, and dragons believing they owned me.

"His magic was linked with mine," I pointed out. "If he'd left of his own volition, he'd have gently extricated himself from our bond. He didn't. It was ripped asunder. He also would have told me he was leaving."

"Perhaps ye doona know him as well as ye believe," Ceirrot suggested with a snide intonation I didn't like at all.

"While we're sitting here batting worthless words back and forth, Bjorn may be fighting for his life," I snarled. "He's not immortal like we are. He needs us. Or at least he needs me. I'm going to look for him."

"How?" Zelli's question was soft and non-accusatory. She was on my side.

I clenched my teeth so I wouldn't howl or scream or do something else that wouldn't help in the least. Once I got hold of myself, I said, "I have no idea, but maybe if I start with Odin or Nidhogg, one of them will be able to sense Bjorn. Assuming he's still here in the Nine Worlds."

"I believe he is," Zelli said.

"Why?" I glanced up at her. Hope teased the edges of my soul. Maybe she'd gotten more out of her perusal of the pillar than I had.

"The dark power has Jotunheim stamped all over it. The giants' realm is wild, chaotic. It surrounds the more civilized portions of the Nine Worlds, but is sunk in perpetual winter."

"What are we waiting for?" I asked. "If we know where he is, let's go." I chewed my lower lip. I'd never been there, so I'd need someone to either show me or take me. Preferably show me. I needed a break from dragons, and I'd kicked myself roundly for not leaving during the brief hiatus when they were gone.

"'Tis only where the evil sprang from," Zelli clarified. "'Tis unlikely they'd have taken Bjorn there. Not against his will, and not if they ever wished his assistance again."

"But we have to do something," I argued. "We can't just sit here and hope for the best."

"Ye're the only one who's worried about him," Ceirrot muttered.

I made myself as tall as I could and stared him down. "Leave. Now. I'm done dancing about like a trained seal. I might not be done permanently, but I'm certainly finished for today."

"Nidhogg specifically instructed—" Ceirrot began.

"I don't give a jolly fuck what he instructed. If he's unhappy about the outcome of his marching orders, he should be here himself." I paused for emphasis and repeated, "Leave."

I stared at Ceirrot. He stared back. It got old fast, so I said, "Very well, then, I'll leave."

"Where will ye go?" Zelli asked.

If anyone but her had asked, I'd have snapped it was none of their affair where I went or what I did.

She must have sensed my inner turmoil because she said, "Hop on, Dragon Heir. We shall go together."

"Halt! Ye only had permission for the one flight," Ceirrot sputtered.

Zelli ignored him. Twisting her head atop her sinuous stalk of a neck she looked meaningfully at the spot on her back where I'd sat once before. I didn't wait for a second invitation. A small magical assist settled me firmly astride the copper dragon.

"Some of you might consider ensuring Nidhogg knows our boundaries have been breached by those who wish us ill," Zelli said and spread her wings.

"Ye doona issue orders," Ceirrot snarled.

"'Twasn't an order, merely a suggestion." Zelli bent forward and added, "Naught more to be done here today. The Dragon Heir and I are leaving, and the master sorcerer is gone as well."

Our transition from ground to air was seamless. As we gained altitude, the same sense of exhilaration and joy raced through me. I tried to talk myself out of my worries about Bjorn. The man was centuries old. He'd been taking care of himself for a long time, but I had a sneaking hunch whatever had happened today was somehow related to my presence in

Vanaheim.

"*Where are we going?*" I asked once we were well clear of Bjorn's courtyard.

"*I was considering that,*" she replied. "*Perhaps Bifrost is our best starting place. If Bjorn used the bridge recently, I'll sense his presence.*"

I didn't have any better ideas. Except hunting down Odin. I wasn't especially keen to do that, but he'd been far more pleasant when he and Nidhogg and Ysien had shown up in Inverlochy Castle than when he'd cornered me in his other role as leader of the Wild Hunt.

"*I should steer clear of the bridge,*" I said.

"*Why is that?*"

"*Bjorn told me that my Celtic blood would alert someone or other, and they'd kick me off it forthwith.*"

"*We are not going to ride it anywhere,*" she informed me. "*I'm merely going to poke my head through one of the many portals and see if he's been there. Besides, Bifrost shouldn't reject you. It will detect your dragon half. We have free rein in the Nine Worlds.*"

I tried to resurrect when Bjorn had told me to avoid Bifrost. He must have known about my dragon side then. He eventually fessed up and told me he'd sensed that part of my bloodlines the second he laid eyes on me. I gave a mental shrug. Everyone interpreted power differently. For now, I'd stick with the conservative approach.

I wanted to ask Zelli why she'd befriended me, but didn't. Instead, I settled for, "*Will you get in trouble for taking off with me?*"

Laughter blatted from her in fire-laced gales. Once she

was done chortling, she said, *"Millennia have passed since I was a hatchling. No one will rebuke me. I'd be surprised if anyone even mentioned this. Ceirrot likes to throw his weight around. So does Ysien."*

"How about Nidhogg?"

"He is far more judicious about how he employs power."

That was a relief. Kind of. "Why wasn't he here today?"

"Because the Celts are arriving in Asgard for an important meeting."

Crap. I'd planned on crashing that meeting. Bjorn and I hadn't been invited, but I deserved a seat at the table, being half Celt and all. I made a snorting sound, but it was jerked away by the wind. By now, the others had probably disowned me, given my mother's fall from grace.

Regardless, I'd show up and find out for myself. Gwydion had actually apologized, told me had he known what a wasteland my childhood was, he'd have intervened. And Arawn had mentioned Dewi would be devastated she hadn't known about me. Words weren't important, though. Their actions when we met next would tell me where they truly stood.

We were circling to land in a small area surrounded by towering evergreens. They looked ancient. "Do you know Dewi?" I shouted into the slipstream.

"Aye."

I waited, but Zelli didn't add to her affirmation, so I asked, "What's she like?"

Zelli thumped heavily onto the ground, and I jumped down. What was it about flying that felt like I'd been born atop a dragon's back? I hustled in front of my new friend, anxious to hear her response.

"She is much like Nidhogg." Zelli nodded as if agreeing with her own statement.

"Thank you." I picked my words with care. "But that tells me less than nothing since I don't know Nidhogg at all."

"Ye lived with Dewi, did ye not?"

My turn to nod. "Indeed I did, but Ceridwen warned me to steer well clear of her."

Zelli tilted her head far back on her long neck and blew fire skyward. I was certain the trees around us breathed a sigh of relief the flames weren't directed at them. After the dragon's ire had run its course, she glanced down at me and said, "Of course Ceridwen would have told you as much. She dinna wish the dragon goddess to sniff out your secrets."

"Yeah, I already figured that part out," I mumbled.

"But what ye really wish to know is if Dewi will accept you, and that I canna answer," Zelli went on. "There's never been a Dragon Heir linked to the Celtic pantheon, and the circumstances surrounding your birth willna endear you to your kinsmen."

I wanted to screech none of it was my fault. Not Ceridwen's tempers or her ill-advised alliance with my dragon father or breaking Midgard. Yet, if I'd never been born, she wouldn't have been driven to drastic measures to herd me back to her side. Measures that had failed abysmally.

It's a funny thing, but when someone treats me like crap forever, I don't exactly jump up and sing when they snap their fingers my way. Ceridwen's pronouncement it was past time for me to reclaim my Celtic heritage had fallen on indifferent ears.

"This portal to Bifrost, where is it?" I was done thinking about Ceridwen and sorry I'd asked about Dewi since she'd pointed the conversation back to my sadly broken mother.

"Right here." Zelli extended her forelegs. Blue-white power arced between them, turning her talons an exotic ruby shade.

The air in front of us took on a glimmering aspect as a gateway formed. Rimmed in fire like many of the dragons' workings, the moment it opened I heard the bridge's song. Low, expressive, enticing. Bifrost's boundaries had been penetrated, and the bridge was intent on luring us onto its rainbow surface. I'd never seen Bifrost, but I'd read about it.

Zelli stalked forward, graceful despite her size, and extended her neck into the portal. The bridge's song intensified, and I took a step forward before I caught myself and erected a ward. I was used to Midgard, where magic was unusual. Here, it was primary. Unless proven otherwise, everything in Vanaheim had enough to cause trouble for me, and I'd do well to remember it.

Zelli was doing her usual thorough assessment. I respected that facet of her. She took her time, didn't rush through things. Because I couldn't resist, I snaked out a thread of magic and opened the place within me that Bjorn slotted into. It was still raw and abraded from how he'd left. He'd never have done such a thing on purpose. He lived for magic. Wielding it with subtlety and grace was important to him.

I'd attempted to explain that to the dragons, but I'd

failed. Zelli was the only one who'd believed me. That the others had dismissed me rankled. Maybe I was done with being the entertainment committee for whomever showed up. I'd been looking for an excuse, and now I had one. No one fought side by side with those they didn't trust.

Dragon magic thickened, turning the air a brilliant array of colors that probably rivaled the bridge. Aware of my warding and of the need to hold myself clear of the bridge, I crept forward a pace. And then one more, hoping for a peek inside. Something about Zelli's power reassured me. She was a formidable ally. I was lucky to have her in my court.

I forced my feet to remain still. Subtle as it was, her coercion spell had nearly snared me. It wasn't focused my way. She was dredging every scrap of information she could out of Bifrost, but some of her casting had slopped toward me.

The portal gleamed silver, and the dragon flames bordering it burned brighter. I caught a whiff of brine and then another. Elation surged. Bjorn smelled like the sea, but then so did Odin, and probably all the other Norsemen I had yet to meet.

Zelli bugled. It snapped me back to attention. Was something wrong? Were we about to face an unknown enemy—another Norseman who also carried the scent of an ocean? I culled power from deep within me and balanced it between my outstretched hands.

Fighting while warded is a neat trick. I have to cut at least a small hole in my shrouding to allow magic to escape. I'd rather be quick on my feet and wield power unimpeded.

There it was again. The smell of the sea. This time, I

caught a hint of sunbaked clay. Frantic I'd miss something, a tiny window that could bang shut any moment, I searched for Bjorn's magic, but I couldn't feel shit through my cloaking. I took a chance and dropped my ward. Most of it, anyway, while I raised my mind voice.

"Bjorn!"

In the space between my indrawn breath and pushing it out, he rocketed into my head. *"Rowan!"*

Relief so heady I almost lost my footing spilled through me. Zelli yanked her head and neck out of the portal. An instant later, Bjorn leapt through. I forgot all about being proper or dignified, and I launched myself on top of him. He staggered to maintain his balance.

Familiar arms closed around me, and he held me like he had other times during our relatively brief tenure as allies and friends. Warm. Solid. Reassuring. Gripping his face between my hands, I kissed him with abandon. He was here. He was safe. We were together, just as we were meant to be. After a brief hesitation, he was kissing me back. Lust and need shot through my body with shocking urgency. If Zelli hadn't been standing over us, I'd have driven him to the ground and hiked up my skirts.

My heart wanted to thump out of my chest. It took gargantuan effort not to string kisses down the open neck of his shirt. Despite my unbridled need to jump his bones, I still could not admit to myself he was far more than just a friend and battle companion.

I could accept friends and allies. I wasn't ready for anything deeper, and I might never be. Reluctantly, I extricated myself from my embarrassing nosedive onto his body. Mine still zinged with sexual heat, but it would recede. Maybe.

Next to us, the portal winked out, and Zelli puffed steam over us.

"Where were you?" the dragon asked without preamble.

I winced. Those should have been the first words out of my mouth. Instead, I'd wasted precious moments indulging myself in the comfort of Bjorn's arms.

He nodded and squared his shoulders. "I got sucked through a gateway. It took me a while to find my way back."

"I found a residue of evil from Jotunheim," Zelli said. "How did you escape?"

Surprise washed over his even features. "Jotunheim, eh? I never got that far. I thwarted the magic that snared me and found my way to Yggdrasil. From there to Asgard, and thence to the bridge." He stopped to take a measured breath and addressed his next words to me. "The Celts have arrived in Asgard. I plan to be part of their council."

"So do I." I nodded crisply.

"We could go there now," he said. "Or right after we clean up a bit."

Zelli shook her head and quit puffing steam. "We must go to Jotunheim. Before the trail grows cold. Whoever dragged you through that fissure was intent on mischief, nothing more, or ye wouldna have escaped so easily. But they snuck in beneath our noses, and managed to leave undetected. Such an event must not happen a second time."

Ash and fire spewed skyward. "I believe today was a test," she went on. "We failed miserably. To ignore such an incursion past our borders is an error. We must address it."

Bjorn raked curved fingers through hair that had mostly escaped the leather bits he tied it back with. "Are three of us enough?" he asked.

"What do ye believe, Master Sorcerer," she tossed back at him.

A grim smile formed, adding a whole new dimension to his almost profane beauty. "Right before I sensed you and Rowan, I was thinking about eradicating whomever had dragged me away from my cottage. About how I'd make them sorry they were ever born." One corner of his smile twisted downward. "Mayhap it's time to put my money where my mouth is. I have friends in Jotunheim. They've summoned me to fix their fuckups on many occasions."

"Good call," Zelli said.

"What do you think?" Bjorn asked me.

I wanted to go to the council meeting, but I trusted Zelli's instincts. Waiting a day or two to show up in Asgard shouldn't cost us much. If this gathering was anything like the ones at Inverlochy when I was a child, it would last for days.

"I'm game. Count me in."

"Excellent." Zelli breathed more steam, the dragon equivalent of praise, and sent a jolt of power to tug the gateway open once again.

"Ro can't use the bridge," Bjorn said.

"I say she can," Zelli retorted. "Her dragon blood will overshadow the Celtic part of things."

"Guess we're going to find out." I sprang lightly through the portal. The same scents I associated with Bjorn hit me broadside. At this level, they were far less pleasant. He followed me onto Bifrost. It reminded me of an acid lightshow in one of the many hippie taverns before the Breaking. Lights washed over me, turning things first one color and then another.

The lights were fascinating. I could have watched them forever. In a distant corner of my mind, I was aware of my free will slipping away, but there wasn't a damn thing I could do about it. Bjorn stood right next to me, but I couldn't even find words to tell him I was in trouble. Or use telepathy.

I felt rather than saw Zelli trudge onto the bridge. "Onto my back," she ordered.

It didn't seem like the time to get into a discussion about why. Or to tell her I didn't take orders from her any more than I did from Ceirrot. I was grappling with magic, trying to get it to do my bidding, when Zelli grabbed me and tossed me over one shoulder. I was no sooner seated in what was starting to feel like my place when her voice filled the narrow channel holding the bridge.

"This one is mine! I name her Dragon Heir, and ye shall allow her passage."

The lights didn't slow down, but my reaction to them snapped back in my face like an overstretched rubber band. Along with the harsh slap came a return of control, and I was myself again.

Thank the fucking goddess for small favors.

The bridge moved forward, rather like a conveyor belt, and I waited to see what would happen next. This was a lot like traveling to borderworlds, but with air to breathe. *"Thanks,"* I told Zelli.

"Pfft. I was wrong about Bifrost, but the problem was

easily solved. Pay attention to the nodes on the wall. They're marked by runes denoting the different worlds..."

I listened, absorbing the knowledge she offered, and snuck a peek at Bjorn. He looked exhausted. Maybe I'd kind of skip over what had nearly happened with Bifrost. The more I thought about it, the better I liked the idea. After all, I had no clue what would have occurred after the bridge hypnotized me.

And I never wanted to find out.

While I recognized the wisdom in Zelli's insistence we go straight to Jotunheim, I would have far preferred retiring to my bed with Rowan. She'd literally hurled herself at me. If I'd had any doubt regarding her intentions, they'd vanished when she crushed her mouth over mine.

All this in front of a dragon, but it hadn't even slowed Rowan down.

She felt like she'd been born to be in my arms, all heat and curves and hunger. Her nipples had formed stiff peaks where they pressed into my chest, and my cock surged to life. As wiped out as I was, my body's immediate response surprised me. Memories of her mouth molding itself to my unruly appendage just made it harder.

I'd begun to think of ways we could excuse ourselves for a short while when Rowan stepped away from me, breaking our intimacy as abruptly as she'd started things. And then

Zelli came up with solid reasons for why we had to proceed to Jotunheim. I might have argued half an hour wouldn't make any difference at all.

If Rowan had still been melded to my body.

She wasn't. The ambivalence she lived with clearly hadn't gotten any better. My distended cock was annoying. It would take time for it to go down, and there'd be a familiar dull ache from having been called into action and cut off before anything could happen. I thought I'd moved beyond being a slave to my sexual side.

Apparently not.

Rowan and I were overdue for a frank discussion. Either we were lovers, or we weren't. She couldn't ride both sides of that street. Meanwhile, she'd ignored my warnings about Bifrost and leapt through the dragon's portal and onto the bridge. Worry about her rashness ate at me. Yeah, color me a sap, but I couldn't not worry. Nothing to do but follow after her as quickly as I could.

In my current state, it felt like I was crawling.

When I joined Rowan on the bridge, she didn't seem quite right to me. I stood next to her but couldn't figure things out. Still irked—and disappointed—by the push-pull of her wanting me, but not, I was just gathering magic to probe her mind when Zelli grabbed her and tossed her onto her back.

When the dragon screeched, "This one is mine! I name her Dragon Heir, and ye shall allow her passage," I knew I'd been right about Bifrost and Rowan. The bridge had done something, but the dragon's power short-circuited its attempt.

Would it be a permanent fix? Or would Rowan always have trouble with Bifrost? Time would answer that question. I turned my attention to our destination. Had the dragon ever been there? Would she take it amiss if I asked?

I didn't care. I needed to know. *"Have you been to Jotunheim before?"* I used telepathy because as I've already said, even my presence on Bifrost is far from a foregone conclusion. I use it, but it's kind of a don't-ask-don't-tell proposition.

"Aye," Zelli answered in kind. *"Wait until we exit Bifrost, and then we shall talk."*

Wise of her. I admit I wasn't fond of any of the dragons who'd taken to camping out on my doorstep, except the black dragon I'd ridden. Zelli seemed to be cut from a different cloth, though. For one thing, she was firmly in Rowan's court. Anyone who befriended Ro was worthy of my trust.

I squeezed my eyes shut and rubbed them. Hot, gritty, dry, they appreciated the brief break. The last time I'd traveled to the giants' realm, it had been to address a sickness that had attacked the trees. Unfortunately, none of the giants had thought to call in assistance until the blight, which turned out to be a magical type of fungus, had wiped out nearly half of a forest.

As I resurrected the memory, a few errant chips slotted together. Trees had roots, often times deep enough to reach the same underlayment the One Tree took its nourishment from. Yggdrasil wasn't ill, but nor was the One Tree its usual vibrant self. Not if it was asking for help from the likes of me.

Perhaps this was how the demise of the Nine Worlds would begin. Through rot spreading from the One Tree's roots. They extended to all the worlds. Jotunheim would be particularly susceptible because 90 percent of that world is thick forest, usually blanketed by snow since winter reigns year round. In the giants' defense, snow had been unusually deep that season and had done a masterful job hiding the blight-stricken trees.

How long ago had that been?

"Get ready." Zelli's words knocked me out of my thoughts. Another fire-rimmed portal took shape. She gestured me to run through ahead of her and Rowan, who still perched on her broad back.

A tiny part of me was jealous. Riding the black dragon had been such an unbelievable experience I'd lacked words to describe it. I could still feel the heat from its scaled hide and the exhilaration as we'd blasted through the skies. Fighting with my feet planted on land would always be lacking from now on, but while Rowan was a Dragon Heir, I am not.

Dragon Heirs from the past had all bonded with dragons, and they'd gone into battle together. Of course, they'd been Norsemen. I waited a couple of meters from the portal for Zelli and Ro. Cold surrounded me; snow drifts rose on all sides, some as high as three meters. A brisk wind pushed chilly air into every chink in my clothing.

If I'd been thinking, I'd have insisted we stop by my house to get warmer garments for Rowan and myself. Well, perhaps not for her. She had Zelli. I cleared my mind before jealousy established too deep a grip. I wanted my own dragon, but I may as well want Vanaheim's twin moons delivered on a platter for all the good it would do me.

And it wasn't as if Zelli belonged to Rowan. We were fortunate the dragon had found us worthy of her attention. Rowan jumped down and tromped over one of the smaller snowdrifts to where I stood.

"Brrr," she said. "Not as cold as Niflheim, but not far off, either."

I started to take my jacket off, but she pushed it back onto my shoulders. "Absolutely, not," Rowan said firmly. "You're not dressed any more warmly than I am. No point in you turning into an icicle."

Zelli moved in front of us and lay on her belly on the ground. It brought her head about to my eye level. The baked clay smells of dragon magic formed a dome around us, and the air warmed immediately. "I doona know how long we have afore the giants sense our presence and send a greeting party," she said, following it with, "To answer Bjorn's question regarding whether I've been here before, I have, but I dinna remain long. More often than not, the giants decide they should be able to turn us into steeds."

"Seems like a common problem," Rowan muttered, "since the Celts did much the same."

"Aye, 'tis. And none of us are overly fond of it," Zelli replied. "The giants have horses. They're as big as houses, and slow as slow can be. Mayhap 'tis why the giants yearn to fly."

"Do you suppose all the giants were part of the dark magic that snared Bjorn?" Rowan asked.

The dragon shook her head. "Nay. Giants are as slow as their horses. They aren't quick thinkers, either, and they often miss what's right beneath their noses."

Remembering the dead trees, I tended to agree with her about them missing the obvious. I narrowed my eyes and forced my tired brain to function. "Do you suspect other than giants live here?"

"I doona know," she replied, "but 'tis a prime location where evil could flourish unnoticed. The one spot in the Nine Worlds that's rarely visited because the weather is so hideous."

"It's nothing to write home about in Niflheim, either," Rowan muttered.

"Aye, but Hel keeps a close eye on that realm," Zelli retorted. "Not much gets past her and her serpent guardians."

I thought about Zelli's assessment of giants as dull-witted. I'd met King Thrym a time or two, and he was far from stupid. Quite the contrary, he'd been bright enough to scheme Thor out of his hammer. The type of power the giants used was different from any other in the Nine Worlds. Because of that, people tended to underestimate them, which was a mistake.

I felt the inexorable pull of that unusual power as giants approached. Not Thrym, but a greeting party made up of lesser nobles. I'd never totally figured out the giants' pecking order. They kept it under wraps for reasons of their own.

No more time for talk. I drew myself up tall and let magic spill through me. Giants respected strength. This wasn't a time to creep on my belly or pretend to be humble.

Sure enough, the crash and rumble of two—or perhaps three—giants moving nearer filled my ears. It might piss Zelli off, but I planned to take the lead. Hopefully, these would be giants I'd known and worked with before.

Noses working like truffle-sniffing pigs, two men tromped out of the thick tree cover. Standing better than three meters tall, they towered over us all. I noticed Zelli wasn't on her belly anymore, but standing, and the lovely canopy that had warmed us was gone.

Luck was smiling on me. I knew both giants. "Krivar! Brios!" I bowed low. When I straightened, I said, "It's truly good to see you once again."

"Ye as well, Master Sorcerer," Krivar rumbled. His voice was deep and low and reverberated in the pit of my stomach. Black hair tumbled around his shoulders, and dark eyes sat beneath thick, hairy brows. A broad, flat forehead, hooked nose, square chin, and blunt beige teeth gave him a doltish appearance, but I wasn't fooled. He had a mind like a gilded trap.

Brios was quite fair. White hair that had once been blond was skinned back from his forehead and captured in a length of leather. His eyes were an unusual icy blue. When I'd first met him, I'd assumed he was blind, but he isn't. Both men wore leather breeches topped by shirts made of some furry hide. Their feet were encased in wooden clog-like affairs.

"Why are ye here?" Brios asked. "Did ye come to offer us a dragon as a sign of goodwill from Vanaheim?" Laughter burbled from him, sounding rather like the beginnings of an avalanche.

Zelli tossed her head back. Fire shot from her mouth. Every single scale screamed outrage. Before she redirected her fire at the giants and their hair went up like a torch, I hurried to say, "I fear we bring difficult news."

"Aye? What manner of ill tidings?" Krivar asked.

Brios had stopped laughing. He resettled his feet, and the ground shook beneath me. My feet were well on their way to freezing, so I wriggled my toes and added a small stream of magic to keep the blood flowing.

"Something from Jotunheim slipped quietly into Vanaheim not far from my cottage. It was a stealth maneuver, and they spirited me into a void. I escaped by linking with Yggdrasil."

Probably sick of remaining silent, Zelli added, "I tested the residue myself. It was Black Magic, and it began here. I do not believe it originated with the giants because I did not find your energy within it."

"Impossible," Brios sputtered. "If other than our own kind were here, we would know."

"Are ye doubting my word?" Zelli's eyes spun faster.

I stepped between her and the giants. "All we were hoping was that you'd check through your realm for anything...unexpected." Because giants are second only to the elves in terms of their love for gossip, I added, "Midgard is in trouble. Serious trouble. It may founder."

Krivar swung a great arm sideways until his fist connected with a nearby tree. It rocked on its roots, and its boughs soughed louder. "Ye must needs say more than that, Sorcerer. What kind of trouble? Why has Odin not addressed it?"

Rowan stepped out from Zelli's shadow. "I'm afraid the trouble is my fault. Ceridwen is my mother, and—"

"Ceridwen, the Welsh sorceress?" Brios rumbled.

"The same," Rowan told him. "Although she identifies herself as a Celtic deity."

Krivar elbowed Brios and guffawed so loud I wanted to cover my ears. "Same wench who came looking for hot cocks a time or two. I remember her. Not my type."

"I wasn't as picky," Brios told him. "Ye missed out on a decent time. Too small to fuck, but her hands and mouth made up for it." He patted his crotch.

A sidelong glance at Rowan told me she was ashamed her mother had been such a slut, but Ceridwen's bedroom proclivities weren't on the table here. I chopped a hand downward. "That good-time wench is who broke Midgard. She was trying to force her daughter back to the Celtic pantheon and cast a spell that got away from her. Over half the mortals are dead, and evil is leaching in from somewhere. I need to make sure it's not spreading to the other worlds as well."

"Ceridwen may have said the spell spiraled beyond her control, but it might not be quite true," Zelli grumbled.

I'd wondered if Ceridwen was trying to whitewash her perfidy too, but I hadn't given voice to my doubts because of Rowan.

"Say more about this Breaking," Krivar urged. "Word of it has filtered into Jotunheim, but we would have details."

"Piss on details," Brios broke in. "Why has Odin not fixed things?"

"He's tried," I said. "He rides with the Hunt most nights to keep an eye on Midgard, but the damage grows deeper with each passing month."

More fire arced from the dragon. She was doing a reasonable job of steering clear of the treetops. Ash rained down. "Dragons have kept ourselves removed from the affairs of other magic wielders. The threat facing the Nine Worlds is serious enough, Nidhogg has instructed us to take whatever steps we deem necessary."

Krivar whistled, creating a windstorm that intensified the bitter cold. "I've never known him to lift a talon for aught beyond dragonkind."

Zelli nodded briskly. "My point, precisely."

"Could you please hunt through your realm for whatever invaded Vanaheim?" Rowan asked.

Brios squatted and looked at her. The stone-like feel of giant magic blasted toward Rowan. "What else are you?" he growled.

"She is a Dragon Heir," Zelli said firmly.

"Nay." Brios pushed creakily upright. It was akin to watching a tree pick itself up. "She doesna have the feel of any other Dragon Heir."

"Besides, there have been no new Dragon Heirs for a thousand years," Krivar said.

"I am Celtic and dragon," Rowan told the giants. "It's probably why my blend of magic feels unusual to you." She hesitated. "From what I understand, there's never been another like me."

"Who was her da?" Krivar asked Zelli.

Interesting the giant hadn't asked Rowan. Perhaps he intuited she didn't know. Giants were reasonable mind readers.

"We are not free to disclose that information," Zelli said stiffly. "Ye willna ask a second time."

The giants looked at one another, and the crackle of power shimmered between them as they shared thoughts. I wanted to eavesdrop, but they wouldn't take it well, and they'd feel my incursion no matter how subtle I kept my casting. Apparently done conversing, they turned away.

Giants don't do anything fast. Before they got halfway around and started walking away, I said, "Does this mean you'll honor Rowan's request, which is mine as well?"

"We will take the matter to King Thymer," Brios replied.

"Aye, he shall decide our next steps," Krivar added.

"Doona take too long," Zelli cautioned.

Krivar halted his slow about face to say, "Odin has known of this since it happened. He's in no rush to address it. Why should we be?"

"Because darkness from your world targeted me." I put steel behind my words. "I've done naught but good for your people and have asked nothing in return."

Brios was facing me again. "Ye're requesting a boon? In repayment for all ye've done for my kinsmen?"

Oh-oh. Slippery ground. "Partial repayment," I said smoothly. I didn't want them to make a meal—or a prisoner—out of me the next time I showed up. It wasn't a secret that Jotunheim was at the bottom of my priority list, and I only came here when my slate from the other worlds was clean.

A slow grin lightened Krivar's face. "I've always liked you, Master Sorcerer."

"Thanks. You're not a bad fellow yourself. Now about my request—"

"We shall honor it," Brios said. "Our first stop will be the palace."

I bowed my head for a brief moment. When I raised it, I said, "Tell your king there is a gathering in Asgard. The Celts are there, and plans are being crafted to deal with the threat facing the Nine Worlds." I hesitated and then winked. "Don't tell them how you know about it."

Krivar chuckled. "We protect our sources. Many thanks from our king." He and Brios moved slightly faster this time and vanished into the woods. I felt the tug of their power as they teleported away from where we stood.

"Smooth," Zelli told me. "Ye gave them a wee bit of information. It should make them more willing to comply with hunting down whatever has invaded this world. I feel it here. The same malevolence I sensed clinging to the moss on that rock."

Power spilled from me reflexively. No need to hide myself. The giants knew we were here. At first, I couldn't feel anything beyond the giants' magic. It pervaded everything on Jotunheim with its damp stone scent and slight prickly feel. Zelli had sounded certain, so I dug deeper. I'd nearly given up when a faint pulse reached me. When I tried to chase it, it shattered. Almost as if it knew I was hunting it.

I reeled in my seeking spell. "If we can find it," I muttered, "the giants should be able to as well."

"Aye, but 'tis elusive," Zelli said.

"Elusive, but present," I retorted.

"You know," Rowan said. Her words were directed at the dragon.

"Ken what, Dragon Heir?" Zelli's response was glib, polished. I girded myself. Rowan valued candor. The dragon had hedged, and it would piss her off.

"You understood me perfectly," Rowan said. "You know who my father is."

"I do." Zelli nodded.

"But you won't tell me," Rowan persisted.

My heart hurt for her. Pain and persistence took turns shaping her expressive features. My own parents had been kind, supportive. Neither possessed much magic, and I'd often wondered how the combination had yielded me, but such things weren't totally unheard of. Da had been a leather worker, Mum a seamstress. I was their sole offspring. Both were long dead, and my cottage was the same one I'd grown up in.

My folks always made me feel loved and valued. I understood why Rowan yearned for at least one decent parent.

"Nay, I willna," Zelli was saying.

"Why not?"

"Such is for Nidhogg to reveal."

"Why not my father? He can't be dead. Dragons live forever." Rowan wasn't going to let this go, and it wasn't my place to tell her to move on.

"He is no longer part of the Nine Worlds," Zelli said, "and that is the last I will say about this. Shall we return to Vanaheim?"

Rowan nodded morosely. "Yeah. We have a council meeting to crash."

"Is that a euphemism for show up uninvited?" I asked.

"Something like that." She still sounded glum.

"Do you feel up to tackling the bridge again?" I asked her.

She shook herself and stared at me. "You know?"

"Of course. Not much gets by me. What Zelli did fixed the problem. The only thing we don't know is if it will remain fixed."

"If it does not, I shall remedy it," the dragon said. Magic sheeted from her as she called a portal into being.

Rowan's shoulders slumped. It wasn't like her to be dispirited, so I wrapped a hand around her upper arm and murmured, "It will be all right."

"Will it, now?" She twisted to look at me. "Contamination from Earth is spreading. Once Zelli pointed it out, I sensed it here too."

I'd figured she was upset about the dragon's refusal to disclose her da's identity, but her sorrow ran far deeper than that. Soothing words jumped to my lips, but I didn't utter them. I wouldn't lie to her.

I'd begun to shiver, and I'd long since moved past where I could feel my feet. I'd have directed more magic to warm myself, but I'd been afraid to dilute my already watered-down reserves.

In case we needed to make a point with the giants. Fortunately, it hadn't come to that.

Zelli's portal was slower to form than before, but I was grateful when it opened and I could escape to Bifrost's relative warmth. This time, I went first and kept a sharp eye on Rowan.

The dragon followed us inside; her gateway zipped shut.

Both of us eyed Rowan. She glared back. "I'm fine," she said, tightlipped. "And I'm getting off at Midgard."

Normally, I'd have asked if she minded company, but I was afraid she'd tell me no. Instead, I asked, "What about the Norse-Celtic gathering?"

She clamped her jaws in a tense line. "I haven't forgotten. We can go there next. I have to check in on the witches. They're helpless without me. Or close to it."

I inhaled briskly to mask my relief. She'd said we'd be going, not that she'd see me there. It was a small enough thing, but I'd take it.

"Tell me about these witches," Zelli said.

This time, the emotion I rode herd on was surprise. Apparently, the dragon planned to stick with us. It was so unheard of, I couldn't quite wrap my mind around it. Dragons interacted with other dragons. Period. If that was changing, Nidhogg must be far more worried about the Breaking than he'd let on.

Or else he'd decided the stone by itself was insufficient to spy on me, and he'd assigned one of his own to take up the slack.

I was being rude and bitchy, but I was tired. I wanted my cozy little chamber. And my cat. And Tansy to make me a soothing cup of herbal tea infused with her witchy healing powers. Mostly, I wanted a place where I didn't have to be on my guard every single fucking second.

That goddamned giant, the one who considered Mother the original goodtime girl, had pushed an unwelcome message right into my head. Their magic is different enough, neither Bjorn nor Zelli heard him. If they had, they'd have said something.

"Come on, ye hot-bodied darling. Ye know ye want it. I'll be waiting whenever ye return. Or I could come to you. Just say the word."

That was when he'd patted his crotch, and not vomiting had turned into a nip-and-tuck proposition. And then there was my not-so-stellar performance where I'd turned into the slut of the year as I invaded Bjorn's space. I'd been so happy and relieved he was safe, my usual reticence to disclose much of anything personal had scattered to the four winds.

And damn but he felt perfect slathered against me. I wanted him with a singlemindedness that baffled me. The harder I tried to dig through to the bottom of it, the murkier things grew. I'd thought fooling around with him would have taken the edge off my bitch-in-heat routine, but it only made me want more. Lots more.

Guess it placed me squarely in the same court as the horny giant. And my mother. I was confused. And tired. And I had to stop whining and buck up. It had taken time to adapt after the Breaking. Just because all the rules had reshaped themselves again was no reason to pull the covers over my head and pretend my life hadn't changed.

No more looking back. I shook a mental finger sternly in my face.

After we'd established everyone was coming to Midgard with me, no one had said anything. There was a time I'd have been delighted to have help. Hell, I should fall all over myself thanking Bjorn and Zelli for their support and caring. Instead, I'd clammed up.

What in the fuck was wrong with me? Something for sure, but I had too much else going on to figure it out. Meanwhile, I should stencil *Ungrateful Bitch* across my forehead.

I'd been watching the markers carved into pillars on Bifrost's right side. Midgard should be next. I didn't want to miss it and have to stay on the bridge for a whole other joy ride.

I muffled a snort, turning it into a cough. If I missed my

stop, I'd get off at the next one and teleport. Bifrost wasn't a bus, but it reminded me of riding them back before the world broke. I'd missed many a stop. All it meant was I got to walk a bit. Thinking about walking down city streets reminded me I missed mortals. Even though they lacked magic, their unique energy had made Earth a richer place.

"Get ready," Zelli said.

I nodded. No reason to be defensive and tell her I hadn't been a total slacker. I readied power to call a portal into being, but the dragon beat me to it. Next to me, Bjorn's energy pulsed. Warm. Solid. It took a lot not to wrap an arm around him, but I had to cut my spontaneous displays off at the roots.

At least until I figured out what he and I were to each other.

Since I didn't have to worry about the gateway, which was forming nicely, I prepared magic in case we walked into a shitstorm. It had happened before—not from Bifrost, but from teleporting—and I like to be ready. Worry about the witches ate at me. Maybe splitting their forces had been a huge mistake. With a few at Inverlochy and the rest beneath Ben Nevis, they were isolated from one another.

Witches can't teleport. They can't even use telepathy unless they're damned close. So if one group was in trouble, the other would never know about it. I slammed my teeth together. Growing crops in Inverlochy's courtyards had been my idea, and the single item that made it doable, something beyond a suicide mission, was me.

I was the link between the two groups, and I'd been absent.

Granted, I was doing Nidhogg's bidding, but still, it wasn't right. If anything happened to any of my witch family because I couldn't split myself in two, I'd carry the guilt forever.

The portal was open, and I leapt through. Familiar scents washed over me. Earth smelled different than the other Nine Worlds. More like mortals, less like magic. I stopped long enough to inhale deeply.

Zelli walked through last, and the opening shut behind her with a swishing sound. Now that I knew I could access Bifrost from Midgard—and that it wouldn't play fast and loose with my magic—it might come in handy since it required far less magic than a full-on teleport spell.

"Where do you want to go first?" Bjorn asked.

I got my bearings. It took me a moment since we weren't in Scotland. The rainbow bridge had spit us out in what looked like the remains of Cornwall on England's southwestern coast. What had once been a bustling region was just as empty as the rest of the U.K. If mortals remained, they'd gone to ground.

Rusted cars sat at odd angles, and many buildings had fallen in on themselves, creating huge rubble piles. Coyotes and racoons dug through the wreckage, probably intent on unearthing mice. They didn't even break stride to look our way.

Zelli turned in a full circle, taking it all in. "The Breaking did this?" she asked.

"Yup," I answered her. "Tornadoes and hurricanes and torrential rain and earthquakes rolled through for years.

Once the onslaught of unbelievably bad shit let up, this is what was left." I spread my arms wide.

"But 'tis inexcusable." She was still stomping about, using smallish steps to take in the devastation. "I'd heard rumors, but the reality of the destruction is disturbing and sad and heartbreaking." Fire shot from her open jaws. "I'm glad that mother of yours is our prisoner. I will make certain all the dragons in Fire Mountain know the extent of her perfidy."

Mother was the last of my concerns. The day I'd forgiven her—never mind, she didn't deserve it—she'd mostly stopped haunting me. "We need to teleport to get to Scotland," I said. "I can give you coordinates, or—"

"I will take us," Zelli said. "Onto my back."

"What about Bjorn?"

"Him too." The ashy stream that had been spewing from her mouth turned to steam. Clearly, she liked Bjorn.

"I appreciate the kindness, but are you certain it won't tax you?" he asked.

Zelli laughed. "I'm quite certain I can move us all to the Highlands with far less expenditure of effort than three of us traveling separately. Where precisely am I aiming for?"

"Inverlochy Castle. It's north of Fort William."

"I ken it." Zelli's tone was unreadable, but I guessed perhaps she'd had an unpleasant run-in with the Celts there.

I walked to Zelli's side with Bjorn right behind me. Before I got my own magical assist together, his power surrounded me with its brine and clay scents. I ended up astride the dragon with him right behind me. Pressed up against him like that, my back to his front, reminded me of us being naked near my special pool just beyond Inverlochy's boundaries. I'd spent many a day lounging within a ring of standing stones—part of Earth, yet not —watching the water and dreaming of growing up.

Or of being grown up enough to escape my Celtic kin. Then, I'd viewed it as the beginnings of freedom. Brother, had I been young and naïve.

Bjorn wrapped his arms around me and gripped Zelli's horns just above where I'd grabbed them. I was intensely aware of the press of his arms against mine, of his inner thighs curving around my hips and legs. The hard-hewn muscles of his chest pressed into my back, and his breath was warm near my neck. The swell of an erection pressed into my buttocks.

Why did he have to be so gorgeous?

But his looks were only part of my magnetic attraction to him. Men could be pretty and total assholes. Their attractiveness crashed and burned the second they opened their mouths. With a sinking sensation, I understood I'd fallen—and fallen hard—for Bjorn's spirit. For the part of him that shone through every cell of his perfect body. He could have been old and wizened and I'd still crave him next to me.

Oh girl, get a grip.

Dragon magic, clean and pure and laced with heat, turned the air around us into a kaleidoscopic mix of colors. The coyotes and racoons did look at us then. A few errant yips sounded as Zelli's casting transported us north. It was fast, even quicker than I'd expected.

The devastation around Cornwall faded, replaced by an

equally ravaged Carlisle. The castle was still recognizable, or I'd not have known where we were. This part of northern England never supported the sheer numbers of mortals Cornwall did, so there was less rubble. We were still hundreds of kilometers from Fort William and Inverlochy castle, though. Maybe Zelli hadn't known quite where to aim for after all.

Before we could dismount, she said, "I dinna wish to teleport into trouble. We will fly from here. 'Twill be swift since I shall add enchantment to our journey. Once we're closer, we will overfly the castle ruins."

"Excellent," Bjorn said from behind me. "Solid strategy."

Zelli twisted her head around until she could see us. "Why thank you, Master Sorcerer."

He laughed, and the sound warmed me. "Never claimed to be a warrior, but I've been reading about battles since I was able to hold a scroll."

She puffed steam all over us and said, "Many methods must work in concert for us to win. Knowledge of tactics goes a long way."

She spread her wings and turned forward in a single movement. Soon we were skimming through the air. If I hadn't been in a godawful hurry to make sure the witches were unharmed, I'd have asked if we couldn't check out Glasgow. I'd always suspected that if mortals remained, they'd have barricaded themselves into defensible positions in the larger cities. We should pass right over Edinburgh, though. It would be good enough.

"Do ye know if the remainder of Midgard looks like this?" Zelli dipped a wing toward the ravaged lands beneath us. What had once been rich farmland was pockmarked with burn scars, deep fissures left by earthquakes, and standing pools surrounded by the bones of long since rotted corpses. Humans. Cows. Horses. Goats. Pigs.

Crows perched on the remains, cawing their pyrrhic victory as they feasted on death.

"I've always meant to check," I admitted. "Never made it farther than Europe, and it looks pretty much the same as here."

"It was on my agenda as well," Bjorn said, "but I never could clear the time."

Something about viewing the wasted lands from my aerial perch iced my blood. I turned my head a little and said, "It looks worse from up here."

"Know what you mean," Bjorn agreed. "It's the scale of things. When we're standing on the ground, we don't think about the next patch of dirt over."

"Yeah. It's not staring me in the face, so I guess I've pretended there have to be places everything is still like it was."

"Was that why you never teleported to the States or Asia or Australia?" His deep voice tickled my ear.

"Maybe."

Bjorn snugged his legs against mine and let go of one horn to wrap an arm around my waist. Him holding me felt too good to wriggle away. Besides, where would I have gone?

Rhetorical question. If I'd been serious about escaping his attentions, I could have teleported off the dragon's back in the space between two breaths.

"We'll figure something out," Bjorn was saying when I dragged my fickle mind back from its meanderings.

Had I missed something before his reassurance?

"What do you mean?" I asked.

A whoosh of warm air coated my neck when he exhaled briskly. "I'm not saying everything will be fine because my crystal ball is cloudy. I have no idea what the future holds, but there must be a way to defeat whatever is intent on sucking the marrow from Midgard's bones."

"Ye raise a good point." Zelli's voice floated back to us. "It revolves around the word 'whatever.' Until we figure out precisely who our enemy is, we will be at a loss as to how to counteract them."

"We fight what's in front of us," Bjorn said. "Eventually, the mastermind behind the destruction is bound to make a mistake and reveal himself."

"Might be a herself." Zelli shot fire ahead of our flight path.

"Or it might have no gender at all," I retorted, debating whether to give voice to my true worries. They'd only just begun shaping up after our trip to Jotunheim.

"What if the target isn't Midgard at all?" I asked.

"What do ye mean?" Zelli replied.

"What if Mother's miscast spell offered a convenient opening into the Nine Worlds? What if whoever the villain in this piece is was lurking, just waiting for an entry point?"

"If that's true—and I'm not saying it's not"—Bjorn tightened his grip around my waist—"how come it's taken them so long to make a move?"

Before I could develop a reply, Zelli said, "Time is

relative. The years since the Breaking are of no consequence to those like you or me. It might have happened yesterday or a hundred years ago."

"True enough, and grist for the mill," Bjorn murmured.

It was. I'd make a point of floating my suspicions after we got to the council meeting. Unless they kicked us out so fast we never got a chance to say boo. Zelli had been right about it not taking much time to reach Inverlochy. The bulk of Ben Nevis flashed past on our left.

A ripple in the center of a scorched field caught my eye. "What was that?" I pointed.

Bjorn leaned that direction. "What? I don't see—"

The cracked, muddy earth exploded as horrors crawled out of it. Snakelike, they had multiple sets of legs, menacing triangular heads, and scuttled like cockroaches once they were free of the hole. At least they didn't stink of poison. It didn't mean they weren't lethal, but they couldn't burn skin from bones on contact.

Some were black. Some gray. And they varied in length from garden snake size to the largest cobra.

"Hang on!" Zelli bugled. "'Tis going to get rough. Can the two of you close the fissure?"

"Aye, I believe so." Bjorn's power slammed into me with such force I almost fell off the dragon. As our magic slotted together, the whole far greater than the sum of both parts, the raw spots from how he'd been wrenched from me healed on contact.

The sky chose that moment to open up. Lightning forked ahead of us, followed by peals of thunder. Rain followed in huge, punishing gouts that drenched me immediately. The wind howled and shrieked like an entire herd of Banshees had been ejected from the *Dreaming*.

Meanwhile, Zelli focused dragonfire on the snake monsters. Her weapon burned hot and true, impervious to the buckets of rain. I worked with Bjorn, mixing fire and air to deal with the fissure. All the rain wasn't helping. It only made the muddy gash crumbly and harder to address. For every bit of magic we tossed at it, rain made the next part cave in. And for every cave in, ten more snakes slithered out.

They were moving faster now, as if sheer numbers offered them protection and added to their weak magic.

"Hurry!" Zelli cried between two blasts of fire. "The wee bastards are developing wings. I doona wish to deal with them up here."

My eyes widened. I hadn't noticed, but wing buds were indeed forming on the snakes, and growing like the beanstalk from an old children's tale. "We need a different approach," I told Bjorn.

"Aye, and tell me something I haven't already figured out. How about we skip air and fire and simply move earth over the hole, smother it, as it were, and glue things together with magic."

"But then we'll have to keep power flowing to keep it shut," I protested.

"We can do that for a short time. Until we figure out something better. Come on. While we've been talking, twenty more of those fuckers have materialized."

He was right. Zelli was doing a decent job killing the snakes. They must have had oil in their scaled hides because they burst into mini-pyres and were still burning. Ignoring their fallen comrades, others slithered around them.

"Go," I said, and poured magic into Bjorn's casting. No holding back. We'd give this all we had. Once the hole was shut, we could back off. Beneath us, the earth rumbled and groaned alarmingly as we shunted dirt and rocks from nearby locations, funneling everything into the gash.

An enormous boom that made my ears ache was accompanied by air pockets that dragged us first up and then down. Zelli was on top of it, though. Her instructions to hang on had been unnecessary. One of my hands held her neck horn in a death grip. Bjorn clasped my body with his legs, but he'd freed both hands. A steady stream of blueish light raced from his fingertips, skirting our target and encouraging bushels of dirt to pile into the hole.

Meanwhile, Zelli dealt death. Smoke from burning flesh rose despite rain that hadn't let up. It carried the stench of rot and evil. So much so, I breathed shallowly, not wanting it in my lungs. Worry for the witches ate at me. If something like the fuckers below us attacked Inverlochy, the closest thing I had to family would be done for. Maybe the castle's magic would protect them, but I wasn't at all certain of it. Power needed to be renewed to be effective, and the Celts had left their erstwhile lodging behind a long while back.

"Rowan!" Bjorn gripped my upper arm and shook me. "We're done. Stop squandering power."

I reeled in my magic and scanned the smoldering ruins beneath us. Bjorn's suggestion had worked. The hole was not only closed; mounds of dirt were piled over it along with boulders so large, I was impressed we'd managed to move them. A quick check told me Bjorn had laced power over the hummocks. It should hold the fissure shut for a few days. We could return and do a better job later.

Or not. As fast as crap was popping up, this might not be a priority.

One last snake was making a run for it. Zelli's fire caught him broadside, but he kept on trucking. She blasted him once more, and we flew on. "Well done," she bugled.

"You as well," I called to her.

"Och, a mere inconvenience." She scribed circles, and I saw the illusion protecting Inverlochy Castle beneath us.

"Looks as if it hasn't been disturbed," Bjorn said, followed by, "I had no idea how much simpler warfare would be from the air."

"Funny, but you stole my exact thoughts," I retorted. Still scanning the area between where the castle stood and the river, I saw a black dragon lift its head from where it had been drinking from the river's sluggish flow.

"A surprise awaits us." Zelli punctuated her words with steam that wafted around us. I was so wet, the warm mist sizzled when it touched my clothing.

"Is that the dragon Bjorn rode?" I yelled.

"Aye," he answered me. "It is." Excitement threaded into his reply, and I was happy for him.

"If we are going to be beset—and it appears we will be," Zelli said, "we shall wield twice the clout if Bjorn has his own dragon to ride."

"I appreciate the thought," Bjorn said, "but I have no right to claim a dragon steed."

"No one claims us," Zelli corrected him. "We chose

whom we offer a spot on our backs. 'Tis an honor, and one ye canna refuse."

"Who said I was planning to refuse," Bjorn said. "I can't wait to fall on my knees and thank him."

"*No need to overplay things,*" Zelli cautioned, having switched to telepathy. "*Dragons respect power. Come from a position of strength, and ye canna go wrong.*"

"Thank you. I shall," Bjorn said solemnly

I gripped his arm with my free hand, riding the coattails of his eagerness. Maybe he'd been right earlier. Perhaps we'd find the key to slamming the gates to the Nine Worlds. Darkness may have gained a toehold, but we hadn't lost the war. Not yet.

And not ever, if I had my way.

"*See you inside,*" I told them. We were almost on the ground. I fashioned magic into a cushion of air and teleported into Inverlochy Castle. I couldn't wait any longer to make certain the witches were unharmed.

CHAPTER SIX, BJORN

I felt torn, which is unusual for me. Normally, I don't have any trouble at all selecting a path. If it doesn't pan out, I switch things up. I wanted to go after Rowan, but I also needed to renew my acquaintance with the black dragon. He'd probably be offended if I ran off without so much as a greeting, and I did not want to get off on the wrong foot. I still couldn't quite believe he'd shown up, but the exhilaration sweeping through me was too compelling to push aside.

I reminded myself Ro had gotten along fine without me for 99 percent of her life, but it didn't satisfy the part of me that yearned to protect her, keep her safe. I winced mentally. If she suddenly turned into a shrinking violet who required me at every turn, my attraction for her would fritter to nothing. I respected her courage; it was both potent and overwhelming. And her in-your-face rashness was one of the primary elements that had drawn me to her in the first place.

Zelli touched down. Craning her neck around, she said, "I will go inside." A layer of steam blanketed my soaking wet body and garments. It wasn't that it didn't rain in Vanaheim, but rarely with this level of enthusiasm.

"I admit to curiosity about these witches," the dragon went on. "They must be special indeed if they lured Rowan away from the gods."

Batting steam aside, I said, "They are special to her. As I understand it, Rowan walked away from the Celts. It was only later the witches took her in. Accepted her. Offered her everything the Celts failed to."

"Och, I see." The dragon bobbed her head knowingly. "They loved her, recognized her merits. Since no one knew about her dragon blood, the Celts would have considered her inferior."

I hadn't viewed it in quite that light before, but it was true. Much like the Norse gods, the Celts were a terrible bunch of snobs. If you didn't carry royal blood, you weren't worth a crap. To them, Rowan had probably been Ceridwen's half-blood brat. Half breed being the operative term. No one had bothered to look for her after she left. It spoke eloquently to how unimportant she was in their minds.

Another less pleasant insight jabbed me. "Damn Ceridwen," I muttered. "She must have known the others would have treated Rowan far better had they known the truth of her parentage, yet she remained silent."

"One more debit from her badly overdrawn account," Zelli agreed almost cheerfully.

I hoped the dragons were torturing Ceridwen, making her suffer the torments of the damned.

"Well met, Master Sorcerer." The black dragon had joined us from Zelli's other side. Because I'd been lost in vengeful fantasies of Ceridwen roasting over a fire, her flesh renewing itself so she was in constant pain, I hadn't noticed.

The dragon—my dragon?—was half a head taller than Zelli and more powerfully built. Close up like this, his wet scales gleamed with a myriad of iridescent colors overlaid atop the black. Lightning forked down a meter away, but I paid it no heed. The sum total of my attention was on the dragon.

I bowed. "Thank you. I am very glad to see you once more." When I straightened, I said, "Likely you know already, but my name is Bjorn Nighthorse." I waited. Courtesy dictated he should offer his name in return. I hadn't ferreted it out when I rode him.

"Ye would know my name as well." His voice was surprisingly soft for such a large beast. More in the alto than bass ranges. "Fair enough. I am Quade, Lord of Fire."

It was an impressive name, far too impressive for him to be bothering with the likes of me. But Zelli had told me to come in strong, so I said, "Thank you for trusting me with your name. You have my word, I shall not betray your faith in my discretion."

"Nor I, yours," he said solemnly.

"I shall see you within," Zelli said. The air around her shimmered, and she was gone.

Dragon magic scoured me, beginning with my feet and ending with the top of my head. The net effect of all that power swirling around me was unsettling. My skin prickled, and the soaking hair across the back of my head lifted slightly. Apparently, Quade was taking my measure. I pushed my tired shoulders back and stood as straight as I could.

Aye, he might be a dragon, but if we were going to be partners, I'd carry my weight. When we'd flown together before, our power had acted independently. Unlike when Rowan and I fought with conjoined magic, Quade had mostly provided an aerial perch and sent the occasional blast of fire at targets other dragons had placed on the ground.

His magic faded. It had shielded me from the worst of the rain, and I missed it. I waited, but he didn't say anything. I didn't want to push him, but I felt some urgency to follow Zelli inside the castle. If anything was amiss, Ro would have alerted me.

Maybe.

Unless she'd walked into a trap. Her association with the witches was common knowledge, and a perfect way for someone to force her hand. I could see her trading herself for their freedom any day.

More time passed. I shifted from foot to foot and finally cast caution aside. "I'm not trying to rush you or anything," I told Quade, "but I'm worried about Rowan, and I'd like to go inside Inverlochy. In case she needs me."

Laughter rumbled from Quade, along with steam. "She has Zelli. Besides, 'tis only one of the things bothering you. Ye wish to know why I am here."

"I have many questions," I agreed. "Like how all this will work. It surprised me when Zelli went to Jotunheim with us, and surprised me further she hasn't left yet. Is she planning to remain with us forever?" I paused before adding, "Are you? Or did you only show up in case more atrocities appear?"

I made a face. That hadn't come out quite right. Before I could stammer around and correct my clumsy wording, Quade said, "Forever is a long time, Master Sorcerer. For now, all I shall say is dragons are well aware the Nine Worlds are under siege. We are warriors. We have answered Odin and Nidhogg's call to arms."

Should I ask what was in my mind? No harm in trying. "You certainly don't have to answer me," I began, "but surely you knew of the Breaking. What alerted you the Nine Worlds were in deeper trouble than even I guessed? My supposition was the primary problems were here. In Midgard. While I feared they might spread, I wasn't concerned it was imminent until today."

"What happened today?" More steam billowed from Quade. He was doing his dragon-best to encourage me.

"Evil from Jotunheim invaded my world and nabbed me, but I also connected another puzzle piece. A while back, many months, I was called to Jotunheim to deal with tree blight. Now I fear the trees sickened because they drank from the same fountain as Yggdrasil."

Quade leaned nearer, lowering his head. "Ye speak in riddles, Sorcerer."

"Aye, I neglected a critical element. Earlier today—or mayhap it was yesterday at this point—I spent time with Yggdrasil. Its branches, not its roots, but it attempted to absorb me and fought my efforts to leave." I rolled my shoulders back. "In an earlier time, the One Tree would scarcely have registered my presence. I fear the root in contact with Midgard is spreading its poison to the remainder of the tree."

"Ye raise an interesting theory, and ye're not as inconsequential as ye believe," Quade said. Before I could probe what he meant by that, he continued. "'Tis an excellent time for us to move within."

He didn't wait for me to agree. Neither had he answered my query about what had shifted the dragons from watchful and waiting to battle mode. The baked-clay scent of dragon magic surrounded me and whisked us through the illusion keeping Inverlochy Castle hidden from mortal eyes. Not that the original reason for the illusion remained, but perhaps it made the castle less visible to wickedness.

I wasn't sure about that, but the dragons might know.

The rich smell of loam and growing things greeted me as Quade's spell cleared. The witches had been busy. Rows upon rows of greenery stretched in every direction. Inverlochy Castle was huge, and its grounds spanned several square kilometers.

I deployed magic, letting it spill from me as I hunted for Rowan. She'd be with the witches. Sure enough, they were above us. Probably where we'd met with them last time we were here. They'd carved out a cozy living space for themselves. Even though I hadn't spent much time here when the Celts were in residence, I felt certain the witches' homey rooms were an improvement.

Even more than the Norse gods, the Celts went for

splashy, gaudy displays of their power. Their council chamber was a prime example. With all its crystal and marble, it was a study in chilly grandeur.

I started for the stairs. I wasn't certain how Quade would manage, but I didn't want to anger him by asking if he needed help. He didn't. Not from me, anyway. Zelli wasn't milling about in the courtyard, which argued dragons had their own ways of figuring things out that didn't include climbing stairs with their ungainly hind feet.

Now that I was inside, my earlier urgency returned. Why hadn't I heard anything from Rowan? Not so much as a quick telepathic message all was well. She would have let me know. My pace quickened, and I loped up the stairs to the next floor. Skidding around a corner, I hustled straight for the witches' quarters and through an open arched doorway.

Rowan sat on the floor cradling a woman's head in her lap and chanting low. The woman was short and emaciated. Steel-gray hair had been cropped short. The bottom half of her body was covered by a blanket. Blood had spattered her chest and glistened wetly on her flowered top. Dried blood around her mouth and down her chin suggested she'd been coughing it up from damaged lungs.

A much smaller version of Zelli stood off to one side. Red-tinged power flowed from her into Rowan and formed a translucent nimbus around the injured witch. I looked again at the dragon. I'd had no idea they could make themselves smaller if need be. Or was this a projection and the actual dragon was elsewhere?

It didn't matter.

Careful not to displace the shroud around Rowan and the witch, I crouched across from where she sat and carefully threaded my magic in with hers. The shrouding brightened immediately. Tears had formed furrows in the grime streaking Rowan's face. Whoever lay on the floor was dear to her.

I command healing magic, but I usually depend on potions and powders and herbs to augment my ministrations. Such accoutrements weren't available to me here. Closing my earth eyes, I employed my psychic vision to determine what we were dealing with. The woman appeared depleted enough, she might be dying from old age.

Seemed unlikely, given the circle of grim-faced witches ringed around us. I wanted to ask what had happened, but I was afraid breaking into Rowan's concentration would court disaster. She was keeping the witch alive. I felt the woman's spirit hovering. It wanted to be on its way, but something had a firm grip on it.

I dug deeper and found a spreading pool of darkness. Soul sickness was leaching life from the witch, but it had also tethered her spirit to her body. I'd only seen a few cases. They resulted from contamination by the darkest strain of Black Magic. Where in the unholy fuck had the witch stumbled across such a thing? We'd cleared it from the Nine Worlds centuries ago. Or was this somehow related to the Breaking?

Almost had to be.

"Ro. We can fix this," I told her as gently as I could.

"How?" Even in telepathy, her voice was thin, desolate.

I considered how to proceed, discarding options as fast as

they occurred to me. When words came, they were Old Norse, my first language. *"Ye hold her life in your hands. There is no way to transfer that binding or her soul will collapse. Draw on my magic. Feed fire into your spell. All fire to scour the taint from her. Be delicate, though. 'Tis a fine line between eradicating the soul sickness and harming her."*

"I'm not a healer," she protested, *"but I will try."*

"Today, ye are. I will guide your efforts." I infused confidence into my words. If Rowan hesitated now, the witch was as good as dead. As things stood, she was 90 percent gone. Our odds were crap, and this was our only chance.

I tightened my linkage with Rowan, helped her funnel fire into her casting a bit at a time, discarding earth and air as we went. Everything else faded to background noise. The other witches. Zelli. Quade—if he'd even shown up in this chamber.

The witch's spirit pushed harder against its bonds as fire seared the darkness within her fading body.

"We're making her worse." Rowan jettisoned telepathy. All her magic was focused on the prostrate witch.

"Aye, but 'tis necessary. She canna recover otherwise." I didn't add she'd had no chance at all without this intervention, and that we were a long way from success. I also didn't go into the fine points of soul sickness. We had to keep going. Even if the witch died, we were freeing her soul to seek the next world. It wouldn't be able to if we couldn't unshackle her from the illness. Those who succumbed to soul sickness were doomed to wander forever, fettered to the spot they'd died. Unable to move beyond it, they grew hard and bitter. Perfect vessels for Black Magic to co-opt for evil.

Sweat sheened the witch's forehead. I took it as a good sign. She'd been burning up with fever, but it was breaking. Her white face developed blotched places, and deep coughs wracked her thin frame accompanied by bloody froth. The momentary return of activity, something beyond her just lying in an unconscious heap, encouraged me to take a chance.

"I'll take over," I told Rowan. "Remain linked, and mirror exactly what I do."

A quick nod told me she was ready. Gently, gradually, I transitioned the way we were wielding power until I had control of the spell. I couldn't be as cautious as Ro had been. We were running out of time. Despite her brief rally, the witch's body was nearly done.

"Stay with me." I wasn't sure if my words were for Rowan or the witch, but I was back to English.

In a quick, hard burst, I funneled a torrent of fire right into the heart of the blackness. The witch shrieked as pain scorched her, but Rowan's magic didn't falter. She trusted me. Her faith meant everything.

The nucleus of the black place turned clear. I hung onto my spell until all that remained was the thinnest of gray margins. Satisfied I'd done all I could, I cut my casting. I could deal with the remnants in a less destructive way. Sweat flowed down my body, but I was already so wet it scarcely mattered.

The witch's cries had thinned to whimpers. Rowan lay

next to her and gathered her in her arms. "Hilda. Oh Hilda. Come on. Reach for me. You can do this."

I coiled what was left of my casting, neutralizing it. Hilda wasn't strong enough for me to ferret out the remnants of the soul sickness. That could wait. Absent the heart of the thing, it wouldn't keep growing.

A man, Patrick, knelt next to me. "Will she be all right?" he asked in a hoarse voice.

"I hope so. At least she has a chance."

"What was it?"

"Soul sickness." As I said the words, Hilda's spirit left off circling and melted back into her body. Relief rattled from me in a great, shuddering breath. It was the first positive sign she might recover.

Hilda wrapped a thin arm around Rowan and croaked, "It will be all right now, dear. Might I have tea?"

"Of course." Rowan kissed the witch's forehead and started to get up.

"I'll brew a pot for her," one of the other witches said. "You stay put."

Patrick tapped my arm. "Look, mate, I'm not trying to be an arse, but how'd she get it?"

I turned to look at him. Dark circles scribed beneath his eyes. "Has she been outside?" I asked.

"Aye, she went into town to retrieve a few things from one of the gardening shops."

"Alone?" I quirked one brow.

Patrick nodded. "She said it would be fine. Town isn't that far, and—"

"You must be warded if you leave this place." I cut him off. "And it would be better if several of you stuck together."

He set his mouth in a terse line. "Of course we will. From now on. I've never seen anyone sicken so fast, and I've never heard of this soul sickness."

"You wouldn't have. I cleared the Nine Worlds of it centuries before your birth."

Patrick drew his gray brows into a frown. "It returned because of the Breaking, didn't it?"

"It's what I suspect." A quick glance heartened me. Hilda was sitting up. Someone had pushed an ottoman and pillows behind her. Her color was starting to improve, and she was sipping tea. Rowan knelt by her side; relief carved furrows into her forehead and shaped small creases around her eyes.

I stood and walked to her, laying a hand on her shoulder. "Why didn't you call me?"

She tilted her head, and her golden eyes latched onto mine. "Things happened so fast. I'd no sooner teleported inside than I heard the witches Lament for the Dying from upstairs. After that, every scrap of magic and focus was on Hilda. I was afraid if I hesitated for even long enough to use telepathy, I'd lose her."

"Could you sense her spirit hovering?"

"Of course." Rowan hesitated. *"The only other time I've felt its like, the person died. I was plenty scared. Hilda has been like a mother to me. And she's Tansy's aunt."*

She patted Hilda's shoulder and pushed to her feet, wincing as stiff joints and muscles were slow to cooperate. The witches had surrounded Hilda and were offering her bits of food to go with the herbal tea. I wanted to talk with Rowan, but first I scanned Hilda.

The residual shards from the soul sickness were breaking up. It appeared my job was done, but I'd check again before we left.

Hilda looked right at me out of very blue eyes. "Thank you."

My knees weren't overly fond of my next move. They creaked as I hunkered next to her. Placing a hand on her arm, I said, "You're welcome. You had soul sickness. It's a fast-moving taint that would have turned you into a vessel for Black Magic."

Her eyes widened. "Damn. I knew it was bad, but that's horrible. Must have happened yesterday when I went to town. I started feeling puny right after I got back here, and —" She waved a hand weakly to one side. "Could I have infected anyone else?"

"Nay. Doesn't work that way."

"Whew. Thank the goddess for small favors."

I squeezed her arm lightly. "Rest. Luckily, the recovery is nearly as quick as the fall into darkness."

She scootched higher against the pillows. "Thank you again. Ro was doing her best, but she couldn't have saved me without your help."

My mouth curved into a smile. "Cuts both ways, Hilda. Our magic is additive. My intervention wouldn't have been so successful without her."

She smiled back. It made her look young again. "Well then, I've already thanked her, and now I'll offer a prayer to the goddess. Surely She was looking out for me because if you'd shown up even half an hour later, my soul would have been consigned to purgatory."

I stood again. It was a bit smoother than the last time. Beckoning to Rowan, I moved out into the hall. Zelli was nowhere in sight. I had no idea when she'd left. And I hadn't seen Quade since entering Inverlochy.

Rowan stumbled from weariness as she walked to my side. I put an arm around her, and she didn't shuck it off. "This is why I can't be gone for very long," she muttered.

I understood. "When did the dragon leave?"

"Right after you took over the spell. She never was here, but upstairs in the council chamber."

So it had been a projection after all. Made more sense than her being able to alter her physical form. My guess was Quade would be with her. I got us headed for the stone staircase, and we started up it.

I was breathing faster by the time we finished the crap ton of stairs.

"Should've teleported," Rowan panted.

I snorted. "Do you have any magic left? For anything?"

"Probably sufficient to teleport from downstairs to up here, but not much more."

"Mine isn't doing any better," I informed her.

We trudged along the broad upper hall. The tall, imposing doors of the council chamber had been propped open. Zelli and Quade stood at the far end of the enormous room. As I thought about it, this was probably the only space in Inverlochy Castle large enough to accommodate both of them.

Once we'd crossed the expanse of marble floor, Quade patted two chairs. "Sit. Afore ye fall down."

I didn't require a second invitation and slid into one.

"Ye did a nice piece of work downstairs," Quade said.

"It was a joint effort," I replied. It wasn't false humility. With Rowan's magic linked to mine, we'd pulled off a small miracle.

"Thanks for your help," Rowan told Zelli.

The dragon shrugged amid clattering scales. "I dinna do much. 'Twas mostly you."

"Whilst we stood outside," Quade addressed his words to me, "ye asked what had transformed dragons from watching and waiting to preparing for battle."

I nodded. I hadn't asked that precisely, but I had thought it, which told me the dragon had helped himself to the contents of my mind.

"The reason"—Quade paused, perhaps for emphasis—"is her." He pointed a talon at Rowan.

She'd been rubbing her temples. Dropping her hands into her lap, she looked from one dragon to the other. "Huh? I don't understand."

"Ye will," Zelli said firmly.

"Aye, we shall tell you about a prophecy," Quade said.

Something about his tone worried me, and I scooted my chair close enough to Rowan's to lay a hand on her thigh. Ceridwen had also alluded to a foretelling that had to do with Rowan and me.

Rather than pushing me away, she gripped my hand with her own. Together, we waited for something I was fairly certain would change our lives in ways we never could have anticipated. When Ceridwen had nattered on about a revelation, courtesy of her cauldron, I'd figured she was blowing smoke to keep from being imprisoned.

Maybe the canny old bitch had truly known something.

Silence grew long as I waited for the dragons to begin. My eyelids felt like they were weighted down with stones, and every muscle in my body ached, but I could hold on a little longer before I gave in and slept.

Hearing the witches' Lament for the Dying had driven a knife into my heart. I'd been so scared I was too late. And when I saw who they were gathered around, the knife twisted deeper. While I cared for the entire coven, Hilda had always been there for me. She'd kept my tears a secret and shored me up when I needed a swift boot in the ass.

I'd finally told her who I really was, and she'd never breathed a word.

Zelli's magic helped, but I'd had no idea how to stop the spreading sheet of evil creeping through Hilda's body. Even after Bjorn added his magic to the mix, things were far from certain. I knew how exhausted he was, but he ran wide open to save my friend. He didn't stop to ask questions. Nope. He dove in with full afterburners engaged. No escaping it. The man had a generous heart. Some would have considered his altruism a weakness, but I loved him for it.

Yeah, there it was. Every time I turned around I ran smack dab into my growing feelings for Bjorn. Every time we linked our power, it drew me closer to him. When he touched me, offering comfort, I didn't have the strength—or the will—to pull away.

I might be conflicted about him, but I wouldn't leave the witches alone again. Not for more than a few hours. I still had to check on the other group, the ones beneath Ben Nevis. I was dragging, so tired putting one foot ahead of the other was a challenge, but I'd look in on them as soon as we left Inverlochy.

Once Hilda was out of danger, my plan had been to touch base with the dragons and go, but it wasn't going to happen. The dragons part was an affirmative, but leaving wouldn't occur anytime soon. Upstairs, in the council chamber where I'd hidden behind wall hangings as a child, I waited for my fate to be delivered—from two dragons no less. Destinies are strange things. You can run, but you can't hide. Fate always catches up with you, eventually. I'd assumed Mother was lying when she'd said her cauldron warned her about Bjorn and me. But Quade just alluded to a divination with me at its center.

Surely, the two had to be related. There couldn't be two prophecies about me. He hadn't mentioned Bjorn, so perhaps Mother had made up that part. After such a long pause, my worries shot through the roof, Quade settled on his haunches across from us and began to speak.

"Long ago when the world was still very young—" he began.

I leaned forward, lulled by the same words that began all

the old tales. And then I got a grip. This wasn't going to be a sweet story. No happy endings here. Not unless I clawed flesh from bone to make it happen. Even then, I wasn't at all certain anything I could do would make a difference.

I was strong, but far from invincible. If it weren't for Bjorn and his magic and his knowledge, Hilda would be worse than dead. I knew a little bit about soul sickness, and it wasn't pretty...

"Celtic and Norse deities were perhaps not the best of friends," Quade continued, drawing my focus back to him, "but they visited one another frequently. Dragons had only recently ventured beyond Fire Mountain. We were still uncertain of the Nine Worlds and the infinite array of borderworlds stretching through the universe. Yet many of us were hungry to expand our horizons."

"We were distrustful of the gods," Zelli said. "They always wanted something from us. It was as if they viewed us as an exotic type of steed, and they resorted to strong magic to compel us to take them on our backs."

"It dinna work," Quade growled. "All it did was add to our misgivings about interacting with anyone outside of dragonkind. Unfortunately, a few of us dinna view things the same way. They enjoyed mingling with those who weren't dragons. Years passed, mostly without incident."

"Aye." Zelli picked up the thread. "During that time, the first Dragon Heir was born, spawn of a dragon and a Norse warrior."

Bjorn held a hand in front of him, fingers splayed. "May I ask a question?" When Zelli nodded, he went on, "By Norse warrior, do you mean one of the Valkyries?"

"Aye, and it created a major meltdown all around," Zelli said. "Odin was furious. He considered the winged women his personal property. The dragon in question refused to apologize. The resulting child was hidden away for a verra long time."

Bjorn was nodding. "Hel kept him safe in her dominion."

"Ye know the tale?" Quade raised both scaled brows.

"Of course. Hel refused to reveal the Dragon Heir's location until Odin gave her his word he wouldn't harm the lad who'd grown into a fearless fighter."

"Scarcely a lad." Zelli puffed steam. "By the time his identity was revealed, he'd passed his first century."

Bjorn had asked a question, so I assumed it was all right if I did. "What happened to all the other Dragon Heirs? Surely, they're still alive."

"We are getting ahead of things," Zelli told me, "but yes they are. Eventually, all of them wearied of being harangued by the Norse gods and retired to Fire Mountain with the dragons they'd bonded with."

"How many is that?" I risked a second question.

"Six, I believe," Zelli said. "And now, no more questions from either of you until Quade and I are done."

"Nidhogg and our dragon elders made it abundantly clear we were not to breed with anyone other than dragons," Quade said. "Despite that prohibition, some of the gods made it difficult to say no to them. Arianrhod was a prime example. The Celts 'virgin huntress' is a garden-variety slut.

"Dragons claimed she blinded them with magic and seduced them, but I never believed they dinna realize what they were doing. At least she had the good sense not to become pregnant."

"Our council of elders," Zelli continued, "includes two blind seers. One fine day, they raced into our meeting room in Fire Mountain breathless and bent out of shape. They'd seen something in their pool. Both of them looked; both came up with the same conclusions."

Breath caught in my throat, and I grasped Bjorn's hand tighter. Whatever had to do with me, it was nearly here. I felt a shadow hovering, ready to smash down on my head and smother me.

Quade folded his forelegs across his black-scaled chest. "At that time, the few Dragon Heirs had all resulted from matings with Norse women." He sent a stream of ash scudding across the marble floor. "Not that dragons weren't fucking the Celts, but none of them had gotten pregnant."

"Our seers foretold a Dragon Heir born of a Celtic god," Zelli said in a strained voice. "They further predicted her birth would be a harbinger of doom, perhaps presaging the end of all worlds."

Already narrow, my throat closed completed. I gasped for air like a landed fish, but couldn't move any to my lungs. Damn Ceridwen to Hell and back a thousand times. She'd given birth to a disaster. Me. I was the herald of doom. Everything bad that was happening to Earth—to the Nine Worlds—was because of me.

Bjorn's magic washed over me, warm, soothing, calming. The next time my starved lungs made a grab to breathe, air flowed into them. A spasm of coughing followed. When I could talk, I gasped, "Did the Celts know of the prediction?"

"Of course, they did," Quade snarled.

Zelli sent fire whizzing outward. "Aye, we made damn good and sure they understood they needed to rein in their lust."

I covered my face with my hand and fought the bitter sting of tears. What in the unholy fuck was wrong with Mother? She'd known, and she'd done it anyway. When I lowered my hand, I stumbled to my feet and bowed before the dragons. "I am so sorry. You can't kill me, but I could go far away. To a distant borderworld. Maybe if I'm gone—"

"Good of you to offer," Zelli cut me off, "but it willna help."

"Then what can I do?" Desolation scoured me. Guilt tromped over my soul. This might not be my fault, but it scarcely mattered. I was the vector of a disaster that could well wipe out everything.

"We canna undo what your mother set in motion," Quade told me.

"We hoped the divination wasn't true," Zelli said. "Many times they are not. 'Tis why we did nothing for so long, despite knowing of your existence."

"After the Breaking, we brought the matter to our elders. Nidhogg counseled us to wait. To see if Odin could repair the damage," Quade said. "The thing about any prophecy is ye must first view an event, and then evaluate it to determine if 'tis the leading edge of what was predicted."

"The only true test is time," Zelli agreed.

I rocked from foot to foot, feeling dirty, like soiled goods. I had no idea what to do next, but standing here mired in self-pity wasn't going to help anybody. I slapped my forehead with my palm.

"The witches. I have to check on the others."

"There are more?" Zelli sounded surprised.

"Aye," Bjorn told her. "Most of them live beneath Ben Nevis in that cave system the Celts hogged out eons ago."

I tried to stand tall, but my shoulders were too heavy. I folded my hands behind me and said, "Thank you for telling me. I have no idea what I'll do with the information, but—"

"You said the Celts knew of the prophecy," Bjorn spoke over me. "Do my kinsmen know?"

Quade shook his head. "Not unless the Celts told them."

My tired eyes widened. The council meeting. Our attendance was even more critical now. I formed words out of the twisted mess my brain had turned into. "After I make certain the witches are all right, Bjorn and I will crash—er, show up at—a joint meeting in Asgard."

"Who will be at this meeting?" Quade asked.

"Many Celts," Bjorn said. "I was hiding when they arrived."

"Hiding? Why?" Zelli shot him a pointed look out of her whirling eyes.

"It was after I'd been shanghaied. I told you how I ended up in Asgard. The Celts stood between me and Bifrost. I had to wait for them to leave."

The dragon nodded. "I see." She smacked Quade with a foreleg. "Shall we attend this gathering too?"

"I doona see why not," he replied. "We're in this up to our wings as it is. Besides"—more fiery ash shot from his mouth and bounced harmlessly off a crystal wall—"if ye and

I are there, 'twill make it far more difficult for them to refuse to admit Rowan and Bjorn."

I'd been worried about going to all the trouble of showing up in Asgard only to be given the boot. "Thank you. I appreciate it," I mumbled.

"Double thanks from me," Bjorn said. "Odin can be unreasonable, and if things with the Celts aren't going well, he may not be in the mood to listen to anything Ro or I have to say."

My mind was sluggish and well past the point of overload, but something worked its way through. "If the Celts knew of the prophecy, it means at least Arawn and Gwydion put two and two together," I said.

"Why them?" Zelli asked.

Bjorn hit the high points of our impromptu gathering in this very room with Arawn, Gwydion, Mother, Odin, Ysien, and Nidhogg.

"So that is how Ceridwen ended up in Fire Mountain," Quade muttered. "Ysien wasna overly clear about where he found her. Or precisely why she's sharing the Morrigan's cell. And I dinna have time to question him."

"Pfft. He would not have answered you," Zelli growled. "This means Nidhogg will be at the meeting as well. Good. The Celts might be a wee bit on the slow side, but I'm certain they've figured things out."

"I doubt they'll be forthcoming with Odin and his nobles, though. 'Twould make them look bad," Quade said. "Verra bad. She"—he pointed at me—"lived beneath their noses for years, yet no one bothered to look closely enough to figure out who she was."

"What are we waiting for?" Magic bubbled around Zelli. I could almost see her rubbing her talons together as she anticipated confronting the Celts for their moral slippage.

"We have to stop by the caves beneath Ben Nevis," I reminded her.

She rolled her whirling eyes. The net effect made me dizzy. Clearly, the witches might be my priority, but they weren't hers. The dragon clacked her double rows of teeth together. The noise ratcheted through me. Damn, but my nerves were shot.

"We shall stop there first. Both of you. Get on. We teleport from here," Zelli ordered.

"But it's not very far," I protested.

"I am in a hurry," Zelli informed me. "Teleporting is quicker than flying. Now get on."

Bjorn was already astride Quade. A blast of dragon magic moved me to Zelli's back. There'd been a time when I would have protested, told the dragon I made my own decisions about where I went and with whom.

I was tired. Dejection beat a path through me. There had to be a way to remove me from the Nine Worlds. Surely, if that happened, the damaged lands would begin to recover. If I was some kind of magnet for evil, not having me here had to make a difference.

The council chamber's walls turned liquid before they vanished. Almost immediately, the hard-packed dirt outside Ben Nevis's cave system took their place.

"*We shall find a path.*" Zelli's voice reverberated through my skull. "*Ye will come to terms with the knowledge ye've been given.*" After a pause, she started up again. "*Only cowards flee. Ye are far from a craven. Stand tall, Dragon Heir. I am proud to be your bonded one."*

My eyes widened. *"What? So I wasn't just a temporary assignment to rehearse fighting skills?"*

Soft laughter met my question. *"Nay. Much as Ysien would have liked to characterize it as such. When I said I volunteered, 'twas for far more than a single practice session."*

I wasn't sure how many more revelations I could absorb without my head bursting into a million pieces. Jumping down from Zelli's back, I waited for Bjorn to join me. I'd bounded into Inverlochy by myself. This time, I'd be smarter about things.

A staunch *mrowww* rolled from the cave's entrance, followed by Mort giving me nine kinds of shit for abandoning him. Got to hand it to that cat. He totally ignored the dragons as he sauntered to me and wove his furry body around my legs.

I hunkered next to him and scratched his ears. When I held out my arms, he jumped into them and thence to his favorite spot around my neck. Tansy raced outside.

"I knew it had to be you. Mort's been in a funk ever since you left. Whoa!" Her eyes rounded until white showed all around the irises. "Dragons. In the sky is one thing, but—"

I scrambled upright and scooped her into my arms. She hugged me back. All the while, Mort purred like a little locomotive. My heart hurt. I loved the witches. I didn't want to go anywhere. Not Asgard. Not Valhalla. Not Vanaheim. I wanted to stay right where I was.

Yeah. I longed for my life back. The old one where the

biggest excitement in my day was checking on the Breaking spot.

It was never going to happen. Best case, I'd drop by long enough to make sure disaster hadn't struck. Tansy and the witches might understand. Mort never would.

I untangled her arms from my neck and said, "I'd like you to meet the dragons."

"Me! Nah. They don't care who I am," Tansy sputtered.

Zelli puffed steam and said, "We care for all who walk the good side of the road, little witch. I am Zelli."

"And I am Quade." He added more steam to settle around Tansy, Bjorn, and me.

She dropped an awkward curtsey. "Tansy Thorne. P-pleased to meet you."

"I'm guessing if you and Mort are out here, everyone inside is doing all right?" I said.

She nodded, unable to stop staring at the dragons. "Yes. We're all fine. Um, how is everyone at Inverlochy?"

I hesitated. She wasn't paying close attention to me, so I could soft-pedal the truth. "Hilda had a small run-in with—"

My words dragged Tansy around. "She's okay. Right? Not hurt or anything?"

"She will be fine," Bjorn reassured her. "I treated her myself."

Tansy's green eyes narrowed. "You brought Ro back when she was sick and well past the scope of my healing. Thank you for your efforts on my aunt's behalf."

"You are most welcome." Bjorn inclined his head.

"All appears to be well here," Zelli said.

"Aye, we must be on our way," Quade added.

The smile on Tansy's face faded. "You're leaving again? But you just got here."

I shut my eyes for a moment. When I opened them, I stood so I faced her and placed my hands on her shoulders. "I would prefer things to be different. There's nowhere I'd rather be than here, but Earth is in trouble."

I left out the part about it being my fault. Maybe not directly, but consequences were all that mattered. My presence was the catalyst that had spawned...everything.

"I have to leverage my magic to try to undo the damage Mother created. The dragons are my allies. Mine and Bjorn's."

"Will you ever be back here for good?" Tansy asked in a small voice.

I feared not, but I refused to rob both her and me of hope. I tilted her chin upward with a grubby finger. "I want to be here. You wish me to be. Maybe our combined desires will catch the attention of the goddess, and—"

"It's all right." She grasped my hand in both of hers, lowering it. "Do what you have to. I understand. So will the rest of us."

My throat was raw, scratchy, and unpleasantly thick. I refused to cry in front of Tansy. It would really worry her if I did. She might be young, but she was plenty smart enough to read between the lines. Reaching back, I untangled Mort from my neck and held him to my chest. Breathing into his matted fur, I told him how much I loved him.

He'd stopped purring. Almost as if he knew I was moments from deserting him once again.

"I'll take him." Tansy held out her arms.

I placed Mort into them. With the unerring instincts of the young, Tansy turned and walked back inside. Long goodbyes wouldn't change the outcome. All they'd do would tear our hearts out.

Steam blanketed me and Bjorn.

"Onto my back, Dragon Heir." Zelli's tone wasn't sharp, but neither could I ignore her command.

"We're teleporting, right?" I asked her.

"In a manner of speaking. We shall enter Valhalla as befits a Dragon Heir. In all our combined glory with ye riding me."

"Combined glory, huh?" I glanced at my blood-and-dirt-spattered clothing.

"Perhaps the Valkyries will have something for ye to wear," Quade said.

"Ha! Not fucking likely since I killed one of them. Besides, armor isn't very comfortable." I shook myself. No reason to go inside the caves and change. I could give a shit less what Odin thought of me.

Bjorn wrapped a hand around my arm. After a quick squeeze, he headed for Quade but stopped shy of the black dragon. "Am I riding too?"

"Aye, Master Sorcerer, jump on. We shall make a grand entry." Fire shot from his jaws. "Let Odin try to displace us."

"It wouldna be Odin, but Nidhogg," Zelli corrected him.

Quade shrugged. "I've had a bellyful of him too. If he hadn't been so mired in dragons never looking beyond our own concerns, we wouldna be in this mess."

"I suppose he assumes we can retire to Fire Mountain while the rest of the worlds disintegrate," Zelli muttered.

While the two of them spread their wings, I vaulted onto Zelli's back. I was starting to think of her as my dragon, which was probably a mistake. The safest path was still walking tall by myself.

No attachments meant I couldn't get hurt. Leaving the witches behind while I battled for the future of Earth was about all the loss I could stand.

I sat astride Quade as his power soared around us. Somehow, we were teleporting and flying at the same time. At least, that's how it appeared. Magic has a way of masking the obvious, sometimes. A fine, grayish mist surrounded us, different from my usual teleport spells where I floated in a black void. My soul ached for Rowan. I'd seen the pain and hurt and fury when the dragons told her about the prediction surrounding her birth.

I still couldn't believe Ceridwen was as oblivious as it appeared. Even after she'd flaunted the dragons' prohibition, and was faced with the results, she could have done so many things to prepare her daughter. Instead, she made things worse by instigating the rift that had broken Midgard. Was she caught up in the prophecy as well? Merely an instrument, albeit a powerful one, someone else had shaped to do their bidding?

I didn't exactly view the Welsh sorceress in that light.

She struck me as someone who'd come out with claws extended and guns blazing at the first hint anyone was manipulating her. My thoughts ranged to Rowan's mysterious father. Why was he nowhere in the Nine Worlds? Had the other dragons banished him? Had he banished himself?

To put a finer point on it, was he wrapped up in a despicable plot to destroy the Nine Worlds? Men were obviously a weakness for Ceridwen. She'd have been flattered by a dragon's attentions, particularly since the liaison was forbidden fruit.

I probably didn't have much time, so I refocused on the upcoming council meeting. If I knew Odin at all—and I thought I did—he'd be so spun out at the Celts for both Rowan's birth and Ceridwen's misshapen spell, he'd be casting blame in a wide net.

The Celts wouldn't remain defensive—or apologetic—for long. My best guess was the council meeting would have devolved into a shit-slinging contest. *"We need to hurry,"* I told Quade.

"Ye think so?" Sarcasm sharpened his tone.

I switched things up. Worrying about things I had no control over was a waste of energy and magic. *"I understand why Rowan is astride Zelli, but why am I riding you?"*

"So the four of us would arrive at the same time."

Mmph. Meant he wasn't going to tell me. I was fully capable of teleporting and showing up more or less along with them. I clamped my jaws shut. Damn Nidhogg to Faery. He was intent on keeping a very close eye on me.

Clearly, the stone wasn't enough. Not now that Rowan was in full discovery mode and figuring out who she was.

I'd been wrong about Zelli being Nidhogg's latest spy to watch over me. It had to be Quade since it was the only explanation for his sudden presence.

Nidhogg's lack of faith hurt my feelings. And my pride. Did he believe I was so petty I'd turn tail and run at the first hint of danger? I winced. The old me might not have exactly made a run for the gates, but neither did I welcome battle situations.

All that was changing. I was changing. Until Rowan told me to go away, I'd do my utmost to ensure her safety. I didn't fully understand the reasons our magic was so attuned, but I'd bet my last spell book, there was a prophecy around us somewhere.

Ceridwen was a grand mistress of weaving lies with truth. She'd alluded to a divination from that blasted kettle of hers that foretold disaster for everyone else if Ro and I blended our power. I sat on a snort. That bit of foreseeing had boomeranged right back in her face.

Ro and I meeting and working together had indeed spelled her downfall. I considered it a major win—for everyone. Certainly for the witches doing everything they could to coax crops out of the rich soil around Inverlochy Castle.

"Get ready," Quade turned his head and eyed me over one shoulder. Neither green nor silver, his eyes had shaded to many hues of gold.

"As in?" I prodded. *"Ward myself?"*

"Nay. Wards willna help. This next part will be unpleasant but verra brief," he told me.

The warning was timely. Whatever we flew through turned from cold to hot enough to burn if it had been normal air. Concerned with searing my lungs, I cupped a hand over my mouth. Sweat poured down my body as I attempted to adapt. Quade bellowed as we flew through what felt like a phalanx of blades. I expected long rips in my garments, but they came through unscathed. They were also mostly dry, probably from the intense heat.

"What was that?" I shouted, but the dragon didn't answer.

The mists we'd been transiting cleared, replaced by the golden streets of Asgard. Zelli and Rowan soared off to our right. Asgard is truly lovely. I always assumed Odin designed it, which is odd since I've never otherwise viewed him as having a shred of artistic ability or taste.

Unlike the river lands occupied by Vanaheim with mountains in the distance, Asgard is rough country. Built in the midst of mountainous terrain, only the rare byway is level. Valhalla's golden walls soar above the crest of Asgard. An imposing structure with many floors, it's been different every time I've looked at it. Today, its gates stood open. Flags flew from all the parapets. Each of the Nine Worlds has its own flag, but today the Celtic banner blazoned with a roaring lion flew as well.

I took it as a good sign. "Looks as if no one's left yet," I muttered.

"Aye, and a good thing," Quade replied.

Rather than landing and walking through the gates as I'd

assumed we'd do, the dragon circled. It gave me an unprecedented view of just how vast Valhalla is. I'd never been invited within, only stood in the front courtyard.

Sections extended up and down the bluff where the castle perched, some at such precarious angles magic shimmered to hold them in place. A central open area held wondrous beasts, along with Sleipnir, Odin's eight-legged black destrier, and his ravens.

I started to ask Quade what we were doing—why we hadn't landed—but it wasn't my place to question him. Hell, it wasn't actually my place to be astride his back, but it would be counterproductive to complain too loudly. Something about riding him sang to every fiber of my being. I wondered if I'd perhaps been a dragon rider in another life. That's how right it felt, like a serious case of déja vu.

When I glanced at Rowan, she looked as comfortable as me, but she had reasons. I didn't. A staunch bugle brought my head whipping around. Another dragon was somewhere close. It hadn't sounded like Nidhogg, but I wasn't exactly adept at recognizing his dragon noises.

"I wondered if she'd greet us," Quade said. I noticed he'd switched to mind speech.

"She" didn't refer to Nidhogg. I started to search with magic but changed my mind. It would only piss the dragon off. Not Quade, but the one who was close enough for us to hear her. I craned my head about. Quade's neck was a big blind spot, but between him shifting course and my efforts I was able to see around it.

Blood-red scales flashed in the same sun that illuminated Valhalla. The effect was so surreal, it might have been a painting. I put two and two together. The dragon heading for us had to be Dewi, the Celts' dragon goddess. All dragons are grace personified in the air, and she was no exception. Her long neck was held at a jaunty angle, and huge crimson wings cleaved the air. Her eyes were a mix of green and gold.

She bugled again. Quade and Zelli bugled back. I considered raising my hand in greeting, but I was out of my league. Besides, the dragons had moved from trumpeting to steam as they greeted one another. Dewi made a point of flying near and bathing Rowan in billows of it.

I assumed it was as close to an apology as dragons ever got.

Puffy, white clouds thickened until I couldn't see Ro, so I felt for her with magic.

"*All is well.*" Her silvery mind voice reassured me.

Words knocked against each other. So much I wanted to say, but the dragons would hear every word. We'd begun to circle lower. I assumed we were heading for the castle, but Dewi led the way through a steep draw with snow on both sides to a small, green meadow below.

The dragons touched down heavily on thick, wet grass dotted with tiny white flowers. The blossoms that ended up crushed beneath their feet gave off a heady odor. Rose mixed with evergreens is as close as I can come to describing it.

I fashioned a bit of magic into a cushion to soften my egress from Quade's back and ran to Rowan's side. Being next to her felt like my place as much as riding the dragon had. A chilly voice intruded and reminded me I'd do better if I kept my expectations within reason. I might be the master sorcerer for the Nine Worlds, but it scarcely put me in the same league with dragons. Or Dragon Heirs.

Rowan was half dragon. She was claiming her heritage, and I'd support her every step of the way. Even if it meant she moved beyond my star. She extended a hand, and I clasped it. Wonder sheeted from her. I guessed she was still as awestruck about dragon riding as I was.

Dewi lumbered to where we stood, stopping a short distance away and folding her wings across her back. As if by design, Quade flanked her on one side, Zelli on the other. They were beautiful—and deadly. I may have shared Vanaheim with dragons, but I'd never spent any time with them except from a distance.

Until Nidhogg singled me out to spy on Midgard.

"I wished a word in private afore we joined the others," Dewi said. "First, I would offer my apologies to you, Dragon Heir." Her gaze fell on Rowan.

Color rose to her cheeks, and she said, "No reason to apologize. You didn't know. Neither did I."

Dewi angled her head to one side; fire flashed from her jaws. "Aye, but that mother of yours did. 'Twould be a lie if I said I dinna notice ye were different as a hatchling, but I never took the time to look more closely."

More fire flew, and she shook her head from side to side. "I trusted Ceridwen. We have history, she and I. No more. I have wiped her from my mind. If I have my way, she will be expunged from the rolls of the Celtic deities. She doesna deserve to be part of our pantheon. Not after what she did."

"I'm guessing that's the consensus from others at the

council meeting?" Zelli jerked her head toward the draw we'd just flown through.

Ash and smoke blew past Dewi's jaws. "'Tis about the only common ground we've established: a mutual hatred of Ceridwen. She's already begun her punishment—and her banishment shall become permanent. I tried to tell everyone further words were a waste of breath."

"It's simpler to excoriate someone who isn't there than to face the bigger problem, which is what our next steps are," I spoke up. Three sets of whirling dragon eyes zapped me.

Before I could stammer through an apology, Quade said, "He's correct. Have ye made aught in the way of progress?"

Dewi shook her head. "Odin spent the first few hours telling us what a bunch of witless fools we were. After he'd thanked us for coming."

"I'm surprised my erstwhile kin sat still for a dressing down," Rowan muttered. "It's nothing like how I remember them."

Dewi crossed her forelegs over her scaled chest. "Ye got a raw deal, child. Ye never saw the power and the glory of what it means to be a Celtic god. Regardless, we should return. I doona trust what type of deals will be dealt in my absence."

"We weren't exactly invited to this meeting," I said.

She blared laughter. "Since when did that ever stop you?"

I had no idea how to reply. She made it sound as if she knew me from somewhere. I'd have told her she'd mistaken me for someone else, but she might have seen it as rude. I drew magic around me, intent on teleporting to the far side of the draw and Valhalla.

"Uh-uh." Quade shook a talon at me. "Onto my back. A show of strength shall ensure us a seat at the table."

"Pfft." Dewi spread her wings. "No one will tell you to leave. If they try, I shall name you my guests. Besides, since when do dragons concern themselves with others' opinions?"

"We doona," Zelli said. "Neither Quade nor I held concerns about ourselves, but Rowan is a living reminder of…many failings."

She stiffened next to me. "None of those failings are mine."

"While we agree with your assessment," Quade replied in about as mild a tone as I've ever heard from one of the beasts, "others may not."

Rowan stepped away from me and tossed her head back, standing straight. "I will teleport into the castle and find my way to the meeting room. I won't ride in on Zelli's coattails—or anyone else's. According to Mother, whatever is brewing includes both Bjorn and me. We will see you inside."

No need for me to add to what she'd said. I went back to putting a spell together. Nothing fancy. We weren't going very far. While I liked the idea of more time on Quade's back, I appreciated Rowan's arguments. Neither of us were gods. She was a hell of a lot closer than I'd ever be, but still the Norse-Celtic bunch had to accept us on our own merits.

Or not at all.

Dewi had said she'd force their hand by claiming guest rights. Such an action would allow us to sit and listen, but not necessarily to open our mouths. No reason to be there if we couldn't forward opinions. I had a few. I'd probably spent far more time in Midgard than anyone except Odin. His ventures there with the Hunt had a whole different slant than mine.

He was on the prowl for spoils while I was trying to keep Midgard from decompensating further.

My casting was ready. I beckoned to Rowan, and she moved next to me. Draping us in power, I loosed my enchantment. Before the meadow dropped away, I saw all three dragons, wings spread, flying toward Valhalla.

"Gutsy," I told Rowan and draped an arm around her to hold her next to me through our brief travel jaunt.

She fisted a hand and punched the air. "I'll be damned if I end up beholden to anyone. I respect Zelli, but I'm not about to let her start scripting my moves. If I fall into that trap, there was no reason to leave the Celts." She paused for a beat. "Do you know where we're going once we're inside?"

"No, but I trust my magic to lead us right to them."

Rowan laughed, and it lightened the tension flowing from her. "No kidding, huh? All that power concentrated in one room will be impossible to miss."

I tweaked my spell and brought us out on one of the castle's upper floors. The sound of voices reached us as I unwound my casting. "Ready?" I asked.

"Never readier," Rowan replied.

Together, we walked along a scarred wooden floor. Battered armor lined the walls; a collection of mismatched tables and chairs were scattered at intervals. From below me, the voices switched to a raucous drinking song punctuated by the sounds of shouts and scuffling. It had to be the dead who also lived in these halls. A quick scan yielded thousands of souls, all vying for position. I'd heard Odin corralled them in a lower level. Quite a contrast to Hel; the dead entrusted to her care wandered freely.

Maybe a valiant death wasn't such a coup after all. Given my druthers, I'd rather be with Hel than here. At least she allowed her charges unrestricted run of her realm. Most of them, anyway.

A solid door blocked our way. "It's been spelled shut," Rowan said.

I'd figured that same thing out but recognized the binding. "I can neutralize it," I told her.

"Do it," she urged. "It's better than knocking like a couple of beggars. Both Zelli and Quade were big on the whole show-of-strength idea, and I agree with them."

Extending my hands, I felt for the ends of the working that sealed the tall wooden doors. Unlike the ornate ones that barred the Celts' council chamber, these were a far simpler design. But the doors weren't my concern. As I expected, whoever had sealed them hadn't taken a whole lot of care.

Why should they? Asgard had its own set of built-in safeguards. It wasn't the kind of place that encouraged folk to drop in. If Bifrost didn't snare you, Valhalla's main gates held power of their own.

Today was the first time I'd seen them standing open. Perhaps on the way out, I could get a closer look at the moat. If the lore was correct, sea serpents swam in it, and the water was so deep it touched Yggdrasil's roots.

I located the end of the magical latch and tugged. The

high, double doors snicked open with far less fanfare than I'd expected. One moment, they were shut. The next, they swung inward on huge brass hinges.

Rowan grabbed a door handle and strode into the room with me next to her, winding in my magic as I went. Heavy footsteps and the overpowering smells of hot clay told me the dragons were right behind us. How long had they been there? Had they actually exercised restraint while I unraveled the enchantment holding the doors shut?

Restraint was very undragonlike, but not my primary concern at the moment.

The meeting room was as utilitarian as the rest of Valhalla. About twenty gods and goddesses from both pantheons sat at a long, shiny table made from either mahogany or cherrywood.

Every head turned our way. Every eye appraised us. I felt the sting of magic multiple times as those in attendance took my measure.

"Oh for the love of the Fae, stop it," Rowan sputtered. "You all know who I am." She jerked a thumb my way. "He's with me, and he's done more to ameliorate Midgard's problems than any of the rest of you."

Nidhogg lumbered forward from where he'd been standing near the far wall. Zelli, Quade, and Dewi crossed the large room with its rough-hewn wooden beams until they stood near him.

"Is it your habit to leave doors standing open?" Odin snarled. "Ones ye found closed and forced your way through?"

I resisted snarking back at him and sent a jet of magic over one shoulder. The satisfying *thunk* of slamming doors reached my ears. I dusted my hands together. "There. All fixed."

Where were the birds? And then I remembered I'd seen them in an open courtyard along with Odin's horse, a couple of unicorns, and furry creatures that begged me to bury my fingers in their thick pelts.

"Apologies for being late." Rowan stood tall. I was proud of her.

"I doona recall inviting you at all," Gwydion said. Today, the master enchanter was garbed in a white robe sashed in blue.

"Nope," she agreed cheerfully. "I invited myself. If there's a prophecy in play, and it involves me and Bjorn, we need to be here. Don't you agree?"

Gwydion didn't answer.

Odin let his gaze rest on those seated around his table, moving from one to the next.

"At least ye're not squabbling like a pack of hyenas," Dewi told them. "'Tis an improvement over when I left."

"'Tis as much your fault as anyone's," Thor thundered. His hammer was strapped across his back, and he wore the same type of leather jerkin as his father. Fair hair fell down his chest, and huge hands with thick fingers splayed in front of him.

Odin thumped a fist on the table. "Not productive. We canna go backward. Aye, we have a Dragon Heir in our midst. Our august companions missed that pithy item for a few years, but we've had well over a century, and we dinna figure out who she was, either."

He rose slowly to his feet. Crap, he was huge. And imposing with his single eye that happened to be focused on me. Should I offer to leave? Still in my pocket, the dragonstone pulsed encouragingly. I wished the damn thing could talk. Was it pushing me to depart? Or to remain.

Slow, lazy, as if he had infinite time, Odin's magic began at the top of my head and tracked to my feet and then back again. The desire to erect a protective ward was strong, but I probably couldn't block him. And any efforts along those lines would piss him off. I felt marked, somehow. It was confusing, but I'd sort it later.

He nodded and blew out a long breath. "'Tisn't just the Dragon Heir's recently claimed power in play," he announced to the group. "Bjorn Nighthorse, our primary sorcerer, has been so effective because he is a Dragon Mage. I've known about him forever, but he seemed to have found a niche that fit his talents, so I never worried how best to deploy his ability."

My eyes widened; I fell back a step. "What the hell is that?" I ground out. Despite all my reading and study, I'd never come across such a term. Before Odin could answer, I blundered on. "You're mistaken. It's impossible. My da was a tradesman, my mum a seamstress."

"They're who raised you," Hel agreed from her spot on Odin's left. "But they dinna birth you." Black hair fell around her shoulders. Wrapped in skins that covered most of the exposed bones in her body, she offered the closest she ever came to an encouraging smile.

Rowan gripped my forearm. "Steady," she hissed.

I wasn't having any of it. Except Odin's words held the

stink of truth. And I'd always thought it odd how little magic my parents commanded. Not odd enough to mine for details though.

In that moment, I understood I'd been afraid of what I'd find.

CHAPTER NINE, ROWAN

I did my best to infuse confidence into Bjorn. Odin's revelation had shaken him to his bootstraps. Never mind I had no fucking idea what a Dragon Mage was. One thing was certain, though, something about the Dragon Heir-Dragon Mage combo packed a hell of a one-two magical wallop.

Were we the first? Had there been other Mages who'd teamed up with the Norse version of me? I kept my mouth shut and my questions shuttered. Bjorn needed to take the lead here, not me.

"What in the unholy hell is a Dragon Mage?" Andraste growled. Tall. Blonde. Broad-shouldered. She was garbed in buttery-soft tan leather with a bow strapped across her back. "Is anyone going to answer me?" She narrowed her green eyes and surged to her feet.

I remembered the goddess of war all too well. She'd kicked me out of her way a time or two, as if I'd been an errant mongrel. Anger surged. "Now you want answers?" I skewered her with my gaze and held tight. "After pretending I didn't exist for sixteen years."

"Pfft. Blame your mum for that. We followed her lead. Besides, 'tisn't answers about you I'm after."

"Stop discounting my existence. No matter what Ceridwen may have said or not said, are you incapable of thinking for yourself? Mother's example doesn't excuse your actions." I resisted an urge to hustle to where she stood and punch her dead center in her patronizing face.

A thread of fire ran in front of me with another near enough Andraste to make her hair smoke. "Stand down!" Dewi shouted. "We have bigger problems than your hurt feelings."

More fire arced in front of me. Why wasn't the floor burning?

Arawn pushed to his feet too and turned until he looked both Bjorn and me square in the eyes. "I would know more about Bjorn Nighthorse as well. I am widely read, unlike others within my kinship circle"—he sent a pointed glance at Andraste—"and such a term has never crossed my path. I'd have remembered if it did."

Odin rose from his spot at the head of the table and strode to the dragons. "Nidhogg?"

The Norse dragon lowered his head until it was nearly level with Odin's. "What?" His golden scales took on more of a burnished copper tone in the muted light filtering through dirty windows. Keeping things clean had been relatively high on the Celts' list. Never cost them much since they employed magic to tidy up. Apparently, the Norse deities didn't share a need for sparkling windows, clean floors, or dust-free surfaces.

My mind was skittering off on tangents to avoid the sparks flying between Odin and the dragon lord.

"This is your tale to tell," Odin announced. After a quick glance over one shoulder at Arawn and Andraste, he snarled, "Sit down."

Color me surprised when they complied. I'd expected them to ignore him—or teleport out of the room.

Nidhogg raised one scaled brow, and his eyes whirled faster. "Ye're who blabbed," he observed.

"'Twas long past time for him to know," Odin countered.

"If the him is me"—Bjorn shook me off and stalked nearer the group—"I agree. I don't give two fucks about who tells me, but one of you will before I leave this room."

"Watch yourself." Odin transferred his one-eyed stare to Bjorn.

He rolled his shoulders taller and stared back. "Why should I? If this long-buried secret concerned you, you'd want to know about it."

"That's different," Odin sputtered.

"Nay, 'tisn't." Bjorn switched to Old Norse, perhaps to make a point.

Long moments ticked past. Magic thickened in the room, some protective, some aimed at ferreting out secrets. Hel flowed to her feet, and she walked heavily around the table. I remembered reading somewhere her mother had been a giant, and she stood somewhat taller than Odin, although not nearly so broad.

One of her eyes gleamed red, and truth shimmered about

her in a misty cloud. "Shall it be ye or me?" she asked Nidhogg. "We knew a time would come when we could no longer hold our knowledge secret."

"Ye may have known," the dragon said amid smoke and ash. "I hoped that particular bit of divination would never come to pass."

Glancing from one to the other, suspicions formed, but I kept my mouth shut. Right now, no one was focused on me, and I rather liked it that way.

Hel set her mouth in a grim line; the exposed bones in half her face lent her expression a forbidding aspect. "For the Celts who may not be well-versed in our legends, I am Hel. I rule over both Niflheim and Hel, our realm of the dead.

"Once I walked these halls, but my kinsmen"—she spread her arms wide and a bitter laugh bubbled from her —"dinna care for how I looked. 'Twas how I ended up tending the souls who dinna die courageously in battle."

"Ye could have remained," Odin growled.

"Your memory is short," she retorted. "Ye're who banished me."

He glared at her but didn't contradict her statement.

"Shall I continue?" She arched both black brows, but she wasn't asking a question. Not really. I had a feeling Hel did what she wanted, perhaps a byproduct of being fathered by Loki, the original my-way-or-the-highway god.

"Nay. Since ye're determined, I shall pick up our story." Nidhogg pushed around Odin and shuffled to where Hel stood. "I visited Niflheim on many occasions. Hel and I grew...close."

"Ye were there because I called off the serpents and

allowed you blood from the murderers and thieves in my care," Hel noted in dulcet tones.

Nidhogg held out a foreleg. Hel reached up to clasp it. "At first, aye," he agreed, "but after a while, my visits were because of you."

Her harsh expression softened, and I looked away. Whatever passed between the two of them felt personal, private. I shouldn't even be here to witness it, yet I was but one of many. Every eye in the large room was on Hel and the dragon. The din of side conversations had died away.

"I was lonely," Hel went on despite Nidhogg's pronouncement he would be the one to tell their story. "One day—"

"Aye, and I recall it verra well," the dragon rumbled.

"One day," she went on, "I borrowed liberally from my father's magic and tricked you. We dinna mate. Such is forbidden, but I cast a spell and took your seed—"

"Are ye trying to tell me ye're my mother?" Bjorn's voice cracked. He couldn't have looked more flummoxed if a meteor had flamed to life in a corner of the room.

Hel nodded. "At first, I planned to keep you, raise you, but 'twasn't a fit place for a child."

"Why do I remember nothing?" Bjorn demanded.

I started to go to him but changed my mind. We weren't that close—not really—and he'd just been handed a bigger chunk of dead sea fruit to absorb than my whole Dragon Heir thing.

"Why do ye think?" The question was stark, but her expression had softened. Where truth had sheeted from her, now love did. My heart went out to the Norse goddess of the dead.

"Ye wiped my memories." Bjorn hooded his eyes until I couldn't read his expression.

"I had no choice," Hel said. "I located a childless couple in Vanaheim. They'd lost several babies, and I knew they would welcome you. They did. I kept a verra close eye on things for enough time to satisfy myself they'd love you and care for you."

Breath hissed from between Bjorn's clenched jaws; he stretched his hands in front of him, and then curved the fingers into claws. "Look. I understand why no one said shit to me when I was growing up. Or even, perhaps, my first hundred years or so. But if we weren't facing this disaster in Midgard, ye never would have told me, would you?"

"Probably not," Nidhogg agreed. "I dinna know of Hel's trickery for a long while. She barred me from Niflheim during the months of her pregnancy. I'd have sensed ye were part dragon and known it had to be from me."

"I told you eventually." Hel let go of his foreleg.

"Aye, after the lad had been fostered. Ye never offered me a choice in the matter."

"And if I had?" Something cunning slithered behind the question.

"Perhaps we'd have found a home for him in Fire Mountain."

Hel snorted. "Aye, and that's almost as poor a choice as Niflheim for a youngster."

"Ach, for the love of Yggdrasil, would you quit carping at

each other," Odin snarled. "Neither of you had the decency to tell me until the lad was in his twenties."

"I'd not have said aught to you"—Hel stared Odin down—"except Freya came to me. She'd had a vision, one so compelling she felt obliged to share it."

Hel walked to Bjorn. "Ye've never heard of a Dragon Mage afore this day because ye are the only one. 'Tis the combination of dragon and Norse and giant magics. Freya named you and foretold unparalleled power within you. She also saw a great darkness descend on the Nine Worlds. In her vision, ye sat in the center of a maelstrom, glowing with light.

"No one can hide anything from me," she went on. "My Eye of Fire ferrets out truth. I understood then that I had no choice but to tell Odin."

"But not me," Bjorn cut in, his words lined with bitterness.

"'Twas always my intention to tell you someday. Nidhogg and I discussed the proper timing of such a disclosure, and—"

"I've heard more than I want to." Bjorn switched back to English and chopped a hand downward. "More than enough." He shook his head so hard, his brains must have rattled from one side of his skull to the other. "Damn it. All of you. Don't you get it? If I'd had access to this knowledge, I could have prepared for my part in what's looking a hell of a lot like Armageddon. As things stand, I'm dreadfully out of my depth."

"Are ye now?" Nidhogg inquired. "When I left you to

fight, ye slew hundreds. Perhaps ye're selling yourself a wee bit short."

"Not the point," Bjorn gritted out. "No matter how well I comported myself in an unfamiliar environment, I never got within spitting distance of a comfort zone. If I'd known—"

"Aye, then what?" Nidhogg pressed.

"I'd still have assigned you your duties as chief sorcerer," Odin cut in. "No one in the Nine Worlds is better suited to the task."

The ship was definitely listing off-course. I hustled to Bjorn's side but addressed my words to Odin. "If I'm hearing you correctly, there's never been another Dragon Mage. I'm guessing one of you"—I looked from him to Nidhogg to Hel —"made up that title. Or did it come from Freya, and you just ran with it?"

"Well, they had to call me something. Or not." The bitter edge coating Bjorn's tone had deepened.

I flapped both hands in front of me. "Sorry. This is no more on point than when the bunch of you were bickering and casting blame. Is there a prophecy somewhere that names a Dragon Heir and a Dragon Mage in the same bit of divination?"

"Not that I know of," Odin muttered.

"Have you looked?" Bjorn shot back.

"Of course I have, particularly after that Celtic bitch insinuated she had inside information from her kettle." He pulled his black brows together. "We may be related, Son, but it doesna offer you the right to question me."

Bjorn stopped shy of rolling his eyes, but only barely. "How about the two of you?" he asked Quade and Zelli.

"How about the two of us, what?" Quade rumbled.

"Did you know about me?"

"Of course," Zelli replied.

"So that must mean every dragon who's ever overflown my cottage knows too," Bjorn sputtered. "And all the ones in Fire Mountain."

"Nay." Nidhogg was quick to step in. "Quade and Zelli know because I told them."

Dewi had been quiet, but she shuffled closer to Odin. "Explain why these two with mixed blood were kept secret from me. Had I realized, particularly about Rowan, much damage could have been averted."

"I have no excuse," Odin replied, "other than protecting two of my own."

"From what?" Dewi pressed. "Shame is a negligible commodity when our verra survival is threatened. Not mine. I can retreat to Fire Mountain. Where will you bide after the Nine Worlds have fallen?"

"Dewi's query pertains to us as well," Andraste piped up. "We'd have booted Ceridwen from the pantheon years ago. Long afore she took it upon herself to break the world."

"That's a pile of horseshit," I told her. "You'd have patted her on the ass and told her to do better. Don't bother denying it. I lived with you for a long time."

Andraste skinned her lips back from her teeth and hissed at me. I felt like hissing back but refused to sink to her level.

Bjorn looked at Hel. "You've cloaked me somehow since even dragons can't distinguish what I am. Whatever you did that hides my true nature from those around me, undo it. Now."

"I was kind to you—" she began.

"Only on account of you felt guilty. The only true 'kindness' would have been ensuring I knew the truth long before the endgame. Remove whatever you swathed me in." Compulsion threaded into his command. Would it be enough to force her to his bidding?

"As ye will," Hel said.

The air around him brightened into a glowing nimbus that dissipated into violet and silver streamers. I stifled a gasp. The goddess of the dead had employed a glamor on him, one he'd had no idea existed. My magic hadn't sniffed it out, either. His overall appearance didn't change much, except he added perhaps five or six centimeters of height. The major alteration was his energy, which fairly screamed dragon.

And his eyes. While still blue, they turned into the whirling orbs I'd come to associate with dragonkind.

Bjorn rolled his shoulders back. I wondered if he felt different or only looked so to my eyes. Hell, I wondered a lot of things. Like, would he be able to fly? Would this change his nature, make him withdrawn and bitter? Or worse, haughty like the other Norse gods?

Odin stomped back to his spot at the head of the table and fell heavily into his chair. "We have our weapons in place," he announced. "Shall we get back to it?"

I twisted around until I faced him. "Whoa! I'm no one's 'weapon.' What I do or don't do will always be my choice. I never answered to the Celts, and I sure as fuck am not going to start answering to you."

"Ye doona have a choice." Odin's message was pointed.

"You damn betcha I do," I retorted. "I can walk out of here and let you fight your own goddamned battles. It's not my fault my mother was a whack job. It's also not my fault she created the Breaking. I don't need the rest of you to work on fixing it. Bjorn and I can handle it."

"What if we need you?" Hel asked softly.

Her question gave me pause. Her tone was open, unguarded. I've never been any good at telling people no, particularly if they've come out and said they need me.

Power sizzled around Bjorn. It smelled the same, brine and baked clay, but it was stronger. Without a word, he vanished from the room.

Thor thumped a fist on the table. "Someone go and bring him back. This is unacceptable."

"Quade is already gone," Nidhogg said.

I hadn't noticed him leave, but when I scanned the room, the black dragon was no longer there. Not satisfied Quade would provide what Bjorn needed, I readied my power, intent on tracking his spell while the trail was fresh.

"Ye're not going anywhere," Odin told me.

"I'm a free agent. I go where I wish," I retorted.

A set of claws grabbed me from behind and lifted me until I was level with Nidhogg's spinning gaze. "I did my son a disservice. Remain here and allow him time to put things into perspective." The dragon turned me until I perched on a foreleg.

"Quade went after him. Why not me?"

"Quade is a dragon."

I could tell from Nidhogg's voice he was fighting to remain even-handed and patient. Wouldn't take much from me to push him into a far less genteel response. Pointing out I was a dragon too might not be wise. I settled for, "Put me down...please."

To my surprise, he did.

I backed up a few steps, my mind busy. Something about the way Odin had characterized Bjorn and I as weapons meant he knew something he hadn't told everyone. Well, maybe Thor knew, or Loki who'd been asleep since I arrived, head cradled on his crossed arms on the table.

About that time, the ravens, Huginn and Muninn—thought and memory—winged through a gap where one of the windows had been propped open. After a few circuits where they flew around the room cawing like crows, they landed on Odin's shoulders.

"You're a seer," I said to Odin. "What have you seen that you haven't told us?"

A huge guffaw ripped from him. After he was done laughing at me, he said, "'Twould take years, child, for me to detail every vision I've had."

Annoyed at being referred to as "child," I gritted out, "What I meant was you know things. Things about the Breaking and the confrontations we face. We're all here. Never a better time to make a clean breast of it."

"Ye've gone daft, lass—" he began.

"Have I now?" I mimicked his brogue. "Ye identified Bjorn and me as weapons. It means ye've seen something of what we face. Enough to understand the *Dragon Mage* and *Dragon Heir*"—I stressed our titles but might have lapsed into sarcasm, maybe—"have instrumental roles to play."

I thumped my chest. "As Dragon Heir, I demand—"

Odin bolted upright. "Ye will demand naught from me," he shouted. Spittle flew every which way, and it made me grateful I wasn't closer.

So much for reality testing. Following Bjorn's lead, I summoned a hasty spell and teleported out of there. I'd been sick of the Celts before I laid eyes on them again. While I felt sorry for Hel, none of the other Norse players made me want to so much as tell them good morning.

If it weren't for the witches, I'd leave Midgard to rot.

I had to pick a destination for my casting, otherwise I'd still be sitting in Odin's filthy meeting hall listening to his crows castigate everyone. I had two choices. Either Bjorn's or back to the witches in Midgard. I probably should have gone home, but I was worried about Bjorn.

And damn it, anyway. When had I begun to view Earth as Midgard? Not that it mattered, but I needed to stop it. I did not want to weave any of my magic in with the Norse pantheon. They weren't an improvement at all over the Celts. In their own way, they might be worse with their secrets and their exiling their own.

Poor Hel. Odin had conveniently forgotten he'd sent her away.

Shouts followed me, but my power is strong. They faded along with Valhalla and Asgard, replaced by the rolling land of Vanaheim. I set myself to come out perhaps half a kilometer from Bjorn's cottage. Nothing like falling into his lap when he was upset and not expecting me.

For a moment, I caught my breath.

I was still tired, but beyond that, I was angry. Deities, regardless of which pantheon they'd sprung from, were a bunch of assholes. Odin's offhand comment about "his weapons" rankled.

A portal swooshed into being, and Zelli glided through, landing smoothly not far from me. Before she could say anything, I held up one hand. "You don't want to stick around," I told her. "You're clearly part of Odin's scheme to turn us into a weapon."

"I am not here for Odin, but because ye and I are bonded," Zelli replied and tapped her chest with a talon. "Me. And you."

"Nidhogg didn't deploy you to haul me back?" I furled both brows.

She shook her head. "We belong together. Ye left. I followed." She hesitated. "Nidhogg dinna 'deploy' Quade, either. It only appeared so because of Odin's query. Quade left of his own accord to support the Dragon Mage."

Mmph. Maybe she was "my dragon," after all, but I didn't want to ask pointblank. I had so few allies, I couldn't risk alienating those willing to stick by my side. People making assumptions about me annoyed the hell out of me. I wasn't willing to place Zelli in an awkward position by asking something she might not want to answer.

I'd already done that once when I'd demanded to know who my father was.

"Shall we see how Bjorn is?" I asked.

"I'm flying," Zelli said pointedly.

Sudden weariness rose from my feet and swept over the top of my head. "Does that mean you're offering to take me? Or are you just stating your intentions?"

Her jaws parted in what might have been a smile, and she puffed steam until I was coated in clouds of it. "I was giving you a choice. Otherwise, I'd have told you to get on my back."

"Sorry," I mumbled. "It's been a rough few hours."

"Try days," she corrected me.

I twisted a thread of power and rode it until I sat astride her back. She leapt skyward. Before we got close enough to Bjorn's cottage to see it, I heard him bellowing. Even worse—maybe—Quade was roaring right back at him.

CHAPTER TEN, BJORN

I've always prided myself on being even-handed, even-tempered. Maybe I'd falsely taken credit for something that didn't belong to me after all. As soon as Hel yanked the glamour she'd shrouded me with, I wanted to kill her and Nidhogg. And Odin. And Thor. And probably Loki. He'd been snoring off a drunk ever since I arrived at Valhalla.

Why stop there? Freya was who'd spurred Hel into spilling her guts to Odin. Worse, I knew Freya. Sort of. She'd called me in on several occasions, and now I knew the reason. At the time, I'd wondered why she'd bothered with someone with inferior magic.

Ha! My magic was as good as it got. No more misplaced modesty in that regard. No more bowing and scraping, either. I was done with my, "Yes, sire," days. More than done. I wished I could undo every scrap of magic I'd ever worked for the gods. At the time, I'd figured they were doing me a favor, letting me strut my stuff.

Goddess curse them twenty ways from Hel. They had no right to hold the circumstances of my birth secret from me. None. If I'd had full access to my memories and my power, I might have been able to stop Ceridwen. Too late now. What had she called it? Spilt milk.

Spilt, indeed. And rotten as fuck to boot.

No wonder Hel had offered me a place to hide out. She had ulterior motives up the ass. The quorking ravens were the last straw. I had to get out of the meeting room before I did something I regretted. Like thrashing the whole lot of them with lightning.

Not that I'd get very far. The august assemblage would band together, bind me with magic, and toss me into one of the dungeons where I could duke it out with the souls of the dead. I'd be able to cut my way free, but what a horrific waste of time and magic.

Besides, it would appear I had the maturity of a five-year-old. I might not be sure who I was anymore, but I wasn't about to portray myself as a wild card. Hel kept trying to catch my eye, but I refused to look at her. She might be hurt, but she'd done far worse to me.

I'd return to my cottage, grab a few things, and then lose myself in Midgard until my head didn't feel like it was about to blow into a thousand pieces. Magic jumped to my command, and I was gone before anyone could even attempt to stop me.

Good thing. Regardless of how it would have looked, I'd

have employed every weapon available to me had one of them tried to block my exit.

Quade sat in front of my door, tail swishing like a cat's. Well, maybe a very languid cat, if its tail made clicking noises when scales scraped against each other. "What took you so long?" He grinned at me through parted jaws.

I raked my hair back from my face. No reason to be oblique. Dragons didn't deal in subtle. "I need to be alone."

"Ye only think ye do."

Something about his tone rankled, but I didn't want to cut my ties with him. Not yet, and I didn't understand why. Sure, I enjoyed riding him, but I didn't need him. Especially not now. Breath rattled through my teeth, and I realized I'd clenched my jaw so tight the muscles ached.

I blew out a breath and opened and closed my mouth a time or two. "Look. I'm not trying to be unreasonable. I need time by myself to figure out who I am. When Hel ripped off the glamour —or whatever the fuck it was—a whole lot of things changed."

"Of course they did." Quade paused before adding, "Ye're who told her to remove it."

"What's that supposed to mean?" I rocked from foot to foot, too keyed up to remain still.

"Simply reminding you."

"Pah. No one to blame but myself, eh? Thanks. If I want your opinion, I'll ask for it."

"For the love of Y Ddraigh Goch, get over yourself. I am in agreement about leaving here for a while. I was going to suggest a borderworld I know, and—"

"I am not going to Fire Mountain," I spoke over him.

"I've been there, and it's not so different from visiting Hell. The other one, not Niflheim's version. Who's Y Ddraigh what's-his-name?"

"One of many dragon gods. Ye've enough dragon blood, ye'd adapt to Fire Mountain." He waved a foreleg in my direction. "Ye might even come to like it there, but 'tisn't the locale I had in mind. Ye need a lot of empty space and practice. One of the alterations from losing Hel's shrouding is your magic has grown far stronger."

Judging from how rapidly it had responded to my teleport casting, I'd already figured that part out. "It's one of the reasons I need to get out of here," I said. "None of my clients will think anything has changed. They'll come for a spell or a potion or an unweaving, and goddess only knows what I'll end up giving them. I might send some poor, unsuspecting soul so far away, they'll end up tangled in Yggdrasil's roots."

Quade cocked his head to one side and regarded me.

"Go ahead." I made come-along motions with one hand. "You want to say something. I wasn't aware dragons practiced restraint."

He snorted steam. "We doona, but ye've had quite a few difficult events to deal with. I was debating how much more truth ye could tolerate."

"Try me. And then I'm going inside to get a few things together."

He nodded to the accompaniment of more steam. "That other life—the one where ye served as master sorcerer—is over."

"Not according to Odin," I muttered.

"Aye, well he has yet to think things through," Quade retorted. "Once he does, he'll ken it well enough." The steam ceded to a stream of smoke, and the dragon turned his head to one side. "For one thing, ye and I are bonded, and—"

Damn. There it was. I held up a hand. "Please. Stop. I'm not ungrateful. Not at all. And I love riding you, but why are we 'bonded,' and what exactly does it mean? Will we go everywhere together? Like a set of conjoined twins? Furthermore, I already figured out Odin—or Nidhogg— conscripted you to spy on me. If it was Nidhogg, I guess he assumed the moonstone he gave me wasn't enough."

"What stone?" Quade regarded me.

"Pfft. As if you didn't know." I reached into the pocket where the damned thing lived and came up dry. Maybe it had picked another pocket. It scarcely required help from me to move about. After a frantic few minutes where I searched every nook and cranny in my garments, relief washed through me.

I shrugged. "Guess it's gone and good riddance. I hated that blasted thing. Nidhogg crafted it to keep an eye on me."

Quade's great head bobbed up and down. "He may have, but he dinna tap me to spy on you. I'd never have agreed to such a scheme. Ye've claimed your dragon blood. The stone is no longer required. So long as Hel's shielding protected you, your activities were invisible to Nidhogg and the other elders."

I waited, but he didn't say anything else, so I prodded, "There's more."

"There is. Ye willna care for it overmuch."

"For fuck's sake"—I cast a longing glance at my cottage

door. Would I ever walk through it?—"tell me and be done with it."

"Done is relative. Nidhogg is linked to all dragons. If ye even think about doing something he doesna believe wise, he has ways of reaching through that link and—"

"Dewi appears to be immune," I blurted.

"Aye. When she was tapped to become a Celtic deity, she erected wards to keep him out."

"Fine. Means I can do the same thing."

Smoke puffed from Quade's nostrils and out the sides of his mouth. "Silence," he thundered.

"Bullshit," I yelled back. "This is my courtyard. My house. You have no right to order me about."

"Ye may be powerful for someone wearing a man's skin, but as dragons go, ye're weak as last week's gruel."

"Oh yeah? It's past time for you to leave." I planted my feet shoulder-width apart. Once kindled, my anger was raging, burning out of control.

"That would be a mistake," he bellowed back. "Doona make this harder than it already is."

Copper scales caught the edges of my peripheral vision. Damn it all to bloody Hel, I had enough problems without Zelli and Rowan. Why hadn't they remained in Valhalla?

Next thing, one of Yggdrasil's roots would shoot up from the dirt beneath my feet. I needed to be alone. Alone. I wasn't in a fit mood to be calm or nice or even to listen to anyone's voice except my own.

What was wrong with me? If yanking off the shrouding had turned me into a class A dick, maybe I should demand Hel put it back. I had a niggling suspicion it wasn't possible.

Rather akin to stuffing a genie back inside a bottle once enchantment had freed it.

Zelli thunked down a couple of meters from Quade. Rowan jumped to the ground and walked toward me, her forehead furrowed into an appraising expression. Where before, she'd have run to me, wrapped her arms around me, this time she stopped a respectable distance away and asked, "How are things going?"

I didn't bother to mute the snort that blustered past my lips. "Badly. How would you expect 'things to be going'?" I copied her words with a singsong intonation.

"I get it," she said. "Feels like we're living in the midst of our own reality television show called, *Revelations are Us*."

"Not funny," I ground out.

She blew out a breath. "Yeah, it is. What happened to your sense of humor? You used to have one."

"Used to being the operative term," I shot back. "I appreciate you making the effort to check on me, but I need to be alone."

Rowan twisted her mouth into a frown. "The first part of that is an outright lie. You were appalled when you first saw Zelli in the sky. The alone part is true enough, though." She tossed her shoulders back. "Why?"

"Why what?"

"Why the sudden need to closet yourself away?"

My hands curled into fists of their own accord. What in the nine hells was wrong with everyone? Why couldn't they accept I required solitude. A whole lot of it. Maybe years at this point.

"Lot of things to figure out," I muttered.

"Yep. But everything will go a whole lot faster and easier with help."

I'd been avoiding looking at her because I feared I'd weaken. She was smart, though. And savvy enough to understand her power over me. With a few steps, she planted herself square in my field of vision.

"I don't agree." Breath huffed from me as I did my damnedest not to get sucked in by the red-gold hair swirling around her and her golden eyes. A long skirt clung to the lines of her hips and thighs, and the outline of her breasts was visible through the thin weave of her shirt. Maybe if I hadn't seen her naked, touched the curves of her body, lost myself in her mouth and hands...

I shut off images of her long-legged form writhing beneath mine. They weren't helping.

"You may not agree," she said, "but this isn't about you."

"Right now, it is."

She rolled her eyes. "Oh please. Your temper tantrum has the stink of ill-conceived, lone-wolf desperation. You're terrified, and—"

"I am not terrified," I shouted, furious at her labeling my outburst a temper tantrum as if I was still a boy in short pants.

"What would you call it?" Rowan held her ground.

"Not ill-conceived, lone-wolf desperation, either," I said, tightlipped.

The corners of her mouth twitched. "We're establishing how you're not feeling. We can do this via a process of elimination and explore whatever is left."

I wasn't sure quite what changed, but the righteous

indignation stick that had been rammed up my ass crumbled. The anger thrumming through me began to recede bit by bit. While Rowan and I had been sparring, the dragons had moved next to one another. A glowing halo suggested they were conversing in mind speech.

I breathed deep, blew it out, and did it a few more times. Rowan's gaze never left me. In it, I read acceptance and caring. I'd all but told her to leave. She hadn't budged. Neither had Quade.

"Feel like a cup of tea?" she asked.

I nodded. "Tea would be lovely. There's mead left too."

"Perfect." She strode briskly to my door and let herself inside.

The dragons were deep into a discussion. Neither of them said boo when I followed Rowan inside. The familiar walls of my home soothed me. A lot had changed, but some things remained the same. My home was one of them. I walked to my collection of lore books and scrolls and ran my fingertips over them. One look at my hands convinced me I needed to wash up.

My next stop was the pump handle next to the sink where I scrubbed grime from myself until the icy water ran clear. Once my hands were clean, I cupped water into them and bent to wash my face. The cold dunking encouraged a return of rational thought.

Rowan had set up shop on the far side of my kitchen ledge and was adding herbs and honey and mead to mugs. She was quiet as she heated water with magic, and I appreciated her not asking more questions.

I might be feeling a tad more settled, but I didn't have the answers she wanted. Not yet, and maybe not for a long time.

She carried the steaming mugs to my battered table and set them across from one another, the invitation obvious. I shuffled to the table, intent on holding a chair for her, but she'd already seated herself. I sat catty-corner from her and inhaled the herbal mix from the tea and mead.

The scents of flowers and heather tantalized me, made me long for a time before the Breaking when the worst thing that ever happened was a disgruntled client.

"Thank you." I picked up a cup, warming my hands. They were still chilled from their trip through the chilly water delivered by my pump.

"You're welcome." She offered a warm, soft smile that made me want to lean across the table and crush my mouth over hers. "I thought about saying I know what you're going through," she went on, "except it's not exactly true. I went a little nuts when Nidhogg dropped the whole Dragon Heir thing on my head, but our situations are different."

"How so?" I was content to let her talk. For one thing, it put off the inevitable, which was my side of the conversation, for a while longer. For another, I loved the sound of her voice. Rich, low, lyrical, it inflamed and soothed at the same time.

"You've lived among people who've loved and cared about you from your earliest memories," she said. "I was the red-headed stepchild until I ran away, and then it took me years to gin up the courage to ask if the witches would let me stay with them. Not for long, but for enough time to pull myself together. I never, never took their hospitality for granted and always gave more than I got. You see"—she leveled her gaze at me—"I never felt worthy of anyone's love or attention. When that damned cat picked me to be his human, I cried.

"The last few years, I've carved out a place with the witches. One where they accepted me. But it blew up in my face when I found out Ceridwen was behind the Breaking. I had to tell my witch family—and I did. But I wouldn't have blamed them if they'd hexed me, kicked me out of the coven."

Listening to her drew me out of my self-absorbed misery. Feeling like a total jerk, I murmured, "They'd never have done that."

Rowan nodded slowly. "You see that, and the witches did, but I've never believed in myself enough to trust that others' affection toward me ran more than skin-deep."

She stopped to take a measured breath. "As in, if I left they'd never miss me. Don't get me wrong, I have absolute confidence in my magic. And I'll be the first to stand up and shout if I think someone's been mistreated. Beyond that, I've always been a loner. So I understand the thing I accused you of intimately. Because I've lived with it almost every day of my life."

I smiled. "Ill-conceived, lone-wolf desperation?"

She nodded. "Exactly. It's why I had the catchphrase on the tip of my tongue."

Speaking of tongues, the combination of her honesty and the spiked tea had loosened mine. I set my empty mug down and said, "I'm confused. And angry." I shook my head. "All those people who knew about me, yet no one had the simple decency to let me know."

"Yeah. We do have one thing in common. Both our mothers knew the truth, but at least yours made certain you had a normal childhood."

I thought back to my trips to Niflheim and Hel proper. "Hel was right," I mumbled.

"About what?"

"Not trying to raise me in her realm. If the frost giants hadn't nabbed me, the souls of the dead would have preyed on my innocence. Most of the dead in Hel's care were rotters. Murderers. Thieves. Adulterers."

Rowan smiled. "Another thing we would have had in common—if Hel had kept you by her side. No other kids to play with and a collection of fuckers on the adult front."

The comparison was so ludicrous, I laughed. "Better not let the Celts hear you comparing them with Hel's dead."

She leaned forward and adopted a conspiratorial tone. "I won't tell them if you don't."

"Your guilty secret is safe with me. On a more serious note, the Celts seemed genuinely distressed by Ceridwen's treachery. Dewi apologized to you. Dragons never apologize to anyone."

Rowan nodded. "It's a case of too little, too late. Whatever damage was done when I was young can't be canceled out by an apology. My hurt places have made me prickly and my own kind of lone wolf. It's very hard for me to trust anyone." She hesitated and then added, "You have a genuineness about you where you expect the best from people. It's a gift. Try not to lose it with all that's happened."

I thought back to wanting to lay waste to the world in Valhalla's upstairs meeting room. Shame scoured me. I'd been so sunk in feeling sorry for myself, my perspective had flown right out the same window Odin's ravens had used to come inside.

"A lot has changed," I said, "but many things are the same too."

"Same conclusion I came to after we killed the griffon-esque monster. Want to know what I think?"

"Sure."

She narrowed her eyes in appraisal. "Good. You truly meant that. When we stood outside, you wanted all of us to leave, but if we had, you'd have started along the same downward spiral that's turned me into a lonely, bitter woman."

"I wasn't in a good place," I admitted. "And I'll probably stay pissed at all of them for hiding my true nature."

"Not forever," she pointed out.

"Nay. Not forever. Anger takes too much energy to maintain, but it might be forever before I trust any of them again."

"Know what you mean. It's how I feel about the Celts who are suddenly all googly-eyed with apologizing." She exhaled sharply. "All that is beside the point. What I believe is this. There are no coincidences. Midgard—Earth—stands at a nexus. It is close to failing entirely. The only thing that will save my world—and yes, it is mine—will be drastic measures.

"You and me. We're the drastic intervention that will keep Midgard whole and part of the Nine Worlds. Will it be easy? Of course not. Will our job be quick? No to that too. Think about how our magic works together."

"It will be different," I cautioned her. "Mine is a whole lot stronger now."

A fierce smile split her face. "I can't wait to experiment. We are exactly where we are supposed to be. A Dragon Heir, the likes of whom has never before been born. And a Dragon Mage."

"Also an anomaly," I said. "No one has the faintest idea about me or my magic."

"See?" She slapped a hand down on the table. "We're invincible. We can do this. Us and the dragons."

"I want to sign up for your enthusiasm," I said slowly, "but what makes you so certain?"

She turned her hands palms up. "I feel it. Here." She twisted one hand to thump her breastbone. "And my instincts have never been wrong. Also, the enemy we face won't understand how our power works. How could they? We barely do."

I could have catalogued all the problems facing us—and our lack of solutions—but we had each other and the dragons. Maybe it would be enough. I got to my feet and opened my arms. Would she come to me? Needing to hold her, feel her body against mine, drove me so relentlessly I almost couldn't breathe.

Rowan stood and closed the distance between us. Twining her arms around me, she smiled softly. The curve of her mouth was impossible to resist, and I slashed my mouth over hers and held her tight while I kissed her.

CHAPTER ELEVEN, ROWAN

I was relieved when the worst of the anger melted out of Bjorn. I'd been fearful he'd hang onto it, drape it around himself like a banner. Just like I had. Standing in Odin's halls watching Bjorn had been quite the eye-opener. I'd viewed myself as strong, independent, rather like a very small nation more than capable of going it alone. I may have let Mort get his feline claws into me, but it was only recently I'd hewed chinks in my thick armor and trusted the witches enough to drop some of my barriers.

Anger was a small blessing and a huge curse. It was what I clung to when everything else was gone, and it had been what got me through. Anger and blaming Ceridwen. But the cost was high. My self-imposed isolation blinded me to the love and support of those who stuck by me.

All those elements were why I tried so hard to get through to Bjorn. Usually, if someone tells me to get lost, I'm out of there so fast all that's left is my dust.

But Bjorn was hurting. Really hurting. My heart cracked wide open because it was so similar to what I'd gone through. And because I'm an old softie—beneath all my emotional fortifications—I can't stand to see anyone suffer. More important than either him or me, though, was the blackness bearing down on us.

Someone—or something—knew about him. And about me. Not the specifics, but they understood full well our combined power would be a problem. It was the only explanation for the monsters that kept trying to disable our ability. Even absent seer talents, I saw endless battles looming. At least one of my worries had been for naught, though. With a dragon father and Hel for a mother, Bjorn had to be immortal.

I wondered if that had occurred to him, but it was a minor point buried amongst everything else. Once we settled over tea, I began talking. As I'd hoped, me revealing some of my hard-to-admit places encouraged him to do the same. After a while, he was thinking again. Not simply reacting. The anger-saturated stranger departed, and he felt like the man I'd come to appreciate and respect.

And love, if I were honest.

When he pushed back from the table and opened his arms to me, I didn't hesitate. Hunger carved a path through me. I craved his arms around me and his mouth on mine. When he kissed me, I tumbled into a hot tide of heat and need. His lips were the same, yet not. Chiseled and demanding, his mouth held fire and promise.

Maybe it was our dragon natures calling to each other. Or maybe I have a hopelessly romantic streak that I've buried so deep I scarcely recognize it when it comes out to play.

He bit my lower lip. I bit back, adding light kisses atop the place to soothe the sting. When he sank his tongue into my mouth, I sucked on it and teased it with mine. He ran his hands down my back until he cupped my ass, snugging me against his growing erection.

Remembering how he'd tasted in my mouth, how he'd responded to everything I'd done to him made shivers run through me. He rained kisses down my neck and then returned to my mouth. I wanted him to do everything, all at the same time. Kiss me. Lick me. Fuck me. Hell, I wanted to do everything to him. My nipples had pebbled, forming hard peaks. Heat spiraled from my belly outward, slicking my thighs. Desire turned into a live thing, tearing at me, demanding my full attention.

Before, Bjorn had been tuned in to my needs, recognizing my reticence to make love because of what such a binding might mean down the road. That part of him was gone, probably courtesy of Hel removing the glamour she'd hidden him behind.

Both of us were panting as we ground our mouths and bodies together. He kneaded the globes of my ass and thrust the hot, hard length of himself into my belly. I'd all but ripped tracks in his shirt as I dug my fingers into his back on my way down to grapple with his high, tight butt.

He had an ass to die for. Thinking about it added one more item to my menu of wanting everything at the same time. I wanted to fuck him and watch him fuck me so I could get off on the muscles rippling along his back and through his ass.

Apparently, I needed a magical mirror. It could be arranged.

He ripped his mouth from mine. Before I could lunge back into his arms and attack his mouth again, the distinctive feel of his power flared around me. I inhaled like a starving woman, losing myself in the mix of the sea and herb-infused hot clay.

Our garments whooshed from us in a small maelstrom and ended up on the floor. Laughter bubbled from me. "Neat trick."

"I could do it before." His voice was raspy with desire. "Never could get magic to pry my boots off, though. Guess I still can't." He cast a rueful glance downward and bent to grapple with his laces.

I didn't view mine as an impediment. While he divested himself of his shoes, I walked around him, absorbing small changes to his body that went beyond the added height and whirling dragon eyes. His skin glowed a warm copper. Power had always spilled from him, but it was far more pronounced.

He glanced up at me and grinned. "Do I pass inspection?"

"Do I?" I countered.

He rose to his feet, never breaking eye contact. "You are the most beautiful, the most incredible, the most amazing—"

Laughing, I held up a hand. "Enough. All this praise will go straight to my head, and I'll become insufferable."

"Not possible," he informed me and wrapped his arms

around me again. Heat from him seared me as our bodies touched. His cock was the same. Hard. Hot. Big enough I'd needed both hands and my mouth to pleasure him. It was a good idea, and I sank to my knees and ran my tongue around the head of his shaft.

He made the most delightful male sound. It reminded me of a big cat purring. Encouraged, I took him into my mouth. Or the first quarter of him, which was all I could manage. He threaded his fingers into my hair and rocked against my mouth. Our scents and our magic rose around us until the air glistened with desire.

My hands joined my mouth, and I swiped my tongue around the tip at the top of each stroke. His cock expanded, hardened still more as I loved him. The bigger he got, the hotter I got until my nub beat like a second heart. I'd never come with zero direct stimulation before, but an orgasm swirled low in my belly.

He lifted my head and pulled his cock out of my mouth. When I looked up, his eyes were on fire, spinning so fast they drew me into their spell. His nipples had hardened into tiny peaks, and his copper skin had taken on a golden glow.

Welcoming what had to come next, I let him help me to my feet. He picked me up and carried me to his neatly made bed. Laying me down, he stood just looking at me for long moments. "Ye're so beautiful," he said in Old Norse. "So lovely." Bending, he traced a finger from my mouth down my neck to my breasts, stopping to swirl it around each nipple.

Somehow, he ended up first sitting and then lying next to me, and his questing hand had made it to the vee between my legs. The second he spread my sex and touched my nub, the climax that had begun while I was sucking him washed over me. He rubbed harder, intent on pleasuring me, and kept on until I was mostly done. Mostly, because we'd barely begun, and I'd come again before we were through. Maybe a whole bunch of agains.

His mouth crushed down on mine. His tongue pressed into my mouth. Still riding high from my climax, I raked my nails down his back and opened my mouth to his tongue. The kiss didn't last nearly long enough before he pulled away.

"On your knees, wench." He still spoke Norse. Maybe his brain was too addled to bother with English.

"How'd you know I love it that way?"

"I dinna, but sooner or later, we'll do this every way."

"Don't make promises you can't keep." It may have sounded like I was teasing, but I was deadly serious.

"Not about this. Not about you, darling."

He turned me over and tugged until my butt was in the air. I felt the press of his cock at my entrance and wriggled to encourage him to plumb me. We were on the verge of discovery, of sealing our attraction, our lust. I couldn't wait. I wanted him with a single-minded intensity that should have scared the hell out of me.

It didn't. If he'd suddenly crawled off the bed, I'd have followed him and pinned him to the floor while I sank my body over his. We'd passed the point of no return, Bjorn and me. Something bigger than us was in play, driving us, but I didn't care. If he was my destiny, there were far worse options out there.

He spread my ass cheeks and pushed inside, little by

little, allowing me to accommodate his girth. He took his time and waited for long moments once he was all the way inside me. Small muscle twitches provided just enough stimulation to drive me mad. I rocked against him, wanting him to move faster, wanting to savor every moment, wanting him to never leave my body. He reached around my thigh and covered my mound with his hand before fingering my clit.

As slowly as he'd entered me, he pulled back until just the tip of him was inside. More slow strokes. All the way in. All the way out. Meanwhile, he swirled his fingertips around my nub, equally slowly. My frantic need to come again—right now—eased. I relaxed into the rhythm he set. When he upped the cadence, I was right there with him.

Ceding control to another was new for me. Exciting in ways I'd never imagined.

He closed his mouth over the juncture of my neck and shoulder, biting me. It did something, and sexual heat poured through me. Along with the bite, he moved faster and faster, rubbing me all the while. Climax surged, crested, and surged again until my body turned into one long, drawn-out howl of pleasure.

I knew he was close. I sensed it. Tasted it. Felt it in every pore of my existence. Rocking, thrusting, I did everything I could to intensify his sensation. When he came, the contractions spilled through me, pushed me into one more release. Gasping, panting, moaning, we clung to each other as our passion spent itself. He pulled out of my body, leaving an empty place.

I wanted him back inside, but we'd snatched time that

didn't belong to us as it was. He untangled the rest of our limbs and we ended up on our sides, facing one another, still breathing as if we'd run a hundred kilometers.

He touched my shoulder, the one he'd bitten. Magic glowed, and the wound healed over. "Ye're mine," he said, still in Norse.

I nodded. I'd understood making love with him would be a one-way door. We could never go back. And I didn't want to. "You're mine as well," I reminded him.

A slow, lazy smile made him so eerily beautiful, he was hard to look at. I was afraid the image would burn itself into my corneas and everywhere I looked from now on, all I'd see would be him. "I'm good with it," he said in English, followed by, "Why do you suppose the dragons haven't bothered us? Quade was in an almighty rush to sweep me off to some borderworld to familiarize myself with my new abilities."

I thought about it. Surely, the beasts had known what we were doing. We'd made less than zero effort to be quiet, but even if we had, they'd have smelled the pheromones and the sex.

"The only reason they left us be," I replied, "is because they believe we need to be bonded."

"Do you suppose they know things they haven't told us?" He snorted. "Scratch that. Of course, they do. And this could well be one of them."

"I don't want to, but we should get up." I ran a hand down his arm. "I'm tired. I could sleep for days, but I'm sure me zoning out isn't on the dragons' approved activity list."

Bjorn laughed softly. "Probably not." He touched my

bite spot again. "I'm sorry about that. I don't know what got into me. Did I hurt you?"

"I barely noticed. If I did, it just made things more intense."

Color rose to his face. "My guess is I marked you with a dragon's mating bite. I've seen them do much the same in the skies above Vanaheim."

"If my dragon half took exception, we'd have known about it." I kissed his forehead and rolled so my feet were planted on the floor. Once I was confident my legs would hold me, I tottered over to the sink, grabbed a handy cloth, and did my best to pump water and clean myself.

"We can make it warmer if you want to bathe." He'd joined me and was dipping a second cloth under the pump's chilly flow.

"Nah. I'm tough. Besides, I don't want to take the time. Third reason is if I indulge in a warm bath, I'll fall asleep."

He rinsed out his cloth and swatted my butt. "Makes two of us. Sleep won't loom large in our future, though."

I cleaned my own washcloth and hung it from a hook. "Really?" I arched a brow in an imitation of a coquette. "And why not?"

"Because if we're lucky enough to find ourselves prone, we'll have other priorities."

"You think?" I smothered a grin but gave up and let it out. I wanted him to want me. Nothing worse than a lover who beat a hasty retreat before his cock was even deflated. I'd had a few of them. Maybe they'd sensed my magic, and it scared the living hell out of them.

I sorted my garments from his and dragged them on. He

beat me dressing, but he waited until I stood by his side before we went out to face the dragons. I scanned the clearing, but they weren't there. I'd been certain they'd wait for us. "What do you suppose happened to them?" I asked Bjorn.

He pointed upward. Sure enough, they were dipping and swooshing and flying in patterns as they rode both up- and downdrafts. "They don't seem in a hurry to land," he noted and ducked back inside his cottage. When he emerged a few minutes later, he handed me a roll with a chunk of cheese tucked inside.

I didn't realize how hungry I was until I took the first bite and saliva slopped onto the ground. "Thank you," I said once I'd swallowed. "This is good."

"I'd love to take credit, but my clients bring me things. Like the bread. I did make the cheese from goat's milk another customer left me."

"They pay you in goods. That's wonderful."

"It is," he agreed between bites. "They're under no obligation to pay me at all. Access to my magic is an implied benefit."

Before I could ask how that worked, he added, "Odin and his merry band of bastards make certain I have what I need. The cottage belonged to my parents..." He made a face and started over. "The wonderful couple who fostered me. When they died, it became mine. My needs have always been simple enough. A roof over my head. A place to store my magical accoutrements and books."

"Did your parents live into old age?" I asked.

He nodded. "Why are you asking?"

"The reason they never told you they adopted you has to be one of three things." I brushed crumbs from my fingers. "Either keeping your origins a secret was part of the bargain. Or you were a foundling, and they never knew where you came from. Or Hel wiped their memories."

"More likely a combination of two and three. Mum and da were the epitome of decency. I learned so much from my years beneath their roof. Even if it cost them, they did the right thing. Took the moral high ground. They taught me there were far more important things than money or winning. Especially if us winning meant someone else lost."

"I'd have liked to have met them," I said, feeling wistful.

"I'm sorry you didn't." He shaded his eyes from the sun that had finally come out from behind thick clouds. I followed the direction he was looking and saw the dragons heading right for us.

"Break time's over." I grinned at Bjorn.

"Consider us fortunate they allowed us the time they did." His expression turned serious, and he cupped the side of my face in one hand. "You're absolutely correct that the only reason they didn't interrupt us is because they considered making love more important than flying off to Quade's borderworld."

Worry struck a discordant note within me. "Do you have any idea how long Quade expects we'll be gone?"

"Nay."

"I have to stop and check on the witches before I leave to go anywhere. I'm not especially worried about the Celts hassling them anymore, but they're still helpless."

He brushed a calloused thumb over my face, tracing the

line of my cheekbone. "They're not as helpless as you believe, but I agree about making certain all is well."

Zelli landed more lightly than usual about three meters away on the far side of the courtyard. She'd no sooner gotten her hind feet on the ground than she puffed steam our way. It was so thick, I felt rather than saw Quade land next to her. Steam from him joined the party until I could barely see Bjorn standing next to me.

"Enough," Bjorn shouted. "We're ready to leave."

The clouds thinned a bit, and Zelli said, "We are congratulating you on your mating."

I should have thanked her, but a teensy part of me wanted to lodge a protest. It wasn't as if we'd sat through a formal marriage ceremony or anything. Or a witches' handfasting.

I buried my thoughts fifty kilometers under and spaded magic over them. Whatever was wrong with me, I needed to identify it and deal with it. I'd known before we made love it would be the glue that cemented us together. I'd welcomed Bjorn into my body, fully understanding the ramifications. The dice were cast. I should be ecstatic. And I was, except for one tiny corner of uncertainty.

"Thank you," Bjorn was saying. He'd moved to my side, and I laced my fingers with his.

"I need to make a quick stop at home," I told the dragons.

"Why?" Zelli asked.

"Why, indeed?" Quade seconded. "Your Celtic kin willna bother the witches further."

"Earth hosts other threats." I looked from one dragon to the other. "The coven is my family, and right now they're split between two locations. Since they're unable to teleport, it places them in a vulnerable position."

"I doona see the harm in a quick stop," Zelli said.

Anger—my go-to place—crackled to life. I let go of Bjorn's hand. "Look here. We've covered this ground. I do not require your permission to ensure my home and my family are safe. You might be used to running things, but you'll never run me."

Fire streamed from Zelli's parted jaws, replacing the steam. I had to jump to one side to avoid it. I was pretty sure I was immune to dragonfire, given my mysterious dragon father, but I wasn't anxious to test my theory.

"We'll see you in front of the caves beneath Ben Nevis," Bjorn said firmly. Before I could protest I'd craft my own travel spell, his caught both of us up and Vanaheim ceded to blackness.

"Sorry," I mumbled. "My temper has always had a short fuse."

"All this will take getting used to," he said. "We're accustomed to operating independently. The dragons are used to issuing orders. I don't think Zelli meant anything by what she said. She was just being who she is. And so were you."

"Glad one of us is the voice of reason."

I heard grunts and groans and outraged cries before the packed-down dirt in front of Ben Nevis came into view. Bjorn's magic slammed into mine. "Ready yourself." His words held a terse edge.

For some reason, orders from him didn't rankle as much as orders from Zelli.

The dark of the teleport spell yielded to the same pock-marked earth I remembered from when the griffon monster had crawled out of some subterranean portal leading god only knows where. No griffon this time. No goblins, gnomes, or trolls, either. In their place was a huge, batlike thing with a three-meter wingspan. Black wings supported a grotesque fur-coated body. At least it didn't reek of poison. The shrill squeals were coming from it. A quick scan showed at least three more.

I thanked every goddess who'd ever walked—except Mother—I'd insisted on stopping here first.

Power sheeted from Bjorn's outstretched hands. I added mine to the mix. Maybe the dragons would show up. Maybe they wouldn't. Didn't matter. We had this. Or I thought we did until I understood the groans were coming from fallen witches who'd done their best to defend their home.

Fury hammered me until I was pure, white light. Every bat abomination I targeted burst into a stinking, smoking pyre. I had to kill them. Had to. The witches needed me. And Bjorn, too. He was a healer, and some of my family were still alive.

Rowan was fierce and beautiful, like an avenging angel as she lobbed magic-laden death at the bats. Maybe her intuition was working overtime. I'd thought she was being overly conservative about stopping by Midgard, but she'd been right on target. A shrill keening preceded holes ripped in the either, admitting two more of the bat monsters. Apparently, not everything bad originated from the dirt under my feet.

Beyond their obvious relationship to bats, there was something familiar about the winged horrors. I'd never seen their like before, but my memories had expanded. Was I tapping into knowledge from Hel? Or Nidhogg? I hadn't stopped long enough to consider what being directly related to him would mean.

I'd always assumed everyone in the Nine Worlds was loosely related to Odin, but my kinship ties had just grown a whole lot more intimate. What that signified remained to be seen as well. Power flowed through me as if I'd been born to wield it. It felt odd and beautiful and right in a way not much else has in my life. Rowan's magic pulsed alongside mine, a glowing ribbon in shades of blue and violet.

I snatched a nanosecond to scan the familiar surroundings. Witches weren't the only ones scattered on the ground. Why in the hell hadn't they remained within the caves? They would have provided protection. A hairy foot looked as if it might have belonged to a dwarf. What was it doing out of Svartalfheim? Severed wings probably belonged to a sprite. Three pieces of what had been a grossly deformed snake with caterpillar markings were separated by unidentifiable debris.

"I'll clear that side," Rowan yelled and sprinted nearer the cave's entrance. She didn't wait for me to answer. No need. I turned toward the farthest bat. This one was pale, almost white. It was new to the party, and the acrid stench of toxins clung to it.

I could keep right on killing what was in front of me, but it was a shortsighted approach. What I needed to do was close off the entrances. Keeping a close eye on the latest bat to arrive, I reached deep, asked for more from Midgard, from Yggdrasil through its root that touched the world I stood upon. My spell was about halfway built when the foul reek of bat drew dangerously near.

I'd thought I had enough time. I'd been wrong. The light-colored bat was female from the looks of the lines of teats hanging from her belly. Crap. Did these abominations give birth? That wasn't good news. I detached a bit of the power I'd been fashioning, redirected it into a ward, and waited.

The high-pitched squeals bats use to locate prey suggested she was effectively blind in daylight.

Excellent.

She'd zeroed in on me, but she was still zigging and zagging. On one of her course corrections, I sent a lethal blow into her heart. I expected her to fall out of the sky, but it didn't even slow her down. What in the unholy crap? The other bat-things had fallen before my magic, and not even as much as I'd just used.

Fuck. They must be mutating, developing ways to counteract what we raised against them. What kind of creature could do that? Not even magical beings were capable of transforming that quickly. At least none I'd ever run into.

Not that I'd faced off against many hordes before, but the goblins and gnomes and trolls Nidhogg had forced me to deal with hadn't possessed that particular unsettling quality. I let my fledgling ward go and focused all my attention on my adversary. She was closer now. Uncomfortably close.

Close enough to use one of the blades I had yet to pick up. They weren't even smelted yet. It felt as if years had passed since my visit to Hagar's forge, not a mere handful of days.

I resurrected my ward in the nick of time. White exudate spattered it, leaving smoking trails in my shielding. My lungs tightened; my nostrils burned. I poured more magic into my shielding. Before the bat had been an inconvenience, but she'd turned into a personal challenge.

Nothing I couldn't deal with. With parents like my real ones, I had to be immortal. The news should have been exhilarating, but I'd been too busy to absorb the full implications.

Hell, I was still too busy.

If a killing blow right into the bat's heart didn't do the trick, I'd have to try something different. I took the netting I'd manufactured to seal off this part of Midgard from further intrusion and tossed it over the bat. My aim was true. The mesh snared its wings, which should drive it from the air. But I didn't stop there. I wound the weave of my snare tight and then tighter, pushing air and life out of the monster.

I'd expected it to be a quick death, but the only quick part was when it splatted to the ground uncomfortably near where I stood. I could have crawled out from under its belly, but I'd have been saturated with poison. By now, I'd figured out that the rows of what I'd assumed were teats were sacs filled with toxin.

It splattered in a ring around the fallen bat. The ground smoked and rippled, outraged by the crap touching its surface. Good. Midgard was still fighting back. I'd begun to wonder if the world had surrendered to a fate that felt inevitable.

I kept the pressure up, winding my net stiffer, tauter. Why in the fuck wasn't the bat dead? I had things to do besides babysitting its demise. Hanging onto my netting with one stream of magic, I fashioned another into a gleaming spear and punctured both its lungs.

Air hissed from its grotesquely open mouth. I would have bet on toxic gas, but it wasn't worth checking since nothing except me was close enough to sustain injury. I probed, not bothering for subtle, and fist-pumped the air. The goddess damned bat was dead. Finally.

If every adversary took this much thought and effort, Rowan and I would be finished before we even began. We'd never be able to stop fighting. And every time we looked up, more of the enemy would be ranged against us.

As I contemplated that sobering backdrop, I released my warding. Zelli and Quade were circling to land. *"We shut this part of Midgard off from above and below,"* Quade informed me in mind speech.

"Over here!" Rowan screamed before I could thank Quade for his and Zelli's efforts.

I pelted around the bat that had sucked up half an hour of my time and ran to Rowan, dodging bodies and potholes as I went. Had there been an earthquake? Was that why the dirt was riddled with fissures? There were way more of them than there should be. Especially since some of the enemy had come through holes in the sky.

Rowan knelt, cradling a man's head in her arms. His spirit hovered above his body, which was never a good sign. I switched up my magic. In general, healing requires water. Lots of water with a bit of fire and a touch of air. The power I'd been chucking at the bat didn't have any water in it at all.

With my hands hovering over the prostrate witch, I hunted for what was wrong with him. Nothing was broken, but his liver was overflowing with venom and his lungs were barely moving air. When I dug further, his magical center had developed a dark perimeter, as if something had barricaded it off.

Absent magic, his ability to heal himself would be nil.

"Hurry," Rowan urged. "He's slipping away."

I tethered his spirit with a thread of power. It wasn't absolute, but it would buy us a bit of time. The man's face twisted into a grimace. "Sorry, buddy," I said firmly. "Hold on. We're trying to bring you back."

I have no idea if he heard me, but hearing is the last sense to go.

"*What's wrong with him?*" Rowan switched to telepathy.

"*Not sure. Something attacked his magic. If I can clear it, channels will open for him to become whole again.*"

"*Show me.*" She sent a glimmering spar into the witch. I guided it to the place I was working.

A startled gasp told me she understood the problem. When she said, "Why the fuck couldn't I see that on my own?" her gasp took on a whole new meaning. She'd scanned the man. Of course she had, and totally missed the seat of his problem.

The witch's spirit strained at its tether. We didn't have time to muck around experimenting. "Stay with me," I told both Ro and the witch.

"What are we doing?" she asked. Tension sheeted from her. Clearly, she was still upset she hadn't been able to locate his broken places.

"It runs counter to everything I've learned over the years because water is the primary healing element, but we're going to send a very fine line of fire here." I showed her the blackened edge where I planned to begin. It seemed weaker there, and was a logical staring point. I didn't waste more time on explanations. We didn't have any.

If this worked, the fire would glom onto the evil and burn

the taint free, working its way around the perimeter of the witch's magic. If it didn't work, the fire would kill the witch, but he was as good as dead anyway.

I was holding my breath. I blew it out as I threaded fire to the spot I'd indicated. Fire has never been my favored element, but now it leapt to my command. So much so, I dialed back the intensity. If I wasn't cautious about how I applied it, the flame would burn right through the witch, and he'd go up like a torch.

I felt Ro's energy hovering. Beyond her, the dragons were doing something, moving around the field. My flickering spark danced around the edges of the blackened perimeter but didn't destroy it. I added more heat, more destruction, but backed off after every alteration.

Sweat beaded my forehead and dripped into my eyes. It ran freely down my sides. Magic was a jealous mistress. She'd take everything I fed into her and beg for more. I'd discovered as a much younger mage that I had to be careful or I'd get so swept into spells it would take me days to find my way back.

"Look!" Rowan moved the end of her spar to a spot where the perimeter had finally begun to smolder. The touch of her magic was the linchpin. In less than the space between two breaths, the entire barrier around the witch's magical center burned merrily.

The next part happened fast, even for my castings. Flames turned to cinders, and a glowing light pulsed outward from the witch's captive magic. His spirit slammed back into his body. His eyes snapped open, and he thrashed in Rowan's grip.

"Let go of me," he sputtered. "I'm fine. We must help the others."

I didn't wait for him to repeat himself. Now that I understood what to do, it would go a whole lot faster. I could skip the diagnostic part and go straight for the cure.

Rowan joined me where I stood next to the witch. He was struggling to stand, but I wasn't worried about him.

A brisk bugle drew my attention to Zelli and Quade. They'd carried prostrate witches to one of the few level areas left. Zelli laid one more down gently. I ran toward them.

"Why'd they leave the caves?" Rowan wailed.

"We'll find out," I told her. "I'm sure they had their reasons." I was close enough to count eight witches. "Is that all of them?" I yelled to Quade. Even without communicating, the dragons had done the best possible thing. I could do a group casting with Rowan. It would save time and magic.

"One more," Zelli called back and took to the skies again.

By the time she returned, Ro and I stood next to Quade, and I'd done a quick-and-dirty assessment. In case one of them had something different wrong with them and I wiped out their magical essence by mistake. Aye, I know I'd said I could skip the diagnostics, but caution trumped hubris.

A muted cry from Rowan dragged my gaze to the latest addition to the group of witches. It was Tansy. My heart hurt for the young witch. And for Rowan. I took a moment to run magic through her, and then I did it once more.

"She has a different problem," I said.

Blue-white magic, courtesy of Rowan, flickered around

the young witch. When she looked up, her forehead was a mass of lines. "Not magic," she ground out.

"Her hurt places are physical," I agreed and looked from her to the eight witches laid out in a rough circle. Many were in the same spot the witch we'd saved had been in. Their spirits hovered, on the verge of departing for the afterlife. If I took the time to cure them, Tansy would be gone. But the reverse held true as well.

"We can help," Quade rumbled.

"Aye. Tell us what ye did," Zelli said.

I sketched out the exact proportions of fire I'd used with warnings about not overdoing it, and then I turned to Rowan. "You have to help the dragons," I told her. "Your magic is the fulcrum, the addition that made mine work."

She nodded once, sharply. "Take good care of Tansy."

"I'll do the best I can." I slipped a noose around Tansy's spirit as I ran to her and lifted her into my arms. Nothing I could do once a spirit departed this world. I moved the girl well away from the others, so none of their magic would slop over and pervert mine.

As I walked with Tansy in my arms, I triaged her injuries. The worst was something had hit her in the back of her head. She was bleeding into her brain and into the layers of tissue covering it. I tried reaching her with telepathy, and then with magic, but she'd moved to the deepest levels of unconsciousness. Where the next stop is death.

I'd no sooner laid her down and wrapped my hands around her head, intent on ameliorating as much of the damage as I could when Hel shimmered into being right next to us.

Because this was a projection, I saw Hel as she really was, bones gleaming whitely where they were exposed. "She is mine." My mother held out her arms.

"Nay. I will fight you for her."

"The child was valiant." Hel's tone was riddled with compulsion. "Doona deny her eternal rest."

I erected a shield before I replied. A barrier to keep my mother out. There'd been a time I'd never have bothered, figuring my power was no match for hers. No more underestimating my ability. I spared a glance at Hel, at my mother. "The child is just that. A child. She has everything to live for." A thought slammed into me, and I voiced it before deciding if it was a good idea. "Help me. Help me heal her. If we fail, she will enter your realm willingly because I shall escort her myself."

Hel leveled a speculative glance my way. "Done. I may not have raised you, but I'm proud of the man ye've become."

I started to ask if she was only just now figuring that out, but my scrambled relationship with her would have to take a backseat. Tansy needed me—needed us. And her need was urgent.

"If I am going to assist, I canna reach through your ward," Hel said.

I hesitated, but only briefly. Hel may have withheld critical information, but she'd never given me any other reason to distrust her. Finally leveraging water, I poured magic into Tansy's wounded places and released the hold I had on the barrier around us. Healing magic was familiar ground. I'd done plenty of it, and I sank into my usual perspective where I held magic on one side and my sense of my patient on the other, adjusting my interventions accordingly.

Hel's power slid in next to mine, so smoothly I almost didn't notice her. It was as pointed a message as I was likely to get that her magic was my magic. Working in concert with her felt normal, natural. Very different from when I worked with Rowan and our power potentiated itself until we were a hundred times stronger together than apart.

Getting the bleeding to stop was easy. Urging the swollen tissues to retreat a little harder. Once they were more-or-less normal size, Hel and I went to work correcting the damaged places. Tansy's breathing stabilized. Her heartbeat grew stronger. When her spirit crashed into her body with no urging from me, I knew we'd won.

Breath rattled from me, and I began a slow withdrawal from where I'd placed fail-safes through the child's brain. Her eyes fluttered open, and she smiled. "You. I heard you calling me back. I didn't want to come, but you were persistent."

"That I am," I agreed.

Rowan swooped in from one side and sank into a crouch. "Thank all the bloody gods and saints and everyone else, you're all right."

Tansy twisted and wound her arms around Rowan's knees. I pushed upright. No need to ask how things had gone with the dragons and the other witches. If they hadn't pulled through, Rowan would still be over there.

To my surprise, Hel hadn't left. I turned to face her. "Thank you for helping me."

"Thank you for trusting me." She inclined her head

slightly. When she raised it and looked across at me, I realized I'd grown taller once she removed the glamour. "Ye're a talented healer," she said.

"I try. Some cases are harder than others. Tansy was pretty far gone."

A soft smile curved Hel's mouth. "Ye're also mated. To Rowan. I saw it while our magic was joined. Congratulations. 'Tis a strong pairing. Odin will be pleased."

I resisted an urge to snarl, but I did say, "I don't care what he thinks or doesn't think."

She waved a bony finger in front of me. "Doona make that mistake...Son. He is our leader and worthy of respect. Dark times are on the horizon. Darker than we have ever faced afore. Odin will need all our support."

Before I could respond, her image wavered, and she was gone.

"Mrroowwwww," Mort announced and launched himself at Tansy and Rowan.

When she looked up at me, tears streaked her cheeks, and she cradled both the cat and Tansy in her arms.

"I'm okay. You can let go of me." Tansy struggled to sit.

"Why did you leave the caves?" I asked.

After crossing her legs under her, she replied, "There were quakes. Big ones. Rocks and dirt were falling, even inside. And then, there was this horrible booming. Some of the older witches said it sounded like a big airplane. Loren just meant to go outside and check on things, but he'd barely left when he started screaming, and—"

"It's all right." She looked so distressed, I waved her to silence. I'd gotten enough of the picture to understand the witches had been lured into leaving the relative safety of the ancient Celtic stronghold.

"From now on," Rowan said, "No one leaves. We have enough food within. And there's fresh water flowing down the back wall of the furthermost cavern into a pool."

"Did you tell the rest of them?" Tansy asked, followed by, "Aw shit. Is everyone all right?"

Rowan still held Mort in her lap. "Yes. We got here in time."

Tansy got her feet under her and stood. "When will you be back?"

"I don't know," Rowan replied.

The young witch nodded somberly. "Do what you must. We'll be all right. I don't think anyone will be dumb enough to encourage a repeat of today."

Zelli and Quade trudged across the uneven ground, wings extended for balance. "Ye have one more spot to check," Zelli reminded us.

Rowan stood. "Thank you for remembering."

The dragon cocked her head to one side. "'Twasn't a matter of forgetting. I dinna appreciate the extent of our problems, but I do now."

"I didn't, either," Quade said, followed by, "Hop on. We'll fly to Inverlochy."

"Good idea. It will tell us if this"—I spread my arms to encompass the destruction—"is widespread." I was relieved the mini-spat between Ro and Zelli had played itself out. Combat has a way of highlighting what's important—and what isn't.

Rowan tried to detach the cat, but Mort mewled as if

he'd lost his best friend. "Mind if I bring him?" she asked Zelli.

Laughter burbled from the dragon, along with clouds of steam. "Better to ask him if he minds riding a dragon."

"So long as he's with me, he won't even notice." Rowan vaulted to Zelli's back.

I mounted Quade, and we took to the air. The vista beneath his wings was reassuring, but disconcerting too. Clearly, the attack had been focused on the witches' lair because the surrounding countryside, while barren, lacked the fissures, cracks, and holes that had formed around the base of Ben Nevis.

Whatever was behind the attack probably knew about Rowan and her long tenure living among the witches. *"Do you think we should move the Inverlochy bunch back under Ben Nevis?"* I asked Quade.

"Let's wait to see what we find there, shall we?"

The dragon's words were both wise and troubling. Inverlochy might be shrouded in illusion, but it was far more vulnerable than the spot we'd just left.

CHAPTER THIRTEEN, ROWAN

Mort clawed his way up my body until he was draped around my neck. Flying didn't appear to bother him at all. Maybe I'd been right about him not even noticing since the sum total of his kitty-consciousness was fixed on me. Turning Tansy over to Bjorn's care had been gut-wrenching. Not because I didn't trust him. I did.

He's a far better healer than me, but that statement could be said about almost anyone. Even the witch healers are better at manipulating that type of energy than I am.

One of the byproducts of working by myself all these years has been it's spared me from today's kind of decisions. There's only one of me. I can only do so much, so I pick the fire that's burning brightest and go after it. Depending on what happens and if I have any magic left, I'll tackle the next one.

Nobody was more surprised than me when the touch of

my power kindled the spell Bjorn had set in motion over Loren, the first witch we treated. It had looked to me as if the casting was on the verge of igniting, but when I tapped it with my probe, it burst into action. I hadn't encouraged it. Hadn't fed any particular power into it at all. Proximity seemed to be sufficient.

Something about the way my ability braided with Bjorn's was essential for that spell to work. When he told me I had to remain with the dragons to heal the eight witches spread in a circle like spokes in a fragile wheel, I understood.

I didn't like it, but if I'd stuck with Tansy, the other witches wouldn't have pulled through. Working with the dragons was different from marrying my power to Bjorn's, but they were efficient and thorough. They did their part, set up the enchantment and stood aside, making space for me to kick their spell into action.

Because we did everyone together, it required a whole lot more magic to pull things off. Mostly, it affected me. The dragons could have done this all day, but I needed a break so my magic could recover.

Or I thought I did.

Maybe what I needed was an attitude adjustment. Half my blood was their blood. Had I babied myself unnecessarily all these years? With a dragon father and Ceridwen riding shotgun on the other side, I should be plenty strong to power through almost anything.

Mort purred louder and licked my neck with his rough tongue. I tightened my grip on the side of his body. He might be comfy a hundred meters in the air, but I worried he'd try to climb down or do something else ill-advised. I could catch him with magic, but he hated when I used my power on him.

It would be full dark soon. I could still see well enough to ascertain the destruction around the caves only extended half a kilometer or so. I wasn't keen on what that meant. The witches were in danger. Because of me. And in a much more direct way than I'd assumed when I'd kicked Inverlochy Castle open for them to borrow.

Then the worst threat was a Celt with a stick up his ass. I hadn't questioned any of the witches in various stages of recovery back at the caves. Probably should have. While the bat-like things had been the most serious adversary, I'd seen body parts suggesting at least a few dwarves and sprites had shown up. And there'd been one impressive snake carved into pieces.

Pride for my witch family ran deep. They'd been cornered, and they'd fought hard to save their home and themselves. Had any of the enemy pierced the caves? I didn't think so. Tansy would have told me. She'd said they'd dealt with rockfall within, but that Loren had gone outside to investigate. If dwarves or sprites or the snake had entered the caves, the witches would have remained within fighting them.

Something about the ancient Celtic stronghold still repelled evil.

Zelli had been quiet. I owed her an apology. "Sorry about earlier," I said. "I'm bad about jumping to conclusions. And down people's throats."

"Och, my throat is long enough to absorb most anything."

I patted her scaled neck. "Thank you for making light of it. I was pretty awful."

"Doona wallow in guilt. Larger issues are looming. Quade and I discussed a few things earlier. He had thought it prudent to select an off-world location for Bjorn to develop more familiarity with his magic."

"Sounds as if you've changed your minds," I said.

"Aye. Trouble is close. So near, we canna afford to be gone for as much as a fortnight."

I didn't realize how worried I'd been about being gone until she said we didn't have to leave. I had so much to do, I felt as if I were drowning. I'd barely made a dent in the lore books about being a Dragon Heir. Bjorn had those damned blades on a back burner. I'd walked out on Odin—and the Celts. There'd be a price for my arrogance, but I had no idea how or when the hammer would crash down on my head.

Bjorn had left too, but Odin and Nidhogg would like as not offer him more latitude, being closely related to them and all.

There was the Breaking spot to keep an eye on. And the place the bats had been. And the witches. And the growing crops. Just because treachery was staring us in the face was no reason to jettison the work we'd done on the garden so far. Another month, and we should be able to harvest the quicker-growing items. Like spinach and lettuce and kale.

"All those reasons," Zelli went on, proving she lived in my mind when she wanted. "And others as well. Nidhogg has summoned every dragon to a meeting in Fire Mountain. Odin will be gathering his forces as well. Yggdrasil must sign on for this effort. It willna be simple to get the One Tree's attention. Its consciousness is..."

"Elusive?" I supplied. Not that I knew from personal experience, but I gathered as much from Bjorn's accounts of his run-ins with the mighty ash tree.

"Aye, the tree is ancient and canny. It has its own priorities, and they rarely mesh with anyone else's. Another problem will be convincing those who live on the eight other worlds that they must help."

"Beyond the witches, I have no idea if anyone on Earth will lift a finger," I told her. "Mortals have gone into hiding since the Breaking. Where before they didn't believe in magic, now they're scared out of their wits by it. They don't trust anyone or anything with power, and they have less than zero interest in changing their outlook or listening to reason." I stopped to take a breath before adding, "Rather like throwing the baby out with the bathwater."

Zelli snorted laughter. "Interesting choice of words. Baby dragons do not take baths. Not until after their first molt."

The river Lochy flowed below us. I peered downward, doing my damnedest to split the illusion that hid the castle from view. I couldn't see a thing. "When are you and Quade going to this all-dragon meeting in Fire Mountain?" I asked.

Zelli circled to land. I cast magic in a wide net but didn't sense anything bigger than a rat beneath us. "What makes ye think ye're not coming along?" she asked in as neutral a tone as I'd ever heard from any dragon.

Air caught in my throat; I choked on saliva that headed

down my windpipe. "Why would we?" I blurted. "We're not dragons. Not like you, anyway."

"The other Dragon Heirs will be there."

"Didn't you say they live in Fire Mountain? Besides, you didn't answer my question."

The dragon thumped onto the ground amid a cloud of dust. I waited for it to clear before I jumped down with Mort still wound around my neck. My conversation with Zelli would have to wait. I skipped the crypt entrance and teleported into the castle. My Celtic blood allowed me entry, whereas the witches had to sneak in through an underground tunnel system.

My first stop was the courtyards. The seedlings were doing well. They'd grown a lot since I'd last seen them and had leafed out. I sent seeking magic arcing outward about the same time Bjorn materialized. He sent a questioning look zipping my way.

"They're one floor up," I said. "It's suppertime."

"All present and accounted for?"

"Yeah. Also, the land around the illusion hasn't been disturbed."

He nodded. "I noticed the same thing. Made me hopeful all was well here."

I closed my teeth over my lower lip. "Well" was a relative term. Just because this group of witches had escaped today didn't mean someone wasn't watching them closely. Waiting for an opportunity to strike.

I hustled up the stairs with Bjorn next to me. The witches had sensed our approach because Patrick met us in the corridor, a broad smile on his careworn face. "What a lovely surprise," he said. "Please. Have a bite to eat with us."

"If you're sure you have enough," Bjorn said.

"We do. Remember, we found all those bins of food here."

It felt like a small piece of the world came back into focus as we sat and shared the witches' evening meal. Conversation flowed freely, and I skirted as close as I have lately to believing Earth wouldn't really implode.

Once we'd eaten, Hilda looked from Bjorn to me. "Tell us why you're really here, and congratulations."

"I was wondering about that, but I didn't want to come out and ask. In case I was wrong." Patrick jumped up and offered a hand first to me and then to Bjorn.

"Och, sure and ye're mated," Leif said, his dark eyes shining with happiness for us.

For the next few minutes, the witches toasted us and made plans for a formal handfasting once everyone was back in the caves. Surely by then, the last bit of my resistance not so much to Bjorn, but to tethering myself to anyone for eternity, would have faded. Or at least, I would have made peace with it.

I hoped.

The mention of the caves for a handfasting ceremony was as good a lead-in as I was likely to get. "About the caves," I began, "everyone is fine, but they had a rough go."

Smiles faded, and everyone focused on Bjorn and me as we relayed what had happened.

"Thank Danu you two were there." Hilda lowered the hand she'd placed over her heart.

"Why in the bloody fucking hell was Loren stupid enough to go outside?" Patrick snarled.

"They were lured out," I said pointblank. "But they won't fall for that trick again. Not after today."

"I hope not," Patrick's tone had softened. "Those caves provide innate protection from evil. Earlier today proved that. The witches who remained within were unharmed."

"Maybe unharmed physically," Bjorn said, "but if I know aught of your kind they're eaten up with guilt because they didn't offer their assistance."

"We must go to them. Reassure them—" Leif began.

"Nay. Our task is finishing what we've begun," Patrick cut in. "The seedlings require our presence. We've employed sufficient magic to urge them to grow a wee bit faster, but not so much as to harm their nutrients."

"Do you believe splitting our forces will be our undoing?" Hilda asked me. It wasn't the first time the question had come up.

"Not if I can help it." I slapped my hands on the table in front of me. "Me being available was the only favor you asked when you were deciding to send witches here. I haven't been nearly as present as I'd have liked."

"We will do better," Bjorn said. "Between Rowan and me, we'll not let more than a day elapse without checking on you."

I turned to him. "Did Quade tell you about some dragon gathering in Fire Mountain?"

Bjorn furled his brows my way. "What gathering?"

"Mmph. So the answer is no. There's some kind of all-dragon mandatory meeting in Fire Mountain sometime soon.

When I told Zelli I didn't see why I had to attend, she sidestepped me, and then we arrived here. I was in a rush to get inside the castle, and I figured we'd talk more about it later."

"I understand why they'd want you," Patrick said, "but why Bjorn? Is it on account of him being your mate?" Color splotched his weathered cheeks. "No offense meant," he added hastily.

"There have been a few new developments," Bjorn said and sketched out the revelations from Odin's halls.

"So that's why you look different," Hilda murmured.

"Aye," Leif said. "Here I thought perhaps 'twas a trick of the light within this castle. It's a magical place even more so than the caves are. I run up against its enchantment at every turn."

"If we're backed into a corner and have to attend this dragon summit, I don't plan to remain long," Bjorn said. "I've been to Fire Mountain, and it's deucedly unpleasant."

"Hush! Don't let the dragons hear you," I cautioned him. "They see it as a sacred place."

"Because they were forged in fire," Bjorn said. "We weren't."

"Meanwhile," I addressed my next words to the witches, "do you have a pressing need for anything in particular? I believe you're safe so long as you remain within Inverlochy's illusion. But you can't leave. No trips into what's left of Fort William for supplies."

"We have what we need. After I ran into trouble with my last jaunt into town, we've grown cautious," Hilda said.

"Soul sickness is nothing to fool around with," Bjorn told

her. He was sensitive enough not to remind her she'd nearly died from it.

Mort meowed and jumped down, making his way around the table and licking up bits of food remaining on the plates.

"Time for us to get going." I pushed back from the table and stood. Mort sent a startled look winging my way and leapt across the table and into my arms.

"We need to take him back to the caves," Bjorn reminded me.

"I'll do that right now. So long as I'm about it, I'll take a couple more bins of the food stocks from here. Tell the dragons I'll meet all of you outside in a few minutes."

Hilda ran to me and hugged me with the cat squished between us. Patrick shook Bjorn's hand, and then he hugged me too. "Bye," I told them. "I'll be back as soon as I can."

Leif handed me two containers. "Lentils and cornmeal," he said, identifying their contents.

A bevy of farewells followed us as we trooped down the stairs. Once we reached the courtyard, I summoned a teleport spell. Mort yowled. He's never cared for magic touching his body, but I held on firmly, balancing him and the food bins. He'd like teleporting even less. No help for it.

"I'm going to find out what I can about this all-dragon gathering," Bjorn said.

"Good idea. Back in a flash."

The garden shimmered to nothingness, replaced by the entry cavern to Ben Nevis's cave system. I'd tried for a specific destination, and this time, I'd hit it spot on. I wasn't certain if anything else evil was lurking without, and I didn't want to have to fight my way out of something.

Mort was frantic to escape my grasp by the time my travel spell spit us out. After blasting me with a bevy of outraged yowls, he took off like a shot down the long corridor that ran the length of the caverns.

Cat delivered. Check. So far, so good. I headed for the common room to see what I could find out before I rejoined Bjorn and the dragons. As I'd expected, everyone was scattered through the generous room sipping what smelled like mint and anise tea. I set the containers on the first table I came to.

Cheers rang out when I scooted into the room. I raised my hands in front of me and shook my head. "No time, but I have a couple of questions."

"Anything," rose from multiple throats.

Tansy hustled toward me and pressed a steaming mug into my hands. I drank deep, grateful for the fragrant brew. "First, did anything bad get inside the caves."

"No," Loren told me. His black hair had been brushed back from his high forehead. Tall. Rangy. Thin. He'd changed into a clean pair of patched pants and a stretchy black top.

"We were just talking," another witch said. "Those of us who were slow to react, we were trapped inside. We tried to go out and help, but the cave entrance wouldn't budge."

I narrowed my eyes. An interesting bit of information, indeed. "Next question. What did you fight besides bats?"

"Not much," Tansy replied. "I saw a couple of dwarves

and a sprite. A snake tried to get through, but we chopped it in enough pieces it barely got out of the ground."

"Do you have any idea what clopped you in the back of the head?" I asked her. Dwarves were small. Too short to reach that high.

She shook her head. "I wondered the same. I felt something bearing down on me. It made me nauseous and lightheaded. But when I tried to turn around to see what it was, I couldn't. I started to run, but then I knew I'd been hit. Pain took over and I blacked out."

"Did any of the rest of you see anything that hasn't been mentioned?" I glanced from one witch to the next. Everyone was shaking their heads.

"Why couldn't we get out of the cave?" someone asked.

I considered the question. "My best guess is this cave has always held strong magic. It's why the Celts picked it for a stronghold long ago. Between their magic, and the power already here, the cave was sentient enough to seal itself off from the threat that stood at its gates."

"So we truly are safe here?" Tansy asked.

I drained the rest of my tea. "I believe so."

"How are Hilda and the others?" Loren asked.

"They're fine. Nothing has bothered them."

"Thank the goddess for that," Tansy murmured. "Does Inverlochy offer the same protections as here?"

I shrugged. "Honestly, I have no idea. My first presumption would be no, but my kin are a crafty lot. They knew enough to disguise Inverlochy. Perhaps that shield extends to magical beings too. You couldn't sense the castle until I touched it and made it visible."

Mort scuttled to me and wove around my legs. Apparently, he'd forgiven me. I bent to scratch his ears. "I have to leave again," I told him. "I'm sorry. I wish it were different."

Cats are wise. I knew not to make promises I couldn't keep. Like one where I told him I'd soon be back in the caves and we'd return to our old lives. Those days were gone. And I had no idea what the replacement would look like.

I straightened. "I'm sorry, but I have to go. I'll return as soon as I can." I pointed at the containers. "I brought more food from Inverlochy. Meanwhile—"

"Don't worry," Loren cut in. "None of us are leaving here. No matter what we hear outside."

"Aye," someone called from the back of the room. "Those kinds of shenanigans only work once."

My throat thickened. "I love you guys."

Before they could shower me with affection that would surely bring me to tears, I hustled out of the room. I called a travel spell and engaged it. I wanted to spend time in my cozy chamber, but it was an indulgence.

Celtic energy dragged at me, herded me. I'd have ignored it, but it was sabotaging my efforts to leave. Rather than fighting it, I followed a path shot with silvery light right to the shaft where I'd tossed my amulet, ring, and golden circlet. Clearly, they were sick of being buried and useless.

When I let my hand hover over the fissure, the wooden box rose until I could curve my fingers around it. Power pulsed warmly, but it no longer felt like Mother. Was it because she'd been banished and was no longer part of the Nine Worlds?

I opened the box and slipped the onyx amulet around my neck, the ring on my finger, and the delicate gold circle around my brow. They were different. Rather than draping me in Ceridwen's magic, they wove with my own. I looked at the box. It had done its job. No longer magical, it was still lovely, and I laid it on the packed earthen floor. Someone would find it and make good use of it.

This time when I launched a teleport spell, I shot from the cave as if someone had lit a cannon under me. The deserted lands around Inverlochy formed immediately, and I tumbled to a stop next to Bjorn and the dragons.

He draped an arm around my shoulders and snugged me against him. "I was just getting ready to leave and look for you."

Zelli puffed steam; Quade blanketed us too. In a backhanded way, I felt like I'd found a new home.

"*We* were preparing to fly to Ben Nevis," Quade corrected Bjorn.

"Well now you don't have to," I said. "Apologies, but I stopped long enough to talk with the witches. Catch me up on what I missed."

"Appears ye're reclaiming more than your dragon blood," Quade observed.

I touched the onyx amulet. "Once it was a gift from Mother, but now the necklace, ring, and circlet are mine."

"Aye, and a perfect match for your energy. Ye'll have to tell us what the witches had to say," Zelli spoke up, "but later. We should be leaving."

"Aye, we doona want to be late," Quade agreed.

I battled a sinking feeling. "Leaving for?"

"Fire Mountain. Where else?" Zelli sounded delighted. "Ye'll love it there. All dragons do. 'Tis our home."

Bjorn kissed me once, quick and hard, before letting go. We'd talk later, assuming we ever had time to ourselves again. "I'll need teleport coordinates," I began.

"Hop on," Zelli invited. "Dragons have our own ways of traveling. Fire Mountain is barred to all but us."

"Explains why I was able to go there," Bjorn muttered before vaulting onto Quade's back.

"How'd Mother get in?" I asked. Having her out of the way was such a relief, I almost didn't care how it had been finessed.

"Och, that's different. Ysien escorted her and parted the barrier," Quade replied.

I mounted Zelli. "If it's not too much trouble," I said once I was settled, "could you tell me about how Fire Mountain came to be?"

A shrill whistling trumpet told me she'd like nothing better. The baked clay smells of dragon power thickened around us, and Earth dropped away. Rather than the darkness I was used to between worlds, Zelli's casting had heat and light.

And air.

Blessed air. I relaxed and leaned against her neck, listening to the story of dragons and Fire Mountain.

The legend of the beginning of Fire Mountain has always been one of my favorites. When the Dragon Heir—*my* Dragon Heir—asked to hear the tale, I was pleased to oblige. 'Tisn't lengthy as legends go. I shall finish it afore we reach Fire Mountain.

"Long, long ago, there were no worlds at all," I began. "Everything was blackness. A void. The gods were naught but spirit, and they existed as energy without physical form.

"No one knows why, but a sphere shaped itself from nothingness and rioted through the void. Every place it bounced off of marked it, added to its power. Eventually, it caught fire and began to spin. It spun and burned. Mountains formed.

"The mountains became volcanoes that erupted, adding more heat and light to the spinning ball. Finally, it came to a stop. 'Twas still the only world in an endless void, but it was finding its way. The mountains formed a ring, still spewing magma. Caves hollowed out beneath the mountains. Water flowed from deep reserves within the newly quiescent sphere and molded pools within the caves. Fish swam in the pools.

"'Twas never a place for trees or bushes. Too hot and too dry. But the gods heard about the first world to have solid ground to walk upon. They visited and liked it enough to begin building other worlds. The Nine Worlds had their beginning on the flanks of Fire Mountain when 'twas verra young, but that is a different tale."

I blew out a fire-tinged breath. So far, Rowan had listened intently with her head leaned against my neck. "Go on," she urged.

"The gods' forms altered from spirit to bodies once they had a world to walk upon. Stories differ on this next part, but one day the god who ruled the winds found an egg deep beneath the ground. He was hunting for a spring because he was thirsty, and when he came out, he cradled the egg between his hands.

"He sensed life within the shell and took it upon himself to nurture the egg, keeping it at a stable temperature until it began to rock. Cracks ran through the shell, and the first dragon was born."

"Was it Nidhogg?" Rowan asked.

Her question made me smile. Why do people always assume men came first? Reminded me of the bogus Adam and Eve story. "Nay," I replied. "'Twas Dewi. She flourished on Fire Mountain. It provided exactly what she needed. Heat. Light. Fish and small creatures to eat."

"How'd they get there?" Rowan spoke up.

"'Tis a magical world, and it has been sentient from its earliest days. Food sufficient to sustain dragons showed up in much the same way as dragon eggs did. Who knows? The world must have welcomed and accepted its destiny as a home for dragons because it created a place perfectly suited to our needs. Eventually, herds of wildebeests took up residence, but not for many hundreds of years.

"More eggs showed up in roughly the same place," I went on, "but 'twas Dewi who ensured they survived through to hatching.

"More worlds, lots of them, followed on the heels of Fire Mountain. Fully corporeal, the gods had other places to roam. Hundreds of dragons had hatched by then, enough the ones who were grown decided we didn't require more. Not when we live forever.

"We sealed our world off from everyone but dragons after the doomsday prophecy predicting chaos if a dragon took a Celt to bed. Some of us disagreed with such an isolationist approach, but they were overruled. Meanwhile, dragons had sallied forth millennia earlier. Many remained in the Nine Worlds. Some took up residence on distant borderworlds. All of us return to Fire Mountain from time to time. It nurtures us, heals us, makes us whole."

I fell silent. I'd reached the end of the most important parts.

"Thank you," Rowan murmured.

"'Twas my pleasure. 'Tis I who am indebted because ye asked to hear of Fire Mountain's beginnings."

"Why do you suppose Nidhogg summoned everyone?" Rowan asked.

"I have no idea. 'Tisn't something he has done often. And not in a verra long time. We shall discover his intent soon, though. We are nearly home."

CHAPTER FIFTEEN, BJORN

Quade and I didn't talk much on the journey to Fire Mountain. I'd expected something like when I teleported to borderworlds. In other words, an airless abyss to suffer through. But whatever channels Quade tapped into had warmth and light and air. It loosely reminded me of the airliners mortals used to ride before the world broke. I was moving through space, not burning my own magic, and not struggling to breathe.

Several plusses.

I was glad Quade wasn't in a chatty mood. My last jaunt to the dragon's world wasn't one of my better memories. Someone—anyone—could have ripped the lid off the secrets of my birth. Nidhogg had claimed no one knew, but I'm not so sure about that. They all knew about Rowan, so it stood to reason they also harbored solid suspicions about me.

No one had said a word.

Instead, they'd let me stand in full sunlight, with both

suns beating down on my head as sweat poured off me. It had been so long ago, I didn't remember exactly what I'd been doing there. Odin had sent me. For something that hadn't worked out very well.

The dragons hadn't given me whatever it was I'd requested. When I returned to Valhalla emptyhanded, Odin had berated me. I swear, that man has the worst temper. Time hasn't improved it. After Ro and I walked out on him, I kept expecting one of his minions to show up, bind us with magic, and drag us back.

Not that it would have worked very well. I couldn't think of anyone in Odin's employ strong enough to hang onto Rowan and me if we didn't want to accompany them. Even Thor would have had a rough go of it. He's all bluster and brawn, but he doesn't have a tenth of Odin's power.

Loki is another story. He has a mean streak a mile wide. And a memory like a steel trap. You might win today's battle, but he'll never forget and, eventually, you'll pay for crossing him. In ways that make you wish you'd never been stupid enough to tangle with him in the first place.

"We'll be there soon." Quade broke his silence.

"What happens then?" I asked.

"We shall enter the caves in a particular spot, walk past the most sacred of the pools, and thence into the council chamber."

Excellent. I wouldn't have to stand outside under the relentless suns.

"Do you have any idea what Nidhogg has in mind?"

"I do," Quade said, "but such is not mine to reveal."

My cheerful thoughts about not baking beneath the

blistering skies of Fire Mountain evaporated. "Why am I suddenly starting to feel like a lamb being led to the chopping block?"

"I have no idea." Quade's reply was bland. Impossible to read anything beneath it. When I probed the dragon's mind, it was closed to me.

We bounced through a few air pockets and blitzed from the subtle glow of where we'd been into the glare of klieg lights bombarding us with heat and light. Except they weren't lights at all but the twin suns belonging to Fire Mountain. The air smelled hot and dry and burned. The ring of volcanoes still spewed smoke and fire. I'd always assumed the largest of them was Fire Mountain, namesake for this world.

The heat hit me like a wall, but it didn't seem quite as horrible as I remembered. Quade settled heavily on cracked red dirt with rocks scattered about as if the place had been a giant's bowling alley. I jumped down and asked, "Which way?"

"Dead ahead, but let's wait for Zelli and Rowan. That way we can enter together."

I tilted my head and looked up at Quade. "I'm guessing Ro and I will be the only non-dragons there."

'Ye're not exactly non-dragons." Scales clattered as he shrugged. "Odin may show up, given your relationship to Hel."

"Oh? And are we inviting Ceridwen as well? Did she receive a 'get out of jail free card' just for today?"

"I doona think so." Quade's eyes spun faster.

I felt like a jerk. "Sorry. This isn't a comfortable place for me."

"Why not?"

It was a fair question. I took stock. Fire Mountain hadn't changed. The twin suns were still up there. Parched dirt spread in every direction. Where before it had struck me as trashed, barren, my perspective had shifted. The clean, spare lines of the land held a macabre beauty all their own.

In the spirit of honesty, I met Quade's gaze. "It's not as bad as I remembered."

He nodded wisely. "Ye've changed. Hel's glamour kept many things from you."

I wasn't sure I liked the sound of that, but I wasn't eager to stuff foot number two into my mouth, either. Zelli's copper scales caught the suns' reflection as she winged toward us.

Even before the dragon landed, Rowan somersaulted off her back and floated down next to me. "Zelli told me the story of Fire Mountain. It was fascinating."

"It is," I agreed. "Dragons were the first creatures in all the universes."

"So you know the legend?" She raised a brow.

"I do, indeed."

Rowan narrowed her eyes. "Mother's in my head. She must have sensed me as soon as we crossed from the travel space into Fire Mountain."

I didn't care for the sound of that. "What's she saying?"

"Gawk. What isn't she saying? She's weeping and carrying on as if they're murdering her and laying her out for crows to pluck at her liver."

"We shall put an end to that," Zelli said. "Follow us within."

I'd been about to join with Ro and help erect shielding around her mind, but if the dragons had a fix, it was probably better. More permanent. We crossed about fifty meters of dirt to a gash in nearby cliffs. It was deceptive from a distance. Once we were close, I saw that it was easily big enough for a dragon to enter. The temperature dropped a good ten degrees as soon as we stepped within, and the air held moisture.

Both dragons took on a glowing aspect that lit our surroundings. We stood in a rounded cavern that might have been twenty meters across. Its ceiling extended far above us, and the circular chamber was lined with thousands of crystals that reflected the dragons' illumination.

Rowan tugged on my arm and jerked her chin at the dragons' retreating forms. Even though they'd moved through an archway at the far side of the cavern, the crystals still glowed warmly. They must have a way to concentrate and hold onto magic.

We hurried after Zelli and Quade down a gradually sloping corridor. I called a mage light because the lighting system in the entry cave didn't extend beyond it. The dragons were still glowing, but they'd pulled quite a way ahead.

"Leave me alone," Rowan muttered.

I wrapped a hand around her forearm. "Ceridwen?"

"Who else. Damn that woman. I liked her better when she was swimming in pride and paying me the slightest bit of attention annoyed the fuck out of her."

The tunnel zigged first right and then left. The dragons had stopped in a generous side cave. I assumed we were supposed to stop too since I had no idea where we were going. The underground warren of paths was starting to feel like a labyrinth.

"Oooh," Rowan sighed. "That's so pretty."

After scooting around Quade's bulk, I saw a turquoise pool. Fed by a waterfall and lined with shimmering white stones, it shone invitingly. Fish of all sizes flitted about in its waters. About the size of a small loch in the Highlands, it extended perhaps forty meters on a side.

"This is the first pool discovered on Fire Mountain," Zelli said. "As such, we pay it homage. Without water, dragons would not have flourished here."

"Was this near where the god of the winds found Dewi's egg?" Ro asked.

"'Twas." Zelli sounded pleased. "The egg was balanced on that rock outcropping." She pointed with an extended talon.

It was probably rude of me since Zelli had said she'd take care of Ceridwen, but I asked anyway. "How long before Ceridwen leaves off her incessant nattering?"

"Och. Can ye hear her too?" Zelli blew a plume of smoke upward.

"No. Thank all the gods, but—"

"Hey! She's gone," Rowan said. "Whatever you did. Thank you."

"I alerted Dewi. She addressed her kinswoman. It willna be permanent," Quade cautioned. "Perhaps placing her with the Morrigan was a mistake. Both of them hold vast power."

"Enough to escape?" I asked pointblank.

"Probably not," Zelli said.

I stumbled over the probably. I'd wanted her to reassure Ro and me that the two exiled Celts hadn't a prayer of subverting whatever magic bound them.

"We need to hurry." Quade hustled back into the main corridor. We followed him with Zelli behind us. Our configuration had changed. Was it accidental, or were the dragons concerned we'd double back? Make a run for it?

My lack of trust hit me between the eyes. Had I always been so wary? Or was it a recent development? One that had shown up after Nidhogg forced the spying dragonstone upon me?

I still couldn't bring myself to call him Father. Or anything remotely associated with such an intimate connection. I'd had an amazing father. He was dead, and I wasn't interested in finding a replacement.

We continued for perhaps another kilometer, past myriad branching side pathways. The occasional hub was lined with the same glowing chips that had been in the entry hall. This cave system was enormous. Did dragons live down here? It made sense they'd have crafted a retreat from the surface and its heat. If the lore was to be believed, this was but one of many caves.

For the first time, I wondered how many dragons existed. Since they were immortal, at least in principle every one who'd ever hatched was still somewhere. We picked our way down a steep grade. It flattened abruptly and flared into a huge chamber. Torches were spaced at intervals along the walls, crackling with the scent of dragonfire.

A raised dais at the front of the room held several dragons. Nidhogg stood in the middle, watching as dragons milled about. On either side of him were two smaller golden dragons with milky eyes. These must be the twin blind seers referred to in legend. Dewi's red-scaled head was bent as she conversed with one of the seers. Ysien scanned the room. He reminded me of a busybody, always taking notes, casting blame, and looking for problems, but Nidhogg appeared to rely on him.

The rush torches whooshed brighter and formed a burning circle all around the vast enclosure. It had to be some kind of sign the meeting was about to begin because everyone formed rough rows and quit talking among themselves.

I didn't bother counting, but there were a lot of dragons here. In every dragon color. Red, blue, green, copper, gold, black, and a few in-between shadings mostly in the copper-gold spectrum.

The torches retreated to their original configuration. Nidhogg lumbered a few steps nearer the assemblage. "The reason we are here today is—"

A blue glare punctuated with lightning bolts burst outward, showering the dais with streamers. Odin stepped from the gateway. "Damn it. Ye've already begun." He snapped his fingers, and the portal swooshed shut behind him.

I beat back a grin. Leave it to Odin not to apologize for being late. Nidhogg hadn't exactly thanked the dragons for jumping to his command and showing up, either. Maybe manners were a purely human convention.

"As I was saying," Nidhogg continued, "the reason we are here is to discuss the impact of two unprecedented developments."

I wondered what they were. Surely, the Breaking. Perhaps the other was Midgard's failing health.

"The sooner we rid ourselves of the Celtic sluts, the better," a black dragon called from near the front of the room."

"I dinna give ye leave to speak," Nidhogg thundered.

"Apologies, sire." The dragon bowed his head but not for long.

Fascinating. The Breaking wasn't even a blip on the dragons' radar, but babysitting the Celts loomed large. I didn't blame them. I'd do everything I could to avoid Ceridwen's company. From everything I'd heard, the Morrigan was far worse—

"Bjorn!" Rowan elbowed me.

"What?" I kept my voice low.

"Come on. Nidhogg wants us front and center." She grabbed my arm and began towing me toward the head of the room.

I shook free and walked by her side. What had I missed? And why had she and I been singled out. Surely we couldn't be the unprecedented developments. We were supremely unimportant balanced against all the other complications the Nine Worlds faced.

The chamber was even larger than I thought. It took at least three minutes to cross to where Nidhogg stood. Odin had moved back a pace or two to a spot between the assembled dragons and the dais. I've never been able to read his expressions, and today was no exception. He looked like he always did, grumpy and annoyed with the world.

Dewi intercepted us and puffed steam.

"None of that," Nidhogg growled. "Ye've apologized for your oversights when the Dragon Heir was young."

"Ye doona rule me," she growled back. "They're mated. The Dragon Heir and, for want of a better title, the Dragon Mage."

"Of course they are," one of the twin seers piped in a surprisingly high voice for such a large creature. "Such was foretold."

The anger I thought I'd moved past developed new life. What a bunch of bastards. They'd known about me, just as I figured. No one had given me leave to speak, but that had never stopped me before. I tried for a deferential tone and said, "I can see where you'd withhold prophecies from non-dragons, but were you ever planning to reveal anything to me?"

"They couldna see you," Odin said. "Not whilst Hel's glamour protected what ye were from prying eyes."

"You knew about me."

"Aye. As did Nidhogg." Odin stopped there.

Words crowded against the back of my throat, wanting out. Of course Nidhogg had known. He'd sired me, albeit unwillingly. Fine. So the Fire Mountain dragons hadn't known about me. Until right now.

"All of you"—Rowan spread her arms wide—"knew about me. Except maybe Dewi, the one dragon who might have made a difference."

"Why did none of you tell me?" Dewi pushed to her full

height. Such things may have mattered to other dragons, but they were all so much taller than me, it didn't make her any more imposing.

Nidhogg twisted until his gaze fell on her. "Because I instructed them not to. What would ye have done with the knowledge?"

"Why, I'd have—" She broke off abruptly.

"Exactly." Nidhogg nodded. "Ye'd have banished the father. We already took care of it. Naught ye could have done about Ceridwen. Dragon-linked children are impossible to destroy. Had ye called her on her treachery, ye'd have created a deep divide amongst the Celts. She would have ripped the pantheon apart. At least this way, by the time the truth surfaced, the other Celts were more than ready to divest themselves of Ceridwen—and her cauldron.

"We assumed she'd gift her spawn with the truth. She never did." Nidhogg exhaled a fire-laden breath. "Meanwhile, our seers kept coming up with new wrinkles in their future telling."

"Start at the beginning," someone yelled.

"There are two beginnings," Nidhogg replied. "Hel tricked me long ago. Using skills from Loki, her da, she stole my seed and created him." He extended a talon my way.

"I claim kinship bonds to him," Odin boomed. "Just so there is no misunderstanding."

I'd have growled at him, told him how warm and fuzzy his words made me feel, but I wouldn't have gotten through. He was convinced he'd done me a great honor, and I was smart enough not to throw it in his face.

"The second beginning is more complex," Nidhogg went

on. "Ceridwen seduced one of our dragons. She worked long and hard to lull him into believing they could subvert the prohibition against such a pairing. Rowan was the result. I was on the verge of revealing her heritage when Ceridwen cast a spell that had disastrous consequences to Midgard. Hundreds of millions of mortals died, and the energy balance of the Nine Worlds became seriously skewed.

"A vast understatement," Odin muttered.

Nidhogg cast a pointed look his way, but I was certain it wouldn't deter Odin. If he had something to say, he'd say it no matter what the dragon thought.

"Once again," Nidhogg continued, "I cast about for an optimal time to toss the veils about Rowan aside and allow her to claim her rightful title as a Dragon Heir. There has never been a Celtic Dragon Heir afore, so none of us ken the extent of her abilities."

"We foresaw the two dragon hybrids mating," one of the seers interrupted. "It is an important pairing because of how strong their magic is."

"Why is that?" I asked. So long as we were here, and the dragons were gawking at us like circus attractions, I may as well get as much information as I could.

The seer nodded. His milk-white eyes spun slowly. "Between you, ye command the full spectrum of power. All four elements. All four seasons. All the strength of both the Norse and Celtic pantheons. With dragon magic to season the mix."

My eyes widened. I hadn't expected him to answer me, but his reply was enlightening.

Beside me, Rowan said, "Wow. What a lot to live up to."

"Ye'll have plenty of opportunity—" the seer began, but Nidhogg silenced him with a wave of his foreleg.

I straightened my shoulders to make myself as impressive as possible, but it was a joke in a room full of dragons. "If there is something specific that pertains to Rowan and me, I want to know what it is."

"Ye sat in the Celts' council chamber and listened to Ceridwen," Nidhogg reminded me.

"So I did, but she lies."

"And tells the truth too," Odin said. "In this instance, what she said about most prophecies never seeing the light of day is true. We would do you a disservice were we to lay out all the possible roads spread before you."

"What roads?" Rowan's tone was shriller than usual. "Whatever are you talking about?"

"I gathered the dragons for two reasons," Nidhogg said. "The first was so they would recognize you and provide any assistance you request of them. Zelli is bonded to you. Quade shall work with Bjorn, but beyond those two, every dragon here will not hesitate to help. Do I make myself clear?"

Scales clanked as heads nodded.

I had a feeling I wasn't going to like the second reason, and I girded myself for bad news. For Nidhogg to offer up every dragon meant what he had in store for us was far worse than what I figured was already riding in the wind.

To my surprise, Nidhogg motioned Odin next to him. "The second reason"—Odin picked up the banner—"is we have partially identified one of the problems keeping Midgard from healing her broken places."

I gripped Rowan's forearm. This related to us. I was certain of it. Judging by the tension in her muscles, she knew it too.

"What does this have to do with dragonkind?" someone asked.

"Aye," another voice cut in. "We doona concern ourselves with other worlds. Other races."

"In this instance, we do," Nidhogg said.

"Why?" the same voice persisted.

Both seers lumbered around the dais. I couldn't tell them apart. The one on the right said, "'Tisn't the nature of dragons to be apart from our own."

The other said, "Rowan's father has done much damage. He planted the idea for the breaking spell in Ceridwen's mind."

"What?" Rowan shrieked. "They're still talking to each other. What the fuck?" She clapped a hand over her mouth and mumbled, "Sorry."

"Your first task," Odin told her—and I guess me, "is to locate the banished dragon. He slipped beyond our scope long ago."

"Wouldn't a dragon be better suited to hunting their own?" I asked.

"Ye're both dragons," Nidhogg replied. "Start acting as befits your blood."

I planted myself in front of him and Odin. "Nay. I'm the master sorcerer for the Nine Worlds. If there's a 'way to act,' it's predicated on my long tenure compounding potions and dispensing magic."

"Yes, and I've spent years passing as a witch," Rowan

reminded everyone. "Once we find my dastardly father—assuming it's even possible—what do we do with him?" She licked at dry, chapped lips. "I'm a little slow on the uptake, but you tapped me because he and I share blood, and blood-bound spells are powerful."

"Smart wench." Odin beamed at her. I could have punched him.

Rowan's "what do we do once we locate him" question was important. We couldn't kill him. I waited, assuming someone would answer her.

"Ye'll figure it out," Odin said.

"Not good enough," I growled.

He focused his one eye on me. "Cast a spell. Find something to immobilize him. Ye canna kill him, but—"

"If you're not going to be more help than that, be quiet," Rowan told him.

Odin whipped a hand back, ready to slap her for impertinence, but I stepped between them. "She is my mate. Mine. You will not touch her."

Odin burst out laughing and dropped his hand to his side. "Well, well, Son. Ye're finally coming into your own."

He sounded surprised, and it didn't endear him to me. If he'd assumed I'd always be a third-rate sorcerer, why encourage Hel to come clean?

Side conversations had picked up again, and the room hummed with chatter. Rowan and I would be hot topics for many a month, if I knew anything about dragons. Besides, no one had asked them to do anything. Except aid us if we happened to cross their paths and needed them.

Quade trudged the length of the room with Zelli next to

him. Both inclined their heads to Nidhogg. "Our assignment is locating Cadir and defanging him?" Quade raised a scaled brow.

"Mmph. Seems my absentee father has a name." Sarcasm blazed a path through Rowan's words. "What does it mean?"

"Destroyer of Life," I told her as a chill marched up my spine.

"Correct," Nidhogg replied.

"I would accompany them as they seek Cadir," Dewi said.

Nidhogg looked surprised. "If ye wish it, I canna stop you."

Fire flashed from her upturned jaws. "Part of this is my fault. Had Ceridwen not blinded me to truth, I might have been able to intervene afore the widespread destruction that ruined Earth."

"We would welcome your presence," Quade told her.

"Shall we leave?" Zelli asked. It felt as if she was inquiring if we'd been dismissed, but I wasn't in a hair-splitting mood.

"Anytime ye wish," Nidhogg replied.

Rowan winced. "Mother is at it again. If you're not careful, she'll warn Cad—whatever the rest of his name is, and our job will turn from difficult to impossible."

"Strengthen the warding around her," Nidhogg ordered. "And separate her from the Morrigan." Several dragons jumped to comply.

"Get on," Quade told me.

Odin held up a hand. "Afore ye leave, know that I will make whatever resources ye require available."

It was an incredibly generous offer coming from him, the ruler who squatted like a vengeful crow over spoils from the Wild Hunt. I thanked him before vaulting onto Quade. Rowan was astride Zelli, and magic bubbled around us as the dragons prepared to teleport away from Fire Mountain.

"Where are we going?" I asked Quade.

"Where do ye wish to go?"

"Back to Vanaheim. I have blades to collect, and Rowan will want to look in on the witches before we begin hunting Cadir." Something about his name left a sour taste on my tongue.

The walls of the dragons' hall fell away. We'd talk about Rowan's dragon father, but not before we returned home and I could build strong wards around us. I might be wrong, but if the incursion into Midgard was any bellwether, he'd developed a network of spies and allies that spanned the universe.

CHAPTER SIXTEEN, ROWAN

I wanted to talk with Bjorn, but it would have to wait until the dragons' travel spell spit us out. I didn't trust employing telepathy where others could listen in. Hell, I wasn't even sure I could reach him. I'd never traveled through anything like the channels the dragons used to teleport. Was this something special where the destination was always Fire Mountain? Or were all their teleport spells like this?

The onyx amulet thrummed warmly against my chest. The stone in the ring glowed. I'd been right to claim the jewelry pieces. They concentrated my power.

I thought about the dragon father I'd never even suspected existed until quite recently. I could easily see him growing embittered by enforced isolation from his kinsmen. And angry at Ceridwen since her life didn't change at all after she suckered him into her bed.

If the seer dragons spoke true, and he'd been behind the

Breaking, it explained a lot. He couldn't get to either Ceridwen or me directly, but splitting the world asunder was a great backdoor. It had placed Ceridwen in a compromising position and forced the Celts to move to a borderworld. I'd already taken up with the witches, but the Breaking narrowed our existence to bare necessities.

Had he known?

That part didn't matter. My guess was he'd gone mad. Ceridwen always was attracted to men who lived on the ragged edge. The cavalcade of lovers, human and otherwise, she'd taken into her bed would have shocked me if I'd been old enough to know better. By the time it occurred to me something might be amiss with her choices, I was on my way out of the Celtic stronghold, anyway.

Even the other Celts looked askance when she took up with a vampire. She told everyone he'd reformed, but it didn't look like that to me. He always smelled of blood and rot. I didn't see how she could stand him next to her. He was gorgeous, with long silvery hair and emerald eyes. But he stank, and his eyes had this fey aspect lurking in their depths. I'd caught him looking at me as if I were an appetizer at time or two.

Ceridwen was powerful enough to keep him from taking her blood and turning her. I was certain she wouldn't have lifted a finger to protect me, so I spent a lot of time hiding out at my pool with the standing stones. No one could find me there.

I squeezed my eyes shut long enough to rest them a little and blot out images from my youth. Just another charming trip down memory lane. I had zero good memories of my time with the Celts. It was a wonder I'd found the wherewithal to knock on the witches' door. Maybe a small part of me understood how close I'd been to tumbling down a one-way rathole into a place where I stopped caring.

About everything.

"How did ye find Fire Mountain?" Zelli's question dragged me out of the dreary pit my thoughts had become.

"I loved the crystalline walls that hold light. And the pool had incredible energy. I'd like to spend more time there."

"We shall." She sounded pleased. "Hang on. Just a couple of bumps and we'll be back in Vanaheim."

"Is this, uh, method of teleporting unique to Fire Mountain?"

"It is," she confirmed. "Our homeland welcomes us back and ensures the journey willna tax us. If ye dinna carry dragon blood, ye wouldna be allowed in this portal system."

I'd suspected as much. The bumps she'd predicted weren't too bad. Soon we touched down in the courtyard outside Bjorn's cottage. He and Quade had beaten us there, and Dewi was just coming in to land. She skidded to a stop but didn't fold her wings.

"Many of my companions remain in Valhalla. I shall fill them in on the latest news and determine if aught of import has passed since we left Odin's halls."

"We'll either be here, or—" I began.

She waved a foreleg at Zelli and me. "I can find you no matter where ye end up." Her wings were already furled. She crab walked a few meters away and leapt skyward, gaining altitude quickly.

Silly me. Of course she could locate me; all she had to do was cast a seeking spell. I fashioned a bit of magic to cushion my egress and jumped from Zelli's back. So many tasks faced me, I decided I should make a list. Something I hadn't ever done before, but I didn't want to miss anything.

Bjorn joined me on the ground and strode to his cottage. Someone had left a scrawled note nailed to the door. He snatched it and unfolded what looked like deer hide, scanning its contents.

"What does it say?" I'd have just read over his shoulder, but didn't want to be too presumptuous.

"It's from Hagar. Apparently, Nidhogg and Odin paid him for my blades, but I need to show up so he can smelt them."

"What need do ye have for swords?" Quade asked.

A corner of Bjorn's mouth twitched upward. "When I could be using fire? Or magic?"

"Aye. Exactly." The dragon shook himself from head to toe and folded his black wings neatly.

"After my first serious battle, Nidhogg and Ysien sat with me to determine an array of weapons. Nidhogg has always recognized what I am. Presumably, Ysien as well since he seems to know everything. They're who instructed me to commission the blades."

"Interesting," Zelli said, followed by, "Quade and I shall pay Jotunheim a visit."

I remembered when we had stopped there quite well, but I had no idea why she'd want to go back. Before I could dig for details, she continued, "We need allies throughout the Nine Worlds. The giants are a logical starting place."

"'Twill be an uphill endeavor," Quade rumbled. Smoke streamed from his nostrils. "No one will see the need to do aught differently than they have since the dawning of the Nine Worlds."

Bjorn still held onto the deerskin. "So long as you brought it up, be sure to stop by Svartalfheim."

"The dwarves' home," Quade muttered. "Why? They live underground in caverns too small to accommodate us."

"That last battle around Ben Nevis, dwarves were among the fallen," I reminded him. I hadn't realized they had their own place within the Nine Worlds, or I'd have taken more time to examine the dead ones. You can learn a lot from a corpse.

"I should have paid closer attention." Bjorn sounded thoughtful. "And I might have if a bat hadn't singled me out. Dwarves have never joined forces with evil before. Mostly, they are smiths, craftsmen. Many powerful gifts, like Odin's spear, originated from their workshops."

"We should go there first," Quade said.

"Aye, perhaps they require our help." Zelli sounded determined.

"I've rethought this. Better if you go to the giants' world and return," Bjorn suggested. "That way, I can accompany you to Svartalfheim. They know me, trust me. I've treated their ailments. It's unlikely they'll leave their dens to talk with you. Dragons or no, they don't know you."

"Hold up, everyone," I said. "Unless I missed something, our next major undertaking is locating the perfidious dragon who sired me. If we get sidetracked on a hundred other equally worthy tasks, we'll never find the time to go after him."

Bjorn nodded. "Excellent point. My first priority is the blades because Nidhogg believes I'll need them. After that, we can search for Cadir."

I thought about it. "I'm shelving the history lesson and going right for ways to deal with Cad-whoever, once we locate him. That's got to be in your books and scrolls too, right?" I asked Bjorn.

"Should be," he replied.

"What's wrong that I can't seem to remember Father's name?" I muttered.

"Mayhap not something wrong but something right," Zelli said. "His name is evil. Makes my scales crawl, and it has since he cracked the shell of his egg."

"We need to say his name, though, no matter how much it creeps us out," I pressed. "Every powerful spell I've come across to exert control requires use of the subject's true name."

"Aye, but ye doona have to utter it much beforehand," Quade said.

"We have the bones of our first steps in place," Bjorn told everyone. "The dragons will begin informing each world of the need to cooperate." He rolled his eyes and added, "Good luck with that."

"Doona underestimate our powers of persuasion." Zelli's jaws lolled into the dragon equivalent of a smile.

"I'll teleport to Hagar's and return as quick as I can with an assortment of short and long blades," Bjorn went on.

"And I'll see what the lore has to say about capturing

renegade dragons. If I get done before the rest of you are back, I'll check on the witches." I headed for the cottage, intent on getting my teeth into my part of our joint project.

Magic rose behind me. Dragon-laced power that held the scent of Fire Mountain's suns. Dewi had, presumably, flown to Bifrost and taken the bridge, thumbing her scales at the "Norse only" rule. Although, Zelli had said it didn't apply to dragons.

Footsteps followed me into the cottage. By the time I turned to face Bjorn, he was half naked and dropping his stained clothing into a basket near the sink. His nude torso made breath hitch in my throat. He bent over the sink and pumped water into it.

I could use a sponge bath too, but if I took my clothes off, we were doomed. No way I'd be able to keep my hands off him. I was having a hell of a hard time as it was. Muscles played across his back and arms as he wrung out a cloth and wiped dust and grime from his skin. I could have watched him, gape-jawed, forever.

Staring at him wasn't doing anything except making me long to tumble him back into his bed. The cottage still held the scents from our lovemaking, and they stoked my hunger. He dipped his head under the spigot and pumped water over it, bringing some around to wash his face.

Draping a towel around his neck, he used it to soak up the water dripping from the ends of his white-blond hair. When he turned around, his smile melted my heart and set the rest of me on fire. Not that I required any encouragement.

"Feel free to bathe." His grin widened. "After I'm gone.

If you undress, I won't be responsible for my actions, and we have too much facing us as it is."

I swallowed around a dry place in my throat and quit rubbing my thighs together. "So I'm supposed to manage my, um, needs with your shirt off, but bare breasts will be your undoing?"

He held up a hand and walked to a row of garments hanging on hooks. "We'll find time, darling." He dragged a clean tunic over his head, followed by a leather vest, before he covered the short distance to me and wrapped me in his arms. His heart beat double time beneath my ear. I'd kept my gaze above his waist, but I felt the press of him against my belly. Long and hard and hot.

I snuggled against him, but not for very long.

"Before you go," I said, "what did you think about Fire Mountain?"

"They're not telling us everything."

"Why do you suspect that?" My eyebrows shot upward. I hadn't even considered that aspect.

"Just a feeling. Odin was downright convivial—for him. He's never friendly. Never does anything for anyone else. Something is in this for him. Something big, but I can't figure out what."

"It seemed odd to me he was even there." I spoke slowly as I considered what it might mean. "He was the only one without dragon blood."

"Nidhogg is the Norse dragon," Bjorn pointed out.

"He wouldn't have invited Odin."

A snort riffled past Bjorn's beautiful mouth. "Nay. Odin invites himself. I could be really off-base, but for some reason they can't locate this father of yours. So they're using us to do it."

"I'm not worried about finding him," I said. "Now that I've had time to roll it around, it's as simple as putting a blood vector into action. Those types of seeking spells are easy for me."

"Aye. It's not the finding him. It's the what the fuck do we do with him once we do. My biggest concern is we'll open a pathway for him to return to the Nine Worlds. If he could do as much damage as he presumably has from such a great distance..."

Bjorn didn't have to say any more. I got it. Our discussion was disturbing enough, my lust had vanished, replaced by worry. "Maybe I'll unearth something in the scrolls," I muttered.

"Speaking of them." He walked to the shelf that held his source materials and whipped two scrolls and an ancient-looking book bound in cracked black leather from the shelves. "Start with these."

I cast a doubtful glance at what appeared to be months' worth of reading and said, "I'm on it."

"I'll return as soon as I can." He started for the door before swinging in a half circle to look at me. "Do ye have any idea how difficult 'tis to walk away from you? Every cell in my body wishes naught but to remain. To remove your clothing, lay you on yon bed, and—" He'd switched to Old Norse, the language he used when he was too emotional to search for English words.

"You're not making this any easier." My voice was thick, rough with desire. I started toward him but forced my feet to stop right where they were. If we touched each other again, we'd be lost. Both of us knew it.

His chiseled lips formed a mischievous grin. "We can take turns being strong. Won't work forever, but 'twill have to do for now."

Power rose around him in the many shades of the sea. When it cleared, he was gone. The cottage smelled of him, of us. My mind was muzzy with heat and need. Finally, I walked to the sink and did what I could to rinse myself. The icy water helped clear my head—a lot. I didn't have clean clothes here, so I borrowed a shirt from off his rack. I'd grab something from my room when I checked on the witches.

Determined to soldier through the stack of lore and legend, I placed the scrolls and book on the table, made myself a mug of tea, and settled in to read. Every lore book was written in a different language. Most had been penned by hand. I started honestly enough, determined to read every word, but I quickly switched to magic, instructing it to highlight the important aspects.

Hours slid by; the angle of light coming through the cabin's single window dimmed until it told me night was imminent. Unlike Earth, Vanaheim didn't appear to have seasons. Not ones affecting the day-night cycle. At a few points, I helped myself to bread and cheese from Bjorn's larder.

I was most of the way through the book and hadn't found anything particularly useful. Whoever had written the tome —and it was probably more than one mage—shied away from the topic of dragons.

Probably no one had ever set out to capture one before.

Didn't make me feel any better. I rubbed my eyes and raked my hands through hair that had dried hours ago. Maybe this would be a good time to check on the witches. I wasn't getting anything done here. No one was back. The more I thought about it, the better I liked the idea.

This way, I'd be ready to leave for points unknown to scare up Daddy once everyone else returned. I was mildly concerned about Bjorn, but I had no idea how long it took to create magical blades. I wasn't at all worried about the dragons.

Before I could talk myself out of it, I stood and gathered a travel spell to me. My magic has felt a whole lot stronger lately. Nidhogg seemed to think claiming my heritage made a difference, but I didn't buy it. Not entirely. Now I could see where Hel ripping a glamour off Bjorn would have made a difference, but no one had done jack shit squat to change me.

I cut off that line of thought. It made me uncomfortable because it suggested a third party somewhere on the sidelines who'd been yanking my puppet strings for years. For once, I couldn't blame Ceridwen.

The amulet warmed as if reminding me to use its talents. I grasped it and set my spell in motion.

Bjorn's cottage faded, replaced by the illusion around Inverlochy. I didn't plan on staying, so I used subtle threads of magic to do a nose count. Everyone was hale and hearty and inside just like they were supposed to be. I even checked on the plants. They'd gained half a meter. Maybe my magic wasn't the only element running rampant.

Satisfied this contingent of witches was safe, I altered my

destination coordinates and came out in Ben Nevis's entry cave. After making certain everyone was doing all right, I cast an obfuscation spell to discourage anyone knowing I was there and headed straight for my room. Mort was curled on my bed looking so despondent, my heart went out to him. I dropped my invisibility illusion and sank next to him, cradling him in my arms.

Cats are wise beings. He knew I wouldn't be there long, so while he allowed me to hold him, he didn't purr or lick me or jump to his favorite spot around my neck. I reached into his mind and said, *"I'm sorry. I miss you too. A lot. I wish things were different, but I don't know if I'll ever be back here to stay."*

He did meow then, a sad little sound that sheened my eyes with tears. I cuddled him for as long as I thought I could get away with before I grabbed a few items from the hooks where I keep my meager wardrobe and teleported back to Bjorn's house.

It was full dark. Zelli and Quade were in the courtyard. Something about the quality of their silence told me they'd stopped talking the second they sensed my approach. "What?" I asked.

"We will talk once Bjorn returns," Quade said.

"Aye, he'll be here presently," Zelli added.

I sent power in a quick arc and felt Bjorn's energy. Sure enough, he strode through a gateway amid clattering and clanging. Three knives hung from sheaths attached to a leather belt. Two thick swords were encased in scabbards. A thinner blade hung free. That was what was making all the racket.

"Quite a haul," I said.

He took in the clothing draped over my arm and said, "How are the witches?"

"Fine. I checked both places."

He unbuckled various sword belts and laid them near the door to his cottage. "These are heavy. They'll take some getting used to. How'd the lore hunt go?"

"Meh. Not good. It's why I took a break to look in on the witches."

Dragon imbued power blasted out of nowhere and draped around the four of us. When I tested it, I ran into an impenetrable ward.

"Whoa. Impressive," Bjorn said. "I'm guessing you found something you don't want bandied about."

"We did." Zelli didn't sound happy.

"Should we wait for Dewi?" I asked.

"We doona know if we can trust her." Quade got the words out, but I bet they cost him.

"Or anyone else." Fire shot from Zelli's mouth and smoldered, creating clouds of smoke when it ran into the ward. "Sorry. I'll try not to do that."

Breath hissed through Bjorn's teeth. "Come on. Let's have whatever this is. And not in dribs and drabs. Before you begin, you should know that Loki may not look much like a giant, but he began in Jotunheim. He had to scheme his way into Asgard and a seat at Valhalla's head table. He and Odin have played a game of one-upmanship forever."

"Fair enough," Quade replied. "We started in Jotunheim as agreed..."

CHAPTER SEVENTEEN, BJORN

"It took us a while to find anyone," Zelli said. "A storm was raging. Snow. Ice. Sleet. If I'd been alone, I'd have left, but Quade insisted we not leave any rocks unturned. Or in this case, any blocks of ice." She shook her head. "Who chooses a land of eternal winter?"

I restrained myself by not pointing out Fire Mountain wasn't an ideal environment for most individuals, either.

"We pressed on." Quade's deep voice rumbled. "A castle reared up from the storm as if someone had plopped it dead in our path. It might have been there all along, but I believe it was hidden behind powerful illusion. Lights shone through many windows, and music drifted along the wind. I'd been hearing it for a while but assumed it was a trick of the ceaseless gusts."

"I bugled," Zelli continued. "It got someone's attention, although I have no idea how the hell they heard us above the howl of the storm."

"Giants have exceptional hearing," I said.

"Aye, they must," Quade agreed. "But it runs deeper than that. Someone withdrew the enchantment keeping the castle hidden from view, so they must have sensed us. They lowered a drawbridge over a frozen moat, raised the portcullis, and opened their home. It was quite a relief to get out of the storm. Also convenient they're as large as we are. No stooping in their halls."

"Aye, we could stand straight. After we exchanged names, they offered us meat," Zelli said.

"Aye, a succulent young pig for us to share," Quade added.

Damn it. Eating with the giants was almost as bad an idea as eating in Hel's realm. Accepting food gave others power over you, but perhaps dragons were strong enough to resist. Their magic trumped the giants' by a good big bunch.

"We tried to talk with them whilst we ate," Quade went on. "Warning them as it were of evil lurking at our gates."

"They laughed and dismissed our warnings." Zelli shrugged. "I can see where they would. After all, no one in their right mind visits Jotunheim. 'Tisn't as if there's a line of sorcerers anxious to move in and take up residence in a land of perpetual winter."

"We were nearly done eating when Loki popped through a portal," Zelli said. "I recognized him from our earlier meeting in Odin's halls. Except he'd sobered up."

I groaned. Couldn't quite keep it in. Loki was such bad news. Nothing decent ever came of even making eye contact with him. Crap. No wonder we were sitting under a ward, and both dragons were spun out about the world being out to get us. The slimy touch of Loki's magic had that effect on people.

"Let me guess." I shoved my tired shoulders straighter. "He told you Odin is in cahoots with the Celts—"

"Aye, but how did ye know?" Quade lowered his head nearer to mine, eyes spinning like pinwheels.

"I didn't. But Loki is a shit-stirrer. He'll say whatever he thinks you'll swallow and seed it with a believability casting. And laugh and caper all the while, so you don't think too deeply about the line of warmed-over crap he's trying to shove down your throat."

"I dinna trust him on the face of things," Quade said.

"Nor did I," Zelli broke in. "I tossed a truth spell over him once he began nattering on about Odin and the Celts."

"Somehow I can't see him sitting still for that," Rowan muttered.

"He dinna have a choice," Zelli said.

I wasn't so sure. Loki had taken advantage of his time in Asgard to strengthen his magic by borrowing lavishly from the Aesir. I'd watched him take a little here and a little there. I'd even been called on to treat the odd god or goddess who'd fallen mysteriously ill. I quietly fixed things and never told them who was stealing their power. Loki would have denied it. And plotted revenge. Like I've said, I give the trickster god a very wide berth.

"Exactly what did he say?" I prodded.

Quade nodded somberly. "He said Odin has had several meetings with Gwydion, Bran, Arianrhod, Arawn, Andraste, and Dewi since our get-together in the Celts' council hall. According to him, the four winds and Poseidon even took part in a couple of them. Odin has determined the Nine Worlds are finished, and he's questing about for a place the Aesir can run to. By Loki's account, Odin asked whether there might be space for them on the Celt's borderworld."

"The giants dinna like that at all," Zelli broke in. "They fussed and fumed and stomped until the verra floors shook. Loki told them he was joking, but then he winked at me. My truth spell had been acting...oddly, and it quit working at all after that." She blew out a smoky breath. "It gets worse, though. I picked up the same scent wafting about him that I sensed around the pillar that nabbed Bjorn."

I snarled. Tricks like that were vintage Loki. He ran roughshod over anyone he could for his own amusement.

"Moving in with the Celts is a pile of shit," Rowan said. "Odin knows better than to ask. For a couple of reasons. First, the Celt's borderworld is small. Second, they'd have less than zero interest in sharing it with people they've always considered inferior."

I filed the information away. I'd never actually heard anyone say what I'd suspected forever: the Celts viewed themselves as a cut above their Norse counterparts. Wonder how they felt about the Greek and Roman pantheons? Or any of the Asian ones. I circled my mind back to more relevant ground.

"How does Rowan's father fit into the equation?" I asked.

"Loki told us 'twas naught but a red herring to keep us occupied," Quade replied.

"I asked him how he even knew about Rowan's father," Zelli said.

"And?" I leaned forward.

"He left as precipitously as he'd arrived." She rolled her spinning eyes.

Alarm bells tolled deep within me. I'm a truth sayer among my other talents, and none of what Loki said held the ring of facts, except a single item. "They do want to keep us occupied. Or Loki does." I spoke slowly. "But he has plans he's not revealing. Probably something to do with shielding Rowan's dragon father from discovery."

"Do you suppose he's been in contact with him?" Rowan asked.

"I have no idea, but I wouldn't put it past him. He might have been the driving force behind Cadir talking Ceridwen into the Breaking spell. It's something very much in character. The bigger the shitstorm, the better he likes it."

"We need to ask Dewi if she's been part of secret meetings with the other Celtic gods and Odin," Rowan said.

"I hate to anger her, but she canna lie to another dragon," Zelli said. I thought she sounded tired, but I might have been reading her wrong. Or maybe I was projecting because I was weary to my bones. The problems we faced were suddenly a whole lot more complicated than Ceridwen getting a wild hair up her ass and shattering Midgard to drive Rowan back to her side.

This was starting to hold all the appeal of a puzzle with layers hidden inside other layers until you weren't sure where the beginning was. Or the end. Normally, I enjoyed that type of challenge, but not when the stakes were so high and the penalty for a mistake so hazardous.

A ripping, tearing explosion brought me around fast, in

time to see a ruby claw slicing neatly through Quade's ward. "Why are ye hiding?" Dewi punctuated her question with a shrill bugle.

"We are not hiding," Quade informed her.

"Merely being prudent," Zelli said and bugled back.

I raked a hand through my hair. With all the racket the dragons were making, I was certain a lot of Vanheim's residents would come running and hide themselves in the thick trees around my cottage. Dragons in the sky were commonplace, but dragons on the ground talking with you weren't.

Two sets of talons finished off the hole Dewi had sliced in the ward. She began to peel it back, but Quade said, "Doona bother," and withdrew the magic powering his barrier.

I switched to telepathy to shield our discussion from the prying ears I was certain had to be nearby. May as well tackle the crux of this head-on, so I asked Dewi, *"Have the Celts had secret meetings with Odin?"*

"Certainly not."

Breath whooshed from my lungs. She'd not only spoken true, she'd sounded outraged. Her next words proved it.

"Why would ye think such a thing?" Her spinning gaze roved from me to Rowan to the other dragons.

"Loki told us, when we went to Jotulheim to secure cooperation from the giants," Zelli said.

Dewi tilted her head back. Fire shot from her mouth and lit the night sky. *"Ye canna believe a word from that one. Ever. What else did he have to say?"* She listened while Quade outlined the gist of the trickster's message. I've never understood his nickname. Trickster implies someone with a sense of humor. Nothing about any of Loki's antics are the least bit funny to anyone except him. He keeps on keeping on until he's inflicted maximum damage.

"Och. Now I ken why ye built a ward." More fire flew from Dewi's mouth. She appeared to appreciate the necessity of keeping clear of the trees. Perhaps her fireworks display would thin out the crowd of eavesdroppers, but I doubted it.

"How were ye able to defeat my casting?" Quade spoke up. *"My wards are strong."*

"Because I command Celtic power, but now I'm sorry I removed it. We must be free to talk, and there is no time to waste."

"You carry news from Valhalla?" Rowan asked.

"Aye."

Quade's ward had been subtle compared with the ton-of-bricks dragon magic that thumped around us. It took a moment before the pressure inside the dome balanced out and breathing became easier. I narrowed my eyes at the dragons. "No fire. No smoke, either."

"We willna be here long," Dewi said, as if that answered my request. "The other Celts are on their way back to Inverlochy Castle—"

"Nooooo," Rowan cried. "The witches—"

"They willna bother your precious witches," Dewi cut into Rowan's protest. "'Tis important they remain near enough to be available. The world where we settled is at least two hours' travel time."

"Will they explain to Patrick and the others why they're there?" Rowan pressed.

"Probably not," Dewi answered her. "We are not in the habit of explaining anything to mortals."

"Well then, I need to go to them so they're not frightened into leaving, and all the work that went into their garden will be for naught." Power flickered around Rowan as she set a travel spell in motion.

"Remain here!" Dewi thundered.

"But I can't." Rowan added magic to the enchantment flaring around her.

I gripped her arm. "At least stay long enough to hear what Dewi discovered." Rowan's mulish expression told me I hadn't gotten through. "You may not like this," I went on. "I'm not fond of it myself, but you are smack dab dead in the center of whatever happens next. The fugitive dragon is your father. You're who can cast a blood vector to locate him."

She tried to extricate herself from my grip, but I held fast. "I'll make time for the things I need to do," she muttered. At least she'd stopped feeding power into her spell.

"This willna take long," Dewi said. Without waiting for Rowan to reply, she plowed on. "Most of this is secondhand because I flew away from Valhalla shortly after the two of you left. As ye well know, I met you in Fire Mountain.

"Odin stomped about cursing, but then he strode from the room. As soon as he was gone, Loki picked his head up looking a whole lot less inebriated than he'd pretended. Arawn was convinced he hadn't been drunk at all."

Rowan's teleport spell guttered and died. "So he was spying?" she asked.

"'Twas Arawn's guess. Gwydion's too. They were readying themselves to leave, but Thor whistled a few times. Must have been a prearranged signal because servants bearing platters of food marched into the great hall. Thor rose and bowed to my kin, inviting them to break bread with him."

I frowned. "That's not like Thor at all. He has a prodigious appetite, and sharing anything edible isn't his way."

"Bran sensed something amiss," Dewi went on. "Out of us all, he commands the most delicate magic. While everyone was eating and drinking and chatting of this and that, he made a surreptitious round of those who remained in the room."

"What did he find?" Zelli asked.

"Thor is many things, but subtle isn't one of them. He was doing his damnedest to keep Loki from leaving. He doesn't trust him, and Odin's instructions were to keep an eye on Loki. 'Tis a far simpler proposition in Valhalla than following him around the Nine Worlds and hoping he doesn't notice."

"Sorry, but that's old news," I told the dragon. "They hate each other. Loki has always been jealous, and he's made Thor's life miserable with some of his nasty manipulations. Thor's lobbed a few missiles of his own, though."

"Loki left, anyway," Dewi went on. "As soon as he was gone, Thor called on Norse spirits to shield the hall and gathered us close. Us being Gwydion, Arawn, Bran,

Andraste, and Arianrhod. Poseidon and the four winds decided to leave. Thor had had quite a bit of ale by then, so his tale was somewhat disjointed, but according to him, Cadir has been crafting channels from the outer borderworlds to Midgard.

"'Tis where the monsters and evil creatures are coming from. Cadir promised them free range of Midgard."

"What outer borderworlds?" Rowan asked. "I've never heard of them."

I had; icy tentacles slithered around my spine. "I thought they were cordoned off."

"They were," Dewi snapped. Smoke oozed from around her jaws. "Cadir has been busy. He's chewed through three of the blockages, which is no doubt how he escaped from where we imprisoned him."

"Will someone tell me what the fuck they are?" Rowan's voice was shrill.

"In a word, they're the containment cells for all worlds," Dewi said. "When the universe was young, still forming, the gods foresaw the need for a place to corral evil. Some wicked creatures are too lethal to risk keeping on lands where decent souls tread."

"They assigned six very small borderworlds to house dangerous rejects"—I picked up the story—"and cordoned them off from the rest of everything with impregnable blockades."

"What I want to know is how Cadir subverted the work of the gods," Quade growled.

"How else?" Dewi ground her double rows of teeth together until the sound twisted my stomach. "He had help.

Loki added his magic. But even with all that, they needed a fragile spot, a way inside worlds that had been barred to them."

"The Breaking," Rowan snarled.

"Exactly," Dewi said. "This next is conjecture on Bran's part. I'm certain he's deep in the crystals he left at Inverlochy seeking confirmation. But he believes Cadir and Loki hatched up a scheme long before Cadir was banished."

"That blasted dragon," Zelli cried. "He was always too vain for his own good."

"Aye. A definite weak link in the chain," Quade agreed.

I was still arranging those same links and not liking what I came up with. "Bear with me a moment," I said. "You suspect that Loki tapped Cadir, knowing about the prophesied doom were a Celt and a dragon to mate. How'd Ceridwen get involved?"

"Another weak link." More teeth gnashing from Dewi before she went on. "Ceridwen flitted through the worlds. She loved flaunting her beauty—and her power. We believe Loki saw right through her and pushed Cadir into her path."

"Two corruptible entities," I muttered. "The doomsday prophecy would provide a smokescreen for what Loki had in mind for the future, so blame wouldn't fall on his head. He's a master of misdirection. When the dragons banished Cadir, you played right into his hands."

"Pah. Nice to know I was a convenient chip in Loki's board game." Rowan shook her head.

"Ye werena alone. He manipulated us too." Dewi spat the words.

"I actually believe what Ceridwen said that day in the

Celts' meeting hall about the Breaking spell getting away from her," I told Rowan. "If she was conned into casting it, she probably assumed her dragon lover—" Understanding rammed me like a tumbling meteorite.

"What?" Rowan leveled her golden eyes on me.

"This is simple. So uncomplicated, I'm amazed we didn't catch on before," I replied. "Cadir reached Ceridwen from his exile—probably with a generous assist from Loki—and told her if she cast XYZ spell, it would free him and he'd hurry back to her side. He loved her, Missed her. Yada, yada."

Dewi swatted me so hard with a foreleg I stumbled and almost fell over. "That's it," she crowed.

"Sounded true enough to me," Zelli muttered.

Rowan was nodding slowly. "It makes a hell of a lot more sense than Mother going to all the work of casting a spell to drive me back to her side. She never gave two fucks about me."

"We have to locate Cadir," Dewi said. "Immediately."

"What are we going to do with him?" I asked. If an outer borderworld didn't do the trick, nothing would.

"Two choices," Quade spoke slowly, almost as if he was waiting for one of the other dragons to tell him to shut up. No one did, so he went on. "We drag him before the dragon gods and let them pass judgement."

"Or we hold him down and cut out his heart," Zelli said. "He can grow another, but not if we cast the first into the throat of Fire Mountain soon enough."

Shock raced through me. I'd had no idea it was possible

to kill a dragon. Zelli had just revealed what was surely a deeply guarded secret.

"I vote for Plan B," I said. It seemed like a surer bet than a bunch of dragon gods who'd never met Cadir and who might take pity on him. Bastards like that were always really sorry. Willing to promise anything—after they'd been caught and cornered.

"Agreed," Dewi said in a crisp tone that betrayed nothing. "Once he's out of the way, we can look to repairing the pathways he's crafted."

"Not trying to be a naysayer," Rowan spoke up, "but what if I can't find him? Blood vector spells are usually foolproof, but nothing about any of this is normal." She narrowed her eyes. "This cave or cell or wherever Mother's located, clearly isn't shielded from outside communication."

"It should be now," Dewi told her.

"Yeah, but if it isn't, how do we know she's not still talking with the dragon who sired me behind the scenes? Could be really bad if she overhears something."

"We have to assume Loki's claws are sunk into this two-meters deep," Quade said.

"Any chance of returning Ceridwen to the Celts?" Zelli asked.

Dewi shrugged amid clattering as scales rubbed against each other. "We could take her back, but what would it accomplish?"

"What about the Ninth Circle of Hell?" Rowan asked. "Ours, not the one associated with the Nine Worlds. It's supposed to have a gatekeeper."

"Might work," Dewi said. "Meanwhile, the only dragons

who know anything about our suspicions are standing right here, so Ceridwen meddling isn't an immediate problem."

"Cadir is," I said. "Let's go hunting." I headed for my blade collection, but the ward stood between me and the pile of enchanted steel.

"It will take me a bit to cast a seeking spell," Rowan said. "I'm going to dash inside and put these clean clothes on, and then I need to teleport to Earth."

"I'll check on the witches at Inverlochy," I told her. "They know me. It's almost as good as you going." I didn't remind her she'd just been there. The unexpected turn of events with Loki acting as ringmaster made me nervous too.

After a pause where I was certain she'd object, Rowan nodded. "I'll get the blood vectors cooking. They won't be absolute because we'll be leaving the Nine Worlds, but I'll bring them along so we can do course corrections."

I gave her a quick hug. "Thanks for trusting me."

"That's only part of it." She hugged me back and let go. "I have this need to control everything in my wheelhouse. It tends to get the better of me."

The ward split around us and dispersed into red streamers. "We will assist with Rowan's spell," Dewi told the other dragons.

I could tell from the look on her face that Rowan wasn't thrilled by the prospect. I understood. Too many cooks could push a delicate undertaking off course.

After crossing the courtyard, I squatted next to the blades and did a quick recall of which to employ for each variety of enemy. I wasn't expecting trouble in Midgard, but it paid to be prepared. I was in a hurry and couldn't risk a protracted battle like others I'd fought there.

I snatched up one of the broadswords and two shorter blades. Once I'd stood, I attached them to my body with sheaths and a sword belt. Power jumped to my command as I teleported to Midgard. I might not have appreciated the way the circumstances of my birth were revealed, but I sure as hell valued the boost to my magic.

I thought we had the rough progression of events figured out with Cadir and Loki, but what if we were wrong? We'd made a lot of assumptions that painted Ceridwen as vain, stupid, and selfish. I was on board with the vain and selfish parts, but I had a hard time believing she was that dumb. So long as I was going to Inverlochy, I'd see if Bran had any luck with his crystals or whatever he used to bring both the past and the future into focus.

Assuming I could get him to talk with me. He'd barely have noticed the master sorcerer of the Nine Worlds, but I wasn't that man any longer. Bran wouldn't respect my Norse half, but my connection to Nidhogg might buy me an audience.

I could be very persuasive when the need arose.

After all my big talk, magic kept bouncing back in my face. I'd hung Bjorn's shirt in the same spot where I'd gotten it and changed into my own clothes, all the while rehearsing just how to launch my incantation. The dragons were deep in conversation when I returned to the courtyard. Power shimmered around them, concealing their mind speech.

I tugged my dirk from its thigh sheath and sliced a gash in the base of my thumb urging globs of blood to form a line in front of me. When I thought I had enough, I healed my cut and focused on my little row of soldiers. The dragons had said they'd help, but they were ignoring me, which was fine. I work best alone—unless Bjorn and I link up.

I cleared my mind of everything but my blood. I even gripped the amulet to concentrate my magic. In the interest of not mucking things up, I started small and infused a bit of air into the crimson droplets while asking for general information. How far away was Cadir? What direction? What would I need to get there?"

The blobs nearest me smoked; I cut the flow of magic to a trickle. If they caught fire, they'd burn up, and I'd have to start over. I chanted low, urging them to show me where Father was. Maybe not the whole thing. Not right away. But should I head east? West?

I visualized a flame to focus myself and encouraged the drops to slowly circle it. The few other times I'd done this, they'd formed a neat little arrow and pointed right at my objective.

Not now.

What blasted into the blank slate of my mind was Mother. "There ye are. Och, Daughter. Ye've come to rescue me."

I slammed the gates down fast. Too fast. My precious blood drops ran amok. Some burst into flames. Others shot off in several directions. By the time I called them back, I was breathing hard and I hadn't gotten them all. Blood is a lot of things. Powerful. A great tool. But it's also one that could be used against me if it fell into the wrong hands.

Zelli's consciousness crashed into mine. My focus evaporated. "Got them," she told me. A ball crafted from golden strands wove around the remaining blood and dropped into my hands.

I blinked stupidly as the ball folded in on itself and disappeared. "Thanks," I muttered and released my hold on the amulet.

All three dragons were ranged around me. They'd placed me in the center of a rough circle, and I was grateful for their support. "Unanticipated problem," I croaked.

"Ceridwen." Dewi said the name as if it were a curse.

"Not exactly her fault. For once." I was damned if I knew why I was defending Mother. "Blood is blood, and I carry hers too."

"We wondered how that would go," Zelli said.

"Why didn't one of you say something?" I demanded.

"We dinna wish to create doubt," Quade replied. "Magic works best—"

"When the wielder has absolute faith in the results," I cut in. "Sorry. Wasn't meaning to be rude, but I'm not certain what to try next. I can attempt to refine the casting, but Ceridwen must be closer than the dragon. I fear the spell will find her first, no matter how many times I cast it."

"That isna good news," Dewi said.

"Aye, Fire Mountain is a long way from the Nine Worlds," Zelli said and crinkled her copper brows. "So far, I'm having a hard time imagining just where Cadir might be."

"Under our noses," a voice boomed from behind me. I jumped a meter and twisted midair to see Bjorn, Arawn, and Bran emerge from what had been empty ether. If there was a gateway, I hadn't felt it and couldn't see its edges. Bran looked like a brighter version of Gwydion. His hair was a sweep of burnished mahogany braided back from his high forehead. Hazel eyes sat on either side of a hawk-bridged nose. Stubble dotted his cheeks and chin. Unlike the other Celtic gods, he wore black woolen breeches topped by a pale green linen shirt embroidered richly with runes.

A golden signet ring adored his index finger. Tall as Arawn, he was broader. Not a neat trick since the god of the dead was downright lean. I bobbed my head at him and Arawn. I was too stubborn to tell them it was nice to see them again. It wasn't. Arawn hadn't been around much when I was a child. He had the dead to ride herd on. But Bran had been a permanent fixture in Inverlochy Castle with his crystal ball and his pool and the other accoutrements of his seer trade.

I stood tall and faced them down. "I just cast a blood vector spell, and the first candidate to show up was Mother. It's not possible that Fa—the dragon—is closer than she is." I couldn't bring myself to call the bastard dragon Father out loud in front of two men who'd treated me like shit.

Bran inclined his head. When he looked across at me, he said, "Apologies, Dragon Heir. Ye werena treated well at our hands within our halls."

My mouth gaped open. I shut it with a snap. When I searched for words, even something inane like, "thank you," I couldn't push anything past my clenched teeth.

"The reason ye couldna locate Cadir," Arawn cut in smoothly, "is because he is hidden among the dead in my halls. Before ye ask how such a thing could happen, ye must needs understand that our Hell isna a single location. It spans Midgard in nine layers with an infinite number of entrances. Over eons, I've done my best to organize it, but souls doona stay put."

He shrugged; his black robes riffled around him. "My charges have built more chambers, with others tacked on, until Hell is truly a patchwork quilt of hidey-holes. Mostly, souls doona pose any problems even if they wander. I segregate the troublemakers. The truly evil ones, I send beyond the Ninth Gate, but my gatekeeper up and quit the other day. Or mayhap, 'twas last year. He's not been there for a while now."

Arawn exhaled sharply. "Many who should have been contained escaped. I've been running them down, and—"

"Get to the point." Bran snapped his fingers.

Arawn slapped Bran's hand down. I rather liked them carping at each other instead of at me. Arawn cleared his throat. "In the absence of my gatekeeper, many left, but at least two residents moved in. Rowan's blood casting would have been worthless investigating the Ninth Level. 'Tis well-shielded on purpose to keep those beyond the gate from being bothersome."

"How do ye know Cadir is there?" Dewi cut into his rambling description. Maybe it was as annoying and long-winded to her as it was to me.

"How else? One of the other souls ratted on him. When I asked Bran, he looked in his pool and confirmed dragon essence within my realm. Apparently, Loki's been in and out of Hell too. I really need to work on securing more reliable assistants."

"Can you close the gate?" I asked. Seemed by far the simplest solution.

"Aye. Of course. 'Tis the keeping it closed that poses a problem. The latches may require repair. Absent a gatekeeper—"

"We've heard that part," Bran said. "And 'twasn't my

scrying pool, but a series of crystals. Reaching beyond the Ninth Gate is difficult, even for me."

"All right, then. We know where Cadir is," Bjorn said. "Let's get moving. We'll figure out how to spell the gates shut once we get there."

"Och, and he is certain to stay put, waiting meekly while we slam the gates." Quade puffed smoke. "If all of us converge in the lowest level of Hell, we'll create an energy path several meters wide."

"So. We erect wards." I took stock of our combined firepower. Pretty impressive with three dragons, two Celtic gods, Bjorn, and me.

"They doona work within my realm," Arawn said. "Can ye imagine if the dead could cloak themselves? I'd never find them again."

Damn but I was sick of Celts. "Fine. You come up with something," I told him.

"After Bjorn ran me down," Bran said, "and convinced me to hear him out, I spent a few additional moments snatching a quick-and-dirty peek into an array of possible futures."

Ha! He'd spent his fair share of time among mortals before the world broke. His occasional use of human jargon clinched it. Bran was a pretty man; the selection of bed partners amongst the Celts was somewhat limited. He'd like as not posed as a mortal to gain access to a string of willing women—or men.

"Rowan and Bjorn—and their dragons—appear to have the best chance of making it to the Ninth Circle undetected," Bran went on.

"I must accompany them," Arawn protested. "They canna dismantle the blockades between levels."

"The souls in your care don't seem to have any problems with them." My words were probably ill-advised, but I wanted to get moving and confront the father who'd been a willing pawn in Loki's scheming.

"We'll teleport right to the Ninth Gate," Bjorn spoke up before Arawn could react to my criticism. Thank Christ he was more diplomatic than I was.

"Will the Ninth Level truly contain him?" Dewi asked Arawn.

I wanted to know too, so I tossed a truth net over the god of the dead. His dark eyes blazed with annoyance, but he didn't tell me what an upstart bitch I was. That statement would have made it past my spell because it was true more often than not.

"I doona know," Arawn said. "If 'twere only the dragon, then aye, but Loki adds another variable. He shouldna be able to move in and out of my domain, yet he does." After a pause, he added, "Loki is Odin's problem."

"Nay," Zelli said. "He is all of ours. He belongs in Jotunheim, but returning him there will be impossible. I vote with Rowan. We need to get moving. If we wait until we have a perfect plan, we'll never leave."

"I am coming with you," Dewi said. "As the first dragon to draw breath on Fire Mountain, one of the dragon elders, and a Celtic deity, I command sufficient power to journey to Fire Mountain and drop Cadir's heart into the hottest volcano."

"I like it," Quade said. "Cadir will grow a new heart in

that time, but if we remove each one as it forms, we might win."

A rapid intake of breath from Arawn suggested the information about how to kill a dragon was news to him. And well it should be. If we hadn't been painted into a corner, the dragons never would have let that tidbit see the light of day.

"Why not trap him in a travel spell and move him to Fire Mountain?" Bran asked. "That way, ye can cut out his heart once and have done with things."

I offered the god of prophecy points for a cleaner path, but then an even better idea occurred to me. "I've got it," I piped up. "Dewi. You can tell Cadir the dragon council has rethought his banishment, and he must return for his sentence to be commuted. Or whatever term you guys use."

"It might work," Dewi said, "so long as I am convincing." She eyed me. "Ye do realize ye're part of 'you guys.'"

"Still getting used to that part," I mumbled.

"Brilliant." Bjorn slapped me across the shoulders. "A solution worthy of Loki." Power rose around him as he built a travel spell.

"Nay," Quade said firmly. "Ye will ride me. Rowan shall ride Zelli. We can mask your presence until we reach our destination."

"See you at the Ninth Gate," Dewi said. Heat intensified as she drew magic around her. "Take the bridge to Midgard," she said just before her bulk shimmered, first to red light and then to nothingness.

"We shall do the same," Zelli said. "It will shroud our presence until we're much closer to the halls of the dead."

Bjorn laughed. "Poor Bifrost. It may never be the same. I

don't believe it's ever hosted dragons within its channels." He vaulted to Quade's back, while I mounted Zelli. I'd perfected the amount of magic I needed to create an elevator made of air.

"Of course it has," Quade told him. "Ye've used it innumerable times."

"Aye, but the critical parts of my nature were muted."

"Bifrost is sentient and linked to Yggdrasil. Never underestimate either of them," Arawn spoke up. I'd nearly forgotten about him and Bran.

"Aye, perhaps it was so free allowing ye access because it sensed precisely what ye were," Bran said, adding, "We shall return to Inverlochy. If ye've need of assistance, we stand ready to aid your mission."

My mouth fell open for the second time since he'd shown up. I shut it and managed to say, "Thank you." It pays to be nice to your allies. I've had so few, I appreciate the ones who step up to the plate.

Zelli and Quade combined their magic this time. They seemed to know where we were headed, which was a good thing, since I didn't. Even as a child, I'd sensed at a deeply intuitive level that borrowing space to hide in Arawn's realm would be a mistake. I'd feared it would trap me somehow, and I'd never find a way out.

Bjorn's courtyard dissolved, replaced by the feel of the rainbow bridge. We'd subverted the need to access one of its gateways, but I wasn't complaining.

"Almost in Midgard," Bjorn said.

I watched the markers flashing by. We were moving faster than my last time within Bifrost's curved walls.

Perhaps the bridge was in a hurry to jettison us. "The witches were fine, right?"

"More than fine." Bjorn said. "The Celts are helping with their garden. Crops should be ready to harvest very soon."

I bit back a sarcastic rejoinder about guilt being a potent motivator. My kin in the Celtic pantheon could be kind, generous, and compassionate. Just because I'd rarely seen that side of them didn't mean it didn't exist.

Dewi was certainly putting herself on the line to help corral Cadir.

The dragons pushed their still-joined power ahead of us and half-flew, half-lumbered from the bridge. I looked around at a windswept, icy landscape that could have been Jotunheim, if it had trees. An unbroken vista of cliffs rose from the ice sheet we stood upon. Not so much as a bird broke the solitude.

"Where are we?" I asked Zelli.

"The far northern reaches of Midgard. Nothing lives here anymore. Not since the Breaking, but 'tis the simplest access to Hell."

"And we hope the least noticeable," Quade added. "From now until we come out at the Ninth Gate, no talking. Not even mind speech."

I felt Zelli's power settle around me and welcomed the solid feel of her skill. She was warding me, hiding me from discovery for as long as she could. No one had ever taken care of me until I took up with the witches, and it was still an unusual-enough occurrence I treasured it.

Despite my "let's get this show on the road" speech

earlier, I didn't feel ready to come face to face with my father. I rebuked myself for being a fool. At most, the dragon had been a sperm donor. Fathers were the dudes who hung around and made sure you felt safe and loved and—

Awk. I had to get a grip. Geez. Next I was going to start crying because he didn't show up to buy me a puppy for Christmas. I crammed the roiling emotional mess I was turning into down a shaft and buried everything at the bottom of my consciousness. To be on the safe side, I locked the whole shebang behind a magical shield.

If that didn't do the trick, nothing would.

The unremitting dark around us shaded to gray. Meant we were almost there. For some reason, I'd expected it to take longer, but we were covering metaphorical as opposed to physical distances. Enchanted realms were like that.

We burst through a flaming gateway. I considered applauding. The dragons were making a splashy entrance, in the spirit of welcoming Cadir back into the Fire Mountain fold.

Once the ring of fire subsided, I took in a moderate-sized cavern lined with unevenly-sized rocks. Water dripped down on every side, adding a dank aspect to the heat-laden air. The overall effect was rather like a sauna, but the wet variety. Two enormous wooden gates with hammered steel borders hung open a few meters away. From the looks of it, they'd been wrenched from their hinges and never repaired.

It was a sure bet everyone who'd wanted out was long gone.

Torches sat in sconces on both sides of the gates, casting eerie shadows on the walls. Dewi sat across from a black dragon, wings folded along her back. They were on our side of the gate, but it didn't matter. The gate-latching mechanism was clearly broken. Equally clearly, Arawn hadn't set foot here for a long time or he'd have done something besides pay lip service to the damage.

I didn't blame him. It was downright creepy in the Ninth Circle of Hell with the weight of the rest of the realms of the dead bearing down on me. Worse than the Grade B horror flicks I'd watched before the world broke.

"Here they are," Dewi chirped. "Your daughter has come as well. She's been worried ever since she discovered we sent you away."

Oh-oh. I'd suggested Dewi lie but hadn't expected to be drawn into the charade.

"Daughter?" Cadir's great head whipped this way and that. "Ye mean the one I never met because I was banished afore her birth?"

"Aye, she is with me," Zelli informed him, and the warding around me shredded.

I felt naked, but this wasn't an occasion for me to be my usual snarky self. I hopped down from Zelli and walked closer to Dewi and Cadir. Bowing my head, I said, "I am so grateful you're unharmed. Nice to make your acquaintance." After a brief pause, I stuffed, "Father," in as an afterthought.

Now that I was closer, I saw he was a bit smaller than Quade, and some of his scales held a brownish cast. His eyes were deep, dark pools, spinning slowly.

Cadir shuffled around Dewi and moved nearer to me. It took all my self-discipline not to back up. Artifice has never come easy, but I smiled and met his gaze as I felt him probe me with magic.

His touch felt wrong, slimy, but I kept right on smiling. Apparently, the dragons had decided Bjorn should remain hidden.

"Daughter. I like the sound of that. Once I've been returned to my rightful place among my kinsmen"—he stopped and cast baleful looks at the other three dragons —"ye'll move in with me. I shall require a maid to attend to my home."

"Perhaps," I said. "I have a mate back on Midgard."

"Och. Such a shame. Well, I'd allow him to visit."

I rode herd on the anger ratcheting through me. Things were going well, but they could slew sideways in the space between two breaths. "We can talk with him about it." I was still smiling; my face felt stiff and stretched and unnatural.

"Shall we go?" Dewi's words were an invitation, but I read the subtle weaving of compulsion beneath them.

Using the lightest touch imaginable, I slotted a slender thread of magic outward, intent on assessing Cadir's mindset. At first I thought I'd been caught when my power reared back and slapped me, but the blast of unexpected magic was Loki.

The trickster danced through a gash in the ether. His multi-hued hair was mostly red but held bits of black and silver and green. Tall and large-boned as befitted his giant heritage, he was clean-shaven with eyes the shade of curdled cream. When I'd seen him before, he'd had a blue cape tossed over his shoulders. The cape was still there. Tight leather pants sat beneath it, and his chest was bare.

Loki clambered onto Cadir's back. "They're lying to you, Dragon-boy. Take me away from here."

Dewi, Quade, and Zelli bugled outrage. They might be planning to kill Cadir, but it didn't mean they'd sit by while anyone else turned him into a glorified hobbyhorse to order about at their pleasure.

"Get off him," Dewi ordered.

"Celtic whore," Loki bellowed. "What will ye do to me if I don't?"

Instead of answering, she shot a stream of fire-laced ash at Loki. His hair smoldered and would have gone up like a field of dry grass, if he hadn't quenched the flames with magic.

"Might work with fire from one of us," Dewi said, "but three dragons stand ready to defend our fellow."

Something shifted within Cadir. I saw it in his eyes. Where before they'd been crafty and appraising, pride shone from their depths. Magic flickered the length of his back, and he shouted, "Get off me. I dinna invite your presence."

Loki tried to make it appear he dismounted of his own volition, but it was nip and tuck whether he'd fall on his ass on the rocky floor. When he came to a stop, he placed his legs shoulder-width apart and stared at the three dragons. And me.

"Ye're his spawn."

I cocked my head to one side. "Your point?"

"They've suckered you," he addressed Cadir. "Pulled out all the inducements. Sweetened the pie. Do ye actually believe ye'll be welcomed back in Fire Mountain after ye broke Midgard?"

"'Twasn't me but Ceridwen," Cadir spoke stiffly.

Loki rolled his eyes and capered about like a court jester. "Technicalities, Dragon. Technicalities. I floated the idea. Ye liked it. Ye rattled the Celtic bitch's cage..." He turned his hands up and offered a simpleton's grin. "We changed history, Brother."

"And now we shall change it once again and bring him home," Dewi growled.

Cadir glanced from her to Loki. Power flowed from the trickster, thick and cloying as honey. Dewi merely looked at Cadir but didn't employ any spells.

Wise of her, and I believe it made the difference. Loki was trying too hard, but Dewi fell back on the dragon-kinship bond. Smoke puffed from Cadir. "I am ready to return to Fire Mountain," he announced, but then his gaze fell on me. "As is befitting, my heir and daughter shall ride on my back for the trip."

It was the absolute last thing I wanted to do, but neither did I want to throw a wrench in a plan that had gone off swimmingly.

So far.

"As a Dragon Heir, I am bonded to Zelli," I told him, "but I'm certain she won't mind." If things got dicey, I could always teleport the fuck off his back and figure things out later.

"This has turned way too 'Old Home Week' for my taste," Loki announced and disappeared in a cloud of glittering mist.

We hadn't seen the last of him. I was certain of it.

Cadir moved closer to Zelli and inclined his head. "I

would have your blessings on our trip back to Fire Mountain."

She nodded his way. "Ye do, Cadir. Take care with my bonded one."

To my utter shock, his dark eyes sheened with tears that clattered to the dirt as precious gems. "Runa is my daughter. Ceridwen robbed her of her proper dragon name. Do ye know how many days, nights, years, I've dreamt of meeting her?"

I'd been nervous about trusting my well-being to him before, but my apprehension shot through the roof. In his own way, Cadir was as much of a monster as Loki. And of course, he would know my true name.

Dewi puffed steam, creating a pathway for me to mount Cadir. "I shall manage our journey spell," she said.

"Just as well," Cadir told her. "My magic is weak from long disuse."

That bastard! He was lying. He'd broken free of the outer borderworlds, supposedly an impossible task. Dewi's power wrapped around us. I held my mind quiet and built wards around it as the bleakness of the Ninth Gate exploded. It was replaced by the glowing aspect of the dragons' special traveling tunnels that led to Fire Mountain.

At least we'd made it this far. The journey was long; much could go wrong. I floundered as I searched for something to talk about to deflect Cadir from whatever he might be plotting. Requesting the story of how he and Mother had gotten together was the wrong approach. So was asking how things had gone since he'd been banished.

I reflexively felt for Dewi's magic. It wasn't there. Panic

narrowed my throat, and my heartbeat soared. "Where's Dewi?"

"Who knows? She must have left. We doona need her. I can teach you everything ye need to know about being a dragon." He sounded smug, but how in the fuck had he wrenched us from Dewi's casting?

"I'm certain that would be lovely." My mind raced. What should I do next? Play dumb or make a run for it?

"Excellent. Our lessons shall begin now."

The enclosure burst, leaving me in the airless void between worlds. Cadir made a grab for me, but he was clumsy in the absence of air to buoy his bulk. All he got was a hank of my hair. Before he had a chance to try again, I kindled power of my own and launched a travel spell. It wasn't elegant, but it was fast and strong. Once I had it well in hand, I built the strongest ward I could.

If it worked, it would spit me out in Inverlochy Castle. The Celts had promised aid. They were bound by their word. They hadn't lined out what their assistance would look like, but I didn't care as long as they herded my bastard of a father to Fire Mountain where Dewi would cut out his heart.

In many ways, this development was a relief. I'd actually begun to feel sorry for him. "Fuck me once," I muttered despite the lack of air, "shame on you. Fuck me twice, and you're dead."

The amulet pulsed. I held onto it—breathed through it— as I hurtled through the dark abyss between worlds.

CHAPTER NINETEEN, BJORN

I was flabbergasted and furious when Cadir made a bid to take Rowan with him. I couldn't believe it when Dewi and Zelli agreed. I fought against the spell Quade had wrapped me in until he hissed, *"Stop. Ye must remain hidden."* It was in the midst of Loki's antics, so no one heard. I wanted to scream at Quade. Why was it important Loki didn't know about me? I wasn't some kind of top-secret weapon. I struggled some more. In a pitched battle against Quade, I might prevail, but there'd be blood on both sides of the tracks.

The minute the dragons' travel portal closed around us, I was done being quiet. "We just made a big mistake," I told Quade. "I'm going after Rowan."

"Have faith in her," he told me. "And settle down. None of this will take long."

"But it's the better part of an hour to Fire Mountain."

"Aye, but Cadir will show his hand long afore that."

"Show. His. Hand. How?" I growled. "He has Rowan, goddammit to fuck. She's my mate."

"She's also competent. Ye're acting like she hasn't been taking care of herself since she was a child."

"Aye, but—"

The channel or tunnel or whatever surrounded us blew outward amid a deafening roar that I felt all the way to the soles of my feet. Quade still held me within his magic, but it was fading fast. *"Ha! Faster than I expected,"* Quade shouted into my mind. *"Head for Midgard."*

"Not Fire Mountain?"

But the dragon didn't answer. We weren't connected any longer. I was turning head over heels, plummeting through the void between worlds. We'd just left Midgard, so returning to it would be quick. I lined up enough magic to get me headed in that direction and hung on. Breathing is high on my list, and it wasn't possible where I was.

I screamed for Rowan. Extending my mind voice as far as I could. No response. Why hadn't I taken the time to learn about the dragons' travel pathways? Had the whole shebang blown up? I'd bet my last farthing Cadir had engineered the destruction. But how? Dewi was supposed to be in charge of shepherding them to Fire Mountain.

I hadn't believed the dragon for a moment when he'd whined about his power being weak. He hadn't felt weak, and it had been simple enough for him to shuck Loki from his back.

That gave me serious pause. Loki was more powerful than Odin in some ways. I had a tough time believing Cadir could have unseated him without his cooperation? Had the whole thing been one of Loki's elaborate manipulations where we'd been conned into playing our parts?

My lungs were on fire. My head pounded, but I poured as much magic into my spell as I could while still hunting for Rowan. Telepathy might not reach her, but if she was anywhere nearby I should be able to sense her.

Unless she'd warded herself.

I didn't believe Cadir could snare her, but if he was in cahoots with Loki, the two of them could probably make her life miserable. My mind devolved into feverish images that blasted me one after another. They had a common theme: revenge. I'd get back at Cadir and Loki. It might take years, but I'd do it. A pale-gray line showed around the edges of my casting. Midgard was near. Unless I'd screwed up and landed elsewhere.

Not likely.

The next time my starved lungs sucked reflexively, they were rewarded with thin air. It would only get better. *"Rowan!"* I tried again.

"I'm all right." After a pause, I thought I heard, *"Inverlochy."* Made sense she'd head for where she knew she had friends.

Relief socked me in the guts so hard, I doubled over. Bad idea because I'd just crossed Midgard's boundary and was dropping like a stone. Feeling like the greenest sorcerer ever, I made enough corrections to slow my descent and to determine I'd come out in the wasteland that had once been Northern Ireland. A ruined city rose around me, but all that remained were rubble piles. Belfast was my first guess. It had plenty of bombed-out buildings even before the Breaking.

I hadn't taken care to ward myself, and high-pitched shrieks told me my clumsy entrance hadn't gone unnoticed.

"Doona worry," I shouted in Gaelic. "Not staying long."

The boom of an old-fashioned muzzle loader hurried me along. Thank the gods those antiques were nearly impossible to hit anything with. My so-far-unused hardware still hung from various belts. I crafted a ward and a teleport spell, instructing the latter to spit me out somewhere near Inverlochy. I'd been aiming for the ruined castle this time and was embarrassed how far off the mark my magic had been.

Probably a by-product of the dragons' travel pathways blowing up.

Moments later, I tumbled out very near my goal, which had been a grove of willows on the River Lochy half a kilometer from the castle. Black wings blotted out the weak light of a fading day, and I redirected my power fast, fortifying my ward and drawing lethal enchantment to my bidding. A sword would be useless against a dragon, and—

Breath rattled from my lungs once the dragon dropped near enough for me to recognize Quade. Damn it. The beasts should come in more than half a dozen colors. He plopped down next to me and scooped me up with his forelegs, tossing me on his back.

"What took ye so long?" he rumbled. "I've been overflying this whole area hunting for you."

"Midgard is a big place, and I, uh, miscalculated." No reason to go into detail about it.

We were airborne before I was done talking. A staunch blast of magic moved us past the illusion the castle hid behind and into the Celts' council chambers on the top floor. Everyone was there. The Celts. The three dragons. And Rowan.

Not even trying for elegant, I vaulted from Quade's back and ran to her, bundling her into my arms. She held on tight.

"No time for that." Dewi's voice broke into my joy and relief. For just this one moment, the rest of the world could stand down, take a break, or go to hell. I didn't care which. Rowan was in my arms. It was all that mattered.

Claws closed over my shoulder hard enough to hurt. "We need your attention," Quade said in a tone I'd never heard from him. Not for the first time, I wondered about his history. About where he stood in the dragons' hierarchy.

Rowan wriggled out of my arms. A huge hunk of her hair was missing on one side of her head, leaving bloody scalp beneath. For once, the Celts were quiet.

"Where are the witches?" I asked Rowan.

"Downstairs. I only just got here too," she said.

"I reassured them all was well." Gwydion nodded my way. "The influx of strong magic so close was unnerving."

"Where'd Cadir go?" I gazed around the room.

"Not Fire Mountain," Dewi said acidly. "I made certain of that once he attempted to divert the travel pathways."

"You're who sabotaged them?" I stared at her. Today was turning into a collection of unexpected events.

"I did." The dragon's scales clanked when she shook her head. "I have no idea how he managed it, but he altered the endpoint. We were heading for a world I've only visited a handful of times. It sits on the boundary betwixt the outer borderworlds and the remainder of them."

"Loki must be behind this," I growled.

"I doona think so." Odin's harsh voice startled me. I hadn't seen him, because he didn't wish me to. Everyone in the room turned to stare. Apparently, I wasn't the only one he'd fooled. Underestimating his power is a mistake I often fall prey to.

He stomped forward. "I invited myself. Figured ye'd all be here. Thor followed Loki to your version of Hel," he said to Arawn. "Needs a wee bit of repair from the sound of things. Anyway, Thor dinna care overmuch for Loki's performance, but his admission he was the force behind the Breaking, was his undoing."

Odin's nostrils flared, and he drank from one of the horns around his neck. "His undoing for now. That one never remains where we put him for long."

"Where is he?" Gwydion asked.

"Jotunheim. The giants were furious enough to agree to stow him in their stone dungeons. Apparently, his last visit there he told them I was about to walk away from the Nine Worlds." Odin narrowed his eyes. "As if that would ever happen. I am bound to my kingdom, my realms. And they are bound to me through Yggdrasil and magic."

He shook a fist in front of him. "The giants willna be able to hold Loki forever, but we've assigned a dozen elves to periodically siphon his magic. If we can keep it low enough, the stones will mute the rest. For a while. Loki will find a way out. And then we shall return to dancing about one another like angry bears."

I wanted to clap; instead, I bowed to my liege. "Thank you. Even if it doesn't contain him, this was long overdue."

"What happened after ye left Hell?" Arawn asked.

I wanted to hear it told in order too.

Dewi lumbered forward and then turned until she faced the room. "When Cadir made a bid for Rowan to ride on his back, I figured he was planning something. If he meant to go to Fire Mountain, he wouldn't have cared how she got there, despite his show of tears."

"And his protests about how subpar his magic was," I hissed. "Anyone who could break his way past the outer borderworlds is far from weak."

Dewi puffed a cloud of steam toward Rowan and me. Ro might not be in my arms, but I'd threaded my fingers with hers. The steady beat of her presence was the most important thing in my life. It wasn't practical, but I vowed we would never be separated again.

"Aye," Dewi said. "That was my second clue."

"Would have been nice if someone had clued me in," Rowan said in a clear, ringing voice.

"How?" Zelli asked. "If we'd told you, even in deeply shielded mind speech, we ran the risk of Cadir picking up on our deception. He'd have snapped you up and been gone. At least the way things happened, ye were in the center of an entity we had control over."

Something Dewi had said earlier circled to the forefront of my mind. "You knew where Cadir was going, right?" Scales clinked and clanked as she nodded. I went on. "We have to follow him. It's near enough to the outer borderworlds, I bet he built himself a stronghold there. A place to retreat to and plan his next attack."

"The same occurred to me," Dewi said.

Andraste surged to her feet, blonde hair flowing around her. "A battle! We shall all go."

"Most of us," Arawn corrected her. "I have repairs to attend to."

She rounded on him, green eyes alight with enthusiasm. "Why? Everyone who dwelt beyond your Ninth Gate is long gone. Ye'll just have to round them up. Come play with us first. It will be like the olden times."

I thought Andraste was laying it on thick, but she swept her hands to the sides. "Celts and dragons used to fight side by side. I miss those days. Och, the blood and the shrieks as our enemies fell by the wayside only to be caught up in dragonfire."

"We're still going to cut out his heart, right?" Rowan looked at Dewi. "And feed it to Fire Mountain?"

"Aye, child." Dewi's jaws lolled into a grin. "My, ye've turned into quite the savage."

"A Celt to her bones," Andraste declared, followed by, "Fascinating. I had no idea dragons had a fatal defect."

"That secret shall remain within these walls," Dewi boomed.

"Aye. We will honor your confidence." Gwydion nodded briskly and addressed his next words to Andraste. "Of course, Rowan is a Celt. What else would she be?"

"Not how they felt about me when I was growing up," Rowan muttered in telepathy that probably everyone could hear.

"Can you still get to Fire Mountain?" I asked the dragons.

"Of course. The destruction to our travel paths was

temporary. And localized. I'm certain it's mostly repaired itself by now," Quade answered me.

Odin's head snapped up. Norse magic rose around him, thick with the scents of the sea and wet greenery. "Ye willna have to go far to locate the errant dragon." He jerked his chin toward a bank of windows. "Cadir stands just outside the illusion."

"For the love of the gods, why is he here?" Ash streamed from Dewi's open mouth.

"Because his need for his own kind superseded his need to be a bastard," Quade rumbled.

"Pah. He's been alone since we banished him," Zelli said. "Why should it suddenly bother him now?"

Dewi cocked her head to one side. "Even if 'twas a lie, we offered him Fire Mountain. 'Tis everything a dragon could want. And more."

"Yeah, but he threw it in our faces and tried to kidnap me," Rowan said.

"He wasn't thinking clearly," Quade said.

"Long association with Loki tends to addle the mind." Odin looked as if he'd bitten into something rotten.

Distant bugling reached my ears. I have no idea what got into me, but I slipped a broadsword from its sheath and brought it down on the marble floor amid a shower of sparks. "Has blood been spilled in these halls before?"

"Not in my memory," Rowan said.

"First time for everything." Adraste sounded positively cheerful. She drew her blade from its sheath riding across her back and gazed at it as if it were a holy relic.

Dewi shot fire skyward. "I will invite him inside." On the

heels of her words, Cadir's black-scaled form slithered through a portal. The dragon dropped heavily onto the floor at the far end of the large room.

He got his hind legs under him and looked around the chamber. "Excellent, I dinna lose track of you after all." His spinning eyes settled on Rowan. "Daughter. Come to me."

"I think not. Last time I did that, you fucked me pretty good. I'm not in the mood for a repeat. Or for losing more hair." She patted the raw place on her head.

"Watch your language, child." Cadir raised a foreleg, one talon extended.

I offered him points for sounding genuinely outraged. Somewhere along the line, he must have gone to acting school. Or maybe watching Loki had been enough.

"Watch yours," Rowan countered. "We may share blood, but I am scarcely your child."

"How can ye say that?" he went on. "I was bringing you home. A special place I made for Ceridwen and you. She knows about it. Ask her. Why, she..." He scanned the room. "Where is she? Where is my love? She belongs here with the rest of you."

Before anyone could come up with an answer, Cadir roared, "What have ye done with her?"

Fire shot from Quade, Zelli, and Dewi, blanketing Cadir in smoke and ash. The air in the vast room thickened with burning debris that made me cough.

"Not your affair." Dewi moved until she stood nose to nose with Cadir. "As First Born of Dragons and part of our council of Elders, I claim the right to accuse you of crimes against dragonkind."

"I have done nothing wrong."

"Ye will remain silent, or I shall cut out your tongue." Dewi leaned closer until Cadir took a step back.

"Ye bedded a Celt, an act that was expressly forbidden. Once your transgression was discovered, ye were banished for your sins. Ye broke free from your bonds and took up with Loki. Regardless of whose idea it was, ye were instrumental in breaking Midgard."

Dewi hesitated for long moments before she asked, "How do ye plead?"

"There were extenuating circumstances. That Celtic slut pursued me. She wouldna let me alone. Loki too. He—"

"How do ye plead?" Quade thundered.

From the corner of my eye, I saw Andraste circle around behind Cadir, her blade glistening with magic.

"Not guilty." Cadir tossed his head back. "'Tis my right to be heard and tried by a jury of my peers. In Fire Mountain."

"We offered you Fire Mountain. Ye threw it in our faces." Zelli sounded furious. Smoke puffed from her mouth and nostrils.

"So, ye will allow us to shackle you?" Dewi inquired archly. "Haul you to Fire Mountain in chains?"

"Nay. All dragons are innocent until the Elder Council has pronounced judgment."

"They already did," Dewi reminded him. "And excommunicated you."

Something shifted in the craziness spilling from Cadir. I braced myself for what might happen next. The Celts must have felt it too because they surged to their feet and formed a circle around the dragon, blades and magic at the ready.

Rowan yanked her hand from mine and marched until she stood next to Dewi, facing off against her father. "What? You're not satisfied? I can see wheels turning in that great, thick head of yours. You think perhaps you'll fight your way out of the heart of a Celtic stronghold with half a dozen Celts, Odin, and three dragons arrayed against you?"

"Ye'll fight by my side," he insinuated slyly.

"Like fuck I will. I don't blame you for bedding Ceridwen, but I do blame you for the Breaking. You left your mark, all right. Hundreds of millions of deaths."

I guess Odin couldn't resist joining in because he materialized on Dewi's other side with his battle axe, Jarnbjorn, drawn. He drew his lips back from his teeth and gritted out, "Meddling bastard."

Rowan rolled her shoulders back. "You've heard the charges against you and stated you are not guilty. We find that you are lying."

"Go ahead. Daughter." He spread his forelegs invitingly, almost as if Rowan was his lover. I wanted to punch his snout until blood ran from beneath the scales.

Rowan made a grab to link with my power. I threw myself wide open and ran lightly to her side. Whatever she had in mind, I was all in. Red bands of power shot from Dewi, but Rowan said, "Hold. He is mine. I claim kinship rights."

Cadir's cagey expression shaded to relief. "Ye've come to your senses, Daughter. I promise—"

"Shut up," Rowan screeched. "You deserve worse than what I can dish out, but I don't have the stomach for torture."

She gripped her amulet and extended an arm. White light shot from her extended fingers, forming a magical blade. I understood her intent, and it was both bold and brilliant. She was leveraging their shared blood to force his scales to cede to her power. Staring beneath his chin, she sliced neatly through his scales to gut level.

Entrails spilled into a gleaming pile.

Cadir seemed to have moved past shock. Fire shot from his mouth, and he ran it around the room in a broad swath. Damn lucky nothing flammable was in the chamber. Marble doesn't burn. Neither do crystals or rocks.

"Your turn," Rowan told Dewi and moved aside.

The First Born Dragon walked through Cadir's firestorm and cut out his heart. Crimson blood spewed from severed vessels, painting everything in their path a brilliant red. The coppery bite of salt and blood filled my nostrils. In a flurry of heat and magic, Dewi was gone.

If anyone could ferry Cadir's heart to Fire Mountain, it was her. She was ashamed any dragon could do what Cadir had, and wiping him out had turned into a personal vendetta.

Cadir bellowed outrage, but the blood was slowing. My eyes widened. I'd assumed he could grow another heart, but I'd had no idea it would happen this fast. The gash Rowan had opened down his midline was knitting shut.

"I donna think so," Odin cried. He cleaved Jarnbjorn along the same path, opening the wound a second time.

Andraste and Gwydion had their own ideas. The

goddess of war sliced her blade through whatever was nearest, cleaving off talons, a foreleg, and a wing. Everything Gwydion touched with his magic-imbued staff turned black with rot and sloughed off. Cadir bellowed and writhed. Fire and smoke blasted from his mouth. Crazy with pain, he wasn't even bothering to aim.

The fountain of blood had stopped. Losing body parts wasn't much more than an inconvenience for dragons, but if his heart grew back, Dewi's mission would fail. I didn't aim to start over. While I wanted Cadir deader than dead, I didn't relish brutalizing him, either. A clean death wasn't possible, but anything we could do to hasten his would be a plus. He was plenty strong enough to keep fire flowing. His aim sucked. I wasn't about to wait for it to improve. The floor was slick with gore and entrails. He'd probably regrown them too, but they weren't my objective.

I didn't consider which blade to use. Somehow I just knew and dropped the long blade in favor of one of my knives. With its slender, serrated blade, it was perfect for my requirements. I don't know when Rowan joined me, but she was by my side, slipping and sliding in her father's organs.

She repeated her earlier action and sliced through the closing gash over Cadir's heart. Damn, but that dragon's regenerative capabilities were far better than I'd expected. I surged forward and carved the new heart from his chest cavity. I had to borrow heavily from magic since he stood so much taller than me.

Gwydion snatched the still beating heart from my hands, tossed it into the slime heap beneath us and brought his staff down dead in the center. Like everything else the staff touched today, Cadir's heart turned to a shriveled black blob.

Blood shot from the opening in the dragon's rib cage. I blinked it out of my eyes. Fuck, but I hoped we wouldn't have to do this too many more times. Rowan dragged me back out of the way of gallons of blood sheeting from the wreck of her father. At least, he'd stopped spewing fire. I picked up my discarded long blade and sheathed it along with my knife.

The other Celts had piled on Cadir, carving away at various parts of his body and shouting encouragement back and forth in Gaelic. Odin excised an eye and ate it. Shades of the Wild Hunt.

"I hope someone cuts off his dick," Rowan said, but she sounded tired.

The air shimmered across the room. Red wings came into view. "It is done," Dewi announced and flew close to the dragon who'd turned into a dead man walking.

"Geez, that was fast," Rowan whispered in my ear.

I thought the same, but Dewi had been motivated. The longer she was gone, the more ways this whole undertaking could have slid off the rails.

"Get off him. All of you," Dewi shouted. When no one moved, she changed from words to lightning bolts.

"Killjoy," Andraste yelled back.

Dewi hissed at her.

The goddess of war hissed back.

Cadir was still on his feet, but the light had left his one remaining eye. Dewi began a chant. Zelli and Quade, who hadn't taken part in the carnage, picked up the refrain.

Flames, hot clean and bright, formed around Cadir, burning with a vengeance. I moved back from the blast furnace that had formed in our midst. Sweat coated my forehead and dripped into my eyes. The fire dissipated as quickly as it had formed, leaving an empty place where Rowan's father had stood. The blood and organs were gone as well.

Zelli and Quade joined Dewi next to where the flames had ignited, and they completed their incantation. "We sent him to his rest," Dewi said.

"May he make better choices when he is reborn from the bowels of Fire Mountain," Quade intoned.

"The fire will purify him, cleanse his mind of madness," Zelli murmured.

When I looked at Rowan, she was crying. Though her mouth was contorted with grief, she wasn't making a sound. Tears welled and fell as brilliant gems, reflecting light from the council chamber's many crystal surfaces.

I put my arms around her. "Where do you want to go?"

"Home," she snuffled.

"Aye, but which one?"

"Mine."

The Celts and Odin were glad-handing each other. Bottles of mead appeared from somewhere. Victory toasts rang out. The dragons stood off to one side, heads bowed. I felt certain what they'd done was unprecedented, and they were finding a way through it. The Elder Council would absolve them, but they had to clear a path to forgiving themselves.

They'd raised their talons against one of their own, an act

that was forbidden. Whoever had written their laws hadn't foreseen every eventuality, though. I felt certain that long ago scribe wouldn't hold today's events against Dewi, Quade, or Zelli.

No one was paying any attention to us, so I summoned magic and took Rowan and me to her chamber beneath Ben Nevis. Cadir might be dead, but his passing hadn't nullified the Breaking. The Nine Worlds still teetered on the brink of annihilation.

A deep weariness dug its hooks into me. We'd done what we had to, but I took no joy in it. Maybe my dragon half was mourning the loss of a fellow, no matter how corrupt he'd become.

I hung on until the walls of Rowan's room formed around us, and then fumbled with the buckles on my various sword belts. They made thumping noises as they hit the floor. Rowan crawled onto her bed, and I curved my body around hers. The last thing I remember before blackness hit me like Thor's hammer was Mort landing across our bodies and purring like there was no tomorrow.

I don't ever recall being quite this tapped out. Bjorn brought us home, but that's about all I remember for the next twelve hours or so. When I finally opened my eyes, he lay next to me, an arm curved protectively around my body. He was still asleep. Dark circles etched beneath his eyes, and new lines crossed his forehead.

Mort was draped across both of us, making certain we weren't going anywhere. It was the only quiet time I was likely to get, so I used it to think about Cadir. Hopefully, for the last time, although I didn't believe I'd be that lucky.

My father.

Why in the godless hell had I been upset enough to cry? It wasn't as if he'd meant anything to me, as if we'd even known one another. A few things he'd said had passed my "truth test," though. He had built a special nest for Mother and me. And he was besotted by Ceridwen. Not that it earned him points in my book, but that he was able to love anyone—no matter how ill-advised—spoke well for him.

"You're awake." Bjorn's voice sounded rusty, kind of like I felt.

"Barely." I snuggled deeper into his arms.

He smoothed a thumb over my cheekbone. "How are you doing?"

I shrugged. "Not sure. I don't get it. We did what we set out to do. I should be ecstatic. First step in the battle is over. We won. Instead, I wish we could have done something less permanent."

"No place to contain him," Bjorn reminded me, "but this cuts deeper than that."

I nodded. "It does. I was just doing my damnedest to come to terms with...everything. Not knowing who my father was held its own set of problems, but meeting him and seeing up close what a self-absorbed bastard he was..." I stopped to arrange my thoughts. "The whole experience was a million times worse than I imagined."

Bjorn kissed my forehead, giving me space to keep on talking if I wanted.

I laughed, but it came out shaky and shrill. "I suppose the proper term for what I'm feeling is mourning. I'm grieving for the family I never had, for the father who cared even less about me than Ceridwen did, if that's even possible."

"Nay. Ye're wrong." He switched to Old Norse. "Cadir was crazy. I suspect he always flirted with the edges of madness, but he adored your mother, and he wanted to love you. When ye told him off in the Celts' hall, ye hurt his feelings." Bjorn took a measured breath. "He was banished afore ye were born, or he'd have moved worlds to lay eyes on his daughter. He loved you enough to select a name for you. Dragons have verra few offspring. 'Tis doubly true since the dragon council decreed enough of them walked the various worlds."

My throat had thickened, and the tears from last night were back in force. "That's what makes it so awful," I sobbed. "I feel like I stuffed a puppy in a sack and drowned it. My head understands I didn't actually commit an act of unspeakable cruelty. And I also recognize he needed to die. There was no other way, but I hurt. Here." I twisted a hand to tap my breastbone, sweeping the gemstones from my tears out of the way.

"Ye're half dragon, darling. The dragon is mourning the loss of one of its tribe. I feel the same crushing sense of sorrow, but 'tisn't as harsh because Cadir dinna share blood with me.

"Ye were lost in your own pain last night, but the Celts and Odin were exchanging toasts and slapping one another on the back. They were thrilled. They'd engaged an enemy and emerged victorious."

"I noticed all that," I said. "The dragons weren't celebrating. They'd huddled off to one side. Zelli told me she'd find me soon, so I assumed they were leaving."

"My take as well. 'Tis one thing to fight alongside allies, but another when they're whooping and cheering over something that rips your heart out and drills holes in your soul."

Oblivious to everything but having me back, Mort

purred on. I took solace from his simple, feline presence. The rest of my room came into focus. Someone, probably Tansy, had left a teapot and a plate with biscuits on the far side of the room.

"We'll get past this," Bjorn said in English. "We must. Yesterday was necessary, but—"

I placed filthy fingers over his beautiful lips. "I get it. We have a long road ahead. Nothing is promised."

"Except us. We're promised." He kissed my fingers.

"Ick. I'm so dirty. You shouldn't be kissing me." I untangled myself to the accompaniment of an outraged yowl from the cat. In his little world, I should remain in my bed forever with him curled on top of me, protecting me from everything wicked in the world.

"Shall we find a spot to bathe?" Bjorn's mouth curved into an inviting smile.

Twisting, I set my feet on the chilly floor. Part of me voted with Mort and fully agreed remaining in bed was the best choice. I stood creakily and turned to face my narrow pallet. Bjorn's hair spread around him in a shining arc. Gems from my tears twinkled from the spots they'd fallen.

"Damn but you're gorgeous," I murmured.

"The feeling is mutual." He winked broadly and sprang from the bed in a fluid motion that upset the cat.

My body felt like it was a million years old; muscles ached that I didn't even remember having. "Aren't you sore?" I asked Bjorn.

He shrugged. "Used to it."

I rolled my eyes. "Don't be such a guy."

"Bath," he urged and wrapped me in his arms. The warmth of his body soothed and aroused me by turns.

"One of the lower levels has geothermal pools," I told him. "We could walk, or—"

"I vote for teleporting. Faster."

I smiled, my bleak mood from earlier dissipating as Bjorn's cock rose in a column and pressed into my belly. Reaching for my magic, I was pleasantly surprised to find it mostly intact. Either I hadn't run through as much as I thought escaping from my dragon father, or I'd slept enough to replenish my stores. Maybe a little of both.

It took very little to transport us from my room to the warm, steamy cavern that held two hot pools. Bulbs of soaproot lay on a small table along with a collection of motley towels. We had the place to ourselves. I had no idea what time it was, but usually a witch or two was taking advantage of the water to soothe aching joints.

I hated to let go of Bjorn, but it was necessary. Shucking my clothes, I left them in a messy pile with my jewelry on top. Beside me, he'd done the same. "Come on," I said and walked into the warmest of the pools, sighing as the mineral water closed over my legs, thighs, and finally shoulders.

"This feels so good." He sank to the sandy bottom and tilted his head back until all his hair was wet.

I grabbed one of the roots and broke it open, layering the thick, creamy goo on his hair. I scrubbed and rinsed and scrubbed some more until the water ran clear. The astringent scent of soaproot was piquant and pleasing.

"Submerged hot springs feed these pools, right?" Bjorn asked.

I nodded. "They're self-perpetuating. Fresh water seeps up through the sand beneath our feet. The witches built drains to keep each pool from overflowing."

Bjorn settled me across his lap until I straddled him. Reaching for another bulb, he washed my hair, moving down my body with his soapy hands. Both of us were splattered pretty good with Cadir's blood. When the last of the copper smell dissipated, it was a relief.

"I haven't seen soaproot in a long time," he said.

"It's all we have," I told him. "Supplies from all the wrecked stores ran out years ago. No one has the fat and lye to make soap."

"We do in Vanaheim, and elsewhere too. The elves make everything they require. So do the dwarves and giants. I have a feeling the Nine Worlds are about to get a whole lot closer. In years past, Odin never worried Midgard believed themselves an independent entity. I'm pretty sure those days are over."

I thought back to what Odin had said about being connected to all the worlds in his realm. "You may be right about that, but the mortals won't like it. At all. Magic has turned into their nemesis."

"I don't want to talk about Odin or the Celts or anything with future stenciled across it." Bjorn tightened his hold across my back and closed his lips over mine. Steam from the hot water rose around us, reminding me of an approving dragon.

I hugged Bjorn and ran my fingertips over the corded muscles in his back. My breasts pressed against his chest, and desire rocketed through me.

Hot. Sweet. Urgent.

I opened my mouth to his tongue and snaked a hand between our bodies until my fingers curved around his cock. He made a noise like a large jungle cat on the prowl. Part purr, part growl. All savage need. The uniquely male sound kicked the lid off my hunger for him, and I couldn't wait.

I didn't need anything fancy, but having him inside me, filling me, was the most important thing—the only thing—in my universe. He bit my lower lip and then strung biting kisses along the side of my face to my ear and lower to the hollow in my neck. Bending my head, I licked his nipple. I could only reach one of them, but the deep growling purr that aroused the fuck out of me grew more intense.

He gripped my hips and twisted me until I was facing the same direction as him, my back to his chest. I was beyond reason, beyond anything but longing for him that cut to my soul. When he lifted me, forearms against the underside of my thighs, I writhed with anticipation.

His cock seated at the entrance to my body and slid in bit by bit. I wanted him hard and fast, but I'd take fucking him any way I could. Magical bands formed beneath the water's surface. Glowing warmly, they wrapped around my thighs and held me suspended.

Once his hands were free, Bjorn reached around me. He closed one around a painfully erect nipple and plunged the other between my legs. I yelped with pleasure as sensation cascaded through me. The water both slowed things down and intensified my desire.

He took me from behind, driving into me first slow, then faster, then slow again while he rubbed my clit and bit the juncture where my neck and shoulder joined. I reached around and held onto his ass. The play of his muscles as he thrust into me was a whole other high.

Orgasm washed through me, leaving me so stimulated I leapt from crest to crest like a mountain goat pumped up on drugs. In the midst of one of the shallow troughs, Bjorn lifted me from his cock, got his arms under me, and carried me out of the water.

A flurry of magic arranged the towel pile into a rough bed. He laid me down tenderly and knelt between my bent knees. His cock jutted from a nest of spiky blond curls, hot, hard, beautiful. I wanted to take him into my mouth, finish him that way, but he had other ideas.

He raised my legs, placed them on his shoulders, and then slid home. It felt like he belonged inside my body. I never wanted him to leave. Such a beautiful man. Muscles bunched and released as he started fucking me again. His coppery skin had developed a rosy glow; his nipples were tight buds. Hair spilled around him, lending him an ethereal appearance.

He slid his hands beneath my ass, raising me as he thrust deeper, harder. His face contorted into a mask of passion, and I couldn't not have come if I'd tried. Swept into his need and his passion, I joined him in release. Semen jetted into me, and I rocked against him to intensify his pleasure.

Breathing hard, sucking air in great gulps, we clung to each other as our passion subsided. He was still rock-hard inside me, but time with him felt stolen. We'd sated ourselves for now. More stolen moments would find us. Or we'd find them.

"Thank you, darling Rowan," he murmured and tickled my ear with his tongue.

"Och, sure and 'tis I who should be thanking you," I slid into an Irish lilt.

He shook his head. "You'd have no way of knowing, but I stopped briefly in Belfast on my way back from the dragons' tunnel exploding."

"Why there?" I was curious.

"I miscalculated. Anyway, humans scattered like mice. One took a shot at me."

I smoothed errant locks of hair away from his face. "Yeah. Odin's let's-all-gather-at-the-river Kumbaya strategy will be a hard sell."

Bjorn's expression turned serious. "Many problems face us. That one isn't ours. If Odin wants to make nice with Midgard, he'll have to figure something out."

"He can send Loki to do his court-jester routine. Think of the advantages. Convivial. Persuasive. Just before he knifes you in the back and lets slip he was the instigator behind the Breaking." Bitterness lined my words.

"And Loki would agree in a heartbeat to anything that would move him out of Jotunheim, but it's not going to happen. He'll like as not escape, but when he does, he'll lay low."

"Sorry." I held Bjorn tighter. "I shouldn't have brought him up."

Bjorn shrugged. "He's part of what we have to deal with, and—" He angled his head to one side as if he were listening to something. And then I heard it too. Or I heard Zelli. Presumably, the voice in Bjorn's head was Quade.

"Be there soon," I told my bonded dragon.

"Playtime's over," Bjorn said, sounding wistful.

I kissed him a good one, tongue and all, before I wriggled out from under him. "We're lucky we had even this long," I said. After a quick dip back into the pool to rinse myself, I picked up the damp towels and hung them from hooks. That done, I gathered my discarded garments and readied a quick travel spell.

"Ready?" I asked Bjorn. He was on his feet and was cleaning himself with a damp towel.

"I am." He gathered his own clothes, tucked them beneath one arm, and laced his fingers with mine. "You've made me a very happy man."

I swallowed a smartass rejoinder about all men being happy after they've come. It was deflection on my part to distance myself from the scary emotions buffeting me. I was falling in love with him, and it terrified me.

"Ro?"

I opened my mouth, but nothing came out.

"It's all right. I understand," he said.

I leaned into him. "You're amazing. I don't deserve you."

"Nay, my love. We deserve each other. We deserve an island of peace and love and joy, a place to retreat to when the world is too hard to bear. You're that place for me, and I'm that place for you."

His words resonated at a bone-deep level as I transported us back to my chamber. Mort had left. Perhaps he anticipated I'd be leaving, and he didn't want to watch me go. Again.

I had clean clothes hanging from hooks, but they were running thin. "Hold up," I told Bjorn, who'd begun sorting his blood-spattered vest, shirt, and breeches.

"Why?"

"Not keen on the blood stench being part of whatever comes next. Let me drop your garments in the wash kettle and find you something clean." Before he could protest, I snagged his things from their heap on the floor and ran out of the room and down the hall. After leaving his garments in the perpetually bubbling wash cauldron, I culled through the stack of clean clothes until I located things I thought would fit him.

"Thank you." He took the items from me and slithered into them. The trousers were a bit short, but not too bad.

"We rotate clothes," I told him. "Makes what we have last longer."

"I always knew witches were smart."

He sat to put on his boots. I did the same. After grabbing biscuits from the plate near the door, we walked outside into the light of a fading day.

Quade, Zelli, and Dewi stood not far from the entrance to the caves beneath Ben Nevis. "We gave you as much time as we could," Dewi said.

"Aye, 'tis past time to leave," Zelli added.

"Where are we going?" Bjorn asked.

"Many places," Quade replied. "Our first stop is Valhalla. Odin has gathered representatives from eight of the Nine Worlds. Once we are done there, we shall go to Fire Mountain."

I cocked my head to one side. "You just came from there, didn't you?"

"We did." Dewi bobbed her head once.

"We sat before the council and relayed what occurred with Cadir," Zelli told us. "It would have been their right to banish us for breaking one of dragonkind's most sacred laws, but they showed clemency."

"I dinna sit with the council," Dewi informed us. "I remained with Zelli and Quade awaiting the will of the other council members."

My heart hurt for her. "You did the right thing," I said. "The only thing."

"Aye. My way of seeing it too, yet it cost me. I shall never be the same. Although it dinna take long, my trip to Fire Mountain holding Cadir's heart in my claws was the longest journey of my life. It has marked me. Scarred me." She squeezed her scaled lids shut as if sealing out an image she wanted behind her.

"The two of you"—Quade looked from me to Bjorn and back again—"how have ye fared?"

"It hasn't been easy," Bjorn said. "But we have each other."

My heart that had ached for Dewi cracked open. What he'd said was so simple, and so spot on, it knocked reality sideways. Having him by my side made all the difference, and I was a fool for not appreciating the power of our connection.

Zelli's whirling eyes zeroed in on me. Her jaws lolled in a smile, and she puffed steam our way. Clouds of it. Dragon steam made me feel all was right with the world. Bjorn draped an arm around my shoulders.

"Och, ye're right," Dewi said out of the blue.

I batted clouds of fluffy mist aside. "Who's right?" I asked.

"Ye have each other," Quade rumbled, "but eventually ye'll have another to love and care for."

Bjorn's face split into the most incredible smile. Even with that, long moments passed before understanding surfaced. Reeling from shock, I placed a splayed hand over my belly. "It's not possible," I sputtered.

"'Tis brand new." Zelli was still grinning.

"Aye, he wasna there last night. Dragon hatchlings have a way of making their presence known." Dewi bugled. The other dragons took up the refrain until the clearing was filled with steam and trumpets and joy.

Bjorn twisted me in his arms until I faced him. "How can we do this?" I asked as worry about battles and borderworlds filled me.

"We can, and we will. I love you, Rowan. And I love our child. I'll keep you both safe."

He sounded so fierce—and so determined—I pushed my doubts aside. Nowhere was safe and hadn't been for a long time. Nothing about that had changed.

"Hurry," Zelli urged. "Get on. We have to leave."

"Just like that? Business as usual?" I joked to cover my vast insecurities. How could I be a mother? I had no idea what to do.

"Aye. No worries about the bairn. Ye couldn't harm it if ye tried."

I vaulted to Zelli's back as something occurred to me. "This new development"—I stumbled over words—"was it also foretold. Kind of like Bjorn and I were?"

"Ask Odin," Dewi said. "We'll be there soon."

Magic and the beat of Zelli's wings closed around me. I shut my eyes and said a quick prayer to any gods who might be listening to give my son an easier path than the one I'd trod. Now I knew he was there, I felt the faint beat of new life within.

It thrilled and terrified me. I had a hell of a lot of work to do before he was born. The sooner I got cracking, the sooner I could give my child my undivided attention... It was a nice dream, but not much more. As Midgard shattered and bled, I'd be lucky to find time to give birth, let alone moments to raise my child.

I gulped air to steady myself and reminded myself I wasn't alone anymore. My child wouldn't be, either. We had Bjorn, and we'd figure things out as we went.

You've reached the end of *Dragon's Blood*. *Dragon's Heir*, last of the Dragon Heir books will be along soon. Read on for a sample from Chapter One. And yes, I know, what a place to stop. But I have no choice. The parts that come next are a whole other book.

Thanks for loving my stories enough to keep on reading them.

BOOK DESCRIPTION, DRAGON'S HEIR

Rowan hasn't made a dent in coming to terms with her black-to-his bones dragon father when she gets pregnant. The dragon-child isn't even here yet, but everyone's already fighting over his future.

The third (and last) book in a magic-laced, fast-paced, fantasy trilogy. With dragons.

I'm being pulled nine ways at once. Brand new mating. Brand new pregnancy. Stronger magic than I'm used to. The Nine Worlds are failing. Rot that began on Earth has spread to Vanaheim. Odin knows more than he's telling us, and no one has any interest in working together.

The only thing everyone has in common is a sudden, weird fascination with my baby. The dragons want him raised on Fire Mountain. The Celts want us in Inverlochy Castle with them. Hel hasn't weighed in, but I bet she'd like to see her grandson in Niflheim where she can dandle him on her knees every day.

If it weren't for the catastrophe looming over our heads, Bjorn and I would escape to a distant borderworld and never look back. It's always an option. Good to preserve as many of those as possible

Keep your fingers crossed for us. And our son. See you on the other side.

DRAGON'S HEIR, CHAPTER ONE, ROWAN

Odin's gallery in Valhalla was filled to overflowing with delegates from eight of the Nine Norse Worlds. Hel was there representing her realms of the dead and Niflheim. An outraged contingent of frost giants had also staked a claim to Niflheim as their domain. A predictable scuffle ensued that had shifted from curses to the ring of steel on steel. One of Hel's serpents was with her, and its forked tongue lashed in and out, spraying poison at the giants.

Odin crashed a fist down on the scarred wooden table that ran the length of the messy hall. The place had clearly seen better days, and it didn't appear anyone ever cleaned it.

"'Tis not why we are here," he thundered and skewered Hel and three frost giants with his single fog-colored eye. His dark hair was in its customary braids and spilled down his back in many small plaits tied off with colorful bits of leather.

I'd never seen frost giants before, but I understood why they'd been named. Icicles clung to their whiskers and dripped down their chests. They wore skins, carried clubs and flails in addition to swords, and looked rather like my idea of caveman warriors. Big ones, though. Humanity's predecessors had been tiny by Norse standards.

The remainder of the room's occupants were interesting as well. I'd never laid eyes on a living dwarf, either, but I had seen the occasional elf.

Hel bowed in Odin's direction. "I hear and obey, my liege." Her huge, black cobra-esque snake slithered to her side and wound around her ankles much like a cat would have.

"Better." Odin still sounded grumpy. "I'll bring the Hunt in to establish order if I have to."

"We doona want them here," an elf shouted. Raspberry hair fell to his feet, and his gossamer wings were decorated with glittery patterns.

"No one does," Hel told the elf, "which is precisely why Odin threatened us with their presence."

"Ye concede Niflheim to us?" one of the frost giants boomed.

"Nay, I doona." Hel's response was acid enough to curdle milk.

Both Odin's ravens took to the air, cawing as they circled the giants. "I said this topic is closed," Odin's voice was level and even—for once. "If ye canna comply, ye must leave. If ye do, ye will still be bound by today's decisions even though ye had no say in them."

Amid grumbling, the frost giants sheathed their weapons

and lumbered to the edges of the hall. It's ceiling was at least four meters tall and supported by rough-hewn beams.

Odin took a slug from one of the twin drinking horns draped around his neck. Thor sat to his left. Other Norse gods were arrayed around the table. No one had bothered with introductions after learning my name, probably because I was the only one there who didn't know everyone.

Zelli, the copper-scaled dragon I'm bonded to—my right as a Dragon Heir—stood behind me. Dewi, the blood-red Celtic dragon god, was next to her. I felt the occasional flare of magic between them, and was certain they were chatting up a storm about me and my unexpected turn of events.

I quashed a mental wince. Even within my thoughts, I was so conflicted I was having a hell of a hard time saying the word pregnant. I'd done what I usually do when I feel overwhelmed: push the whole mess aside with promises to think about it later.

Not that I didn't have some time. At least I figured I did. I'm part Celtic god and part dragon. Bjorn Nighthorse is sitting next to me. He's my mate. Delight and pride and determination have practically oozed from him since the dragons sensed a hatchling within me. Bjorn carries Norse and dragon blood. I have no flipping idea what this baby will be. I mean, it will look human—probably—but the little creature will be magic incarnate.

We'll probably have to ward the nursery to keep him contained.

I should be paying attention to the meeting, but Odin hadn't said much after censuring Hel and the frost giants. Ha! Of course, I wasn't focused. How could I be? I had so many questions. How long would I be pregnant? Would it be the normal nine months? Or some other variable? Dragons laid eggs. If I remembered right, it took them something like two years to hatch.

Sooooo, splitting the difference meant I had roughly sixteen months before the birth. Or maybe I only had nine. Or perhaps even less. Magical children have their own timetables. I chewed on my lower lip. Less was unacceptable. I had so much to do even eating and sleeping felt like luxuries.

Speaking of dragons, Quade is bonded to Bjorn. I neglected to mention him, but he's huge and black and part of the dragon gabfest unfolding behind me. Probably, they didn't see any reason to focus on Odin, either. So far, all he'd done was act as a referee. After a couple more transits of the hall, the ravens returned to his shoulders.

Huginn and Muninn, Thought and Memory, were beautiful birds. Twice as large as normal ravens, their black feathers glistened, and their dark eyes shone with sharp intelligence. If legends were true, they flew the length and breadth of the Nine Worlds acting as Odin's spies and feeding him knowledge as they gleaned it.

"Why is no one from Midgard here?" one of the Norse women asked. Golden hair swept back from her high forehead and cascaded to the floor around her chair. Her eyes were the color of polished amethyst.

Thor shot her an annoyed look, but she faced off against him and turned her hands palms up. "Midgard is the focal point of the current attack. It's turned into a wasteland. I assumed mortals would care about their fate, but apparently not." An eloquent shrug held a "let them eat cake" flavor.

It annoyed me enough, I spoke up. "Humans didn't believe in magic. Now they're scared shitless of it. Do you blame them? From where they sit—or cower in ruins, more accurately—magic broke their world. Nothing is left of their old way of life."

"Aye?" The unknown Norsewoman raised a golden brow.

An idea flashed through me. "I can secure a representative from Midgard. Probably two or three. They're not mortals, but witches. Would that be good enough?"

Breath whistled through the woman's teeth. "I suppose 'tis better than naught."

I stood, preparing to leave, when Bjorn jumped to his feet. "You're not going alone," he said.

I twisted to stare at him. "Don't be silly. I'll return before you know it."

He stared back. "How were you planning to transport the witches?"

It was a decent question. One I should have an answer for, except I didn't. While I can teleport, witches can't. "Uh, Bifrost?"

"Which is why you need me. The rainbow bridge barely tolerates your presence."

I bristled. Granted, my first encounter with the bridge hadn't been pretty, but it had been resolved courtesy of Zelli's intervention.

"No one leaves," Odin bellowed. "Not until we have crafted first steps to deal with the dark magic flowing unimpeded into Midgard. I've taken care of the witch problem. 'Tis well in hand."

The back of the meeting hall grew indistinct, fluid, and shiny with reds and golds. When they cleared, Nidhogg stepped through a portal. The Norse dragon is pure gold with silvery green whirling eyes. A smaller blue dragon named Ysien followed him into Odin's halls.

The gigantic room was beginning to feel crowded with five dragons and a bevy of Norse gods.

"I heard that last part," Nidhogg rumbled. "I agree with including a witch or two. Eyes on the ground and all that."

Speaking of eyes, I resisted rolling mine. It always slays me when ancient creatures who've been around since the dawn of time spout modern jargon.

I expected the portal to wink out. Instead, it glowed brighter. Patrick and Hilda tumbled through looking frightened out of their wits. I was already on my feet and I sprinted to them. "It's all right," I shouted to get through to them.

Both witches zeroed in on me. Patrick's harsh expression softened, and the taut set to Hilda's shoulders relaxed a bit. "You brought us here?" he asked.

"Nope. It was Nidhogg. I don't command that kind of power." Reaching out a hand, I hauled Hilda to her feet first, and then Patrick. He's short with thinning blond hair and blue eyes. Patched breeks came to knee level, and he wore a plaid woolen shirt. His feet were bare and dirty, which suggested he'd been working in the garden when Nidhogg's magic caught him up.

Hilda is even shorter than Patrick with steel-gray hair

that she keeps cut short. Her blue eyes hold a violet cast that's always reminded me of a field of lupine. A navy blue denim skirt covered her legs and she wore a sleeveless red sweatshirt. Like Patrick, her bare feet were covered with dirt.

"Crap." I shook my head. "The others will be frantic. They must have seen you disappear." The spell I'd started jumped to my call. I'd teleport to the ruins of Inverlochy Castle and reassure everyone.

"I'll take care of it," Ysien said and vanished.

Eyeing the spot he'd stood, I muttered. "Maybe not the best idea." Ysien was far from diplomatic, and I could see him scaring the witches worse than they already were.

"It will be fine." Nidhogg turned his swirling gaze my way. "I instructed him to be gentle."

Gentle and Ysien didn't belong in the same sentence, but I kept my mouth shut and rode herd on my need to control everything. It's always been one of my stumbling blocks.

"Why are we here?" Patrick asked.

"Ye have become the official representatives for Midgard." Odin sounded as friendly as a cornered wolf. "And now the Nine Worlds are complete within these halls, we can begin. And we shall."

"Official representatives to do what?" Hilda tipped her chin up.

I was proud of her. She had to be stunned by the sheer volume of power canting around the room.

"Why, speak with Midgard's inhabitants. What else?" the blonde goddess said. "Tell them they must help."

"We'll figure it out," I told Hilda and Patrick. Mostly, I wanted Odin to get on with things. In the grand scheme of how badly Midgard—Earth—was broken, I didn't see mortals as playing any role at all.

Ysien shimmered back into view and the silvery gateway swooshed shut behind him. I wanted to grill him, demand a blow-by-blow account of his time with the witches, but I'd never get it.

I was used to the way the Celtic gods did things. Most of them hated meetings of any kind, so when they all gathered, it was always short and sweet. Didn't take me long to figure out the Norse pantheon loved to hear themselves talk. The blonde goddess turned out to be Freya. I listened through a long-winded rendition from her of her last few scrying episodes.

Thor and the giants had been reminiscing about a hunting expedition for some mythical beast whose name I couldn't pronounce when Odin's shrill whistle brought their discussion to a halt. It must have signaled someone in the wings because platters of food materialized, carried in by dead warriors.

Many of them stayed and broke bread with us.

I admit I was hungry—feeding two and all that—but I was also frustrated. Not trusting telepathy not to be intercepted, I placed my mouth near Bjorn's ear and murmured, "How much longer."

A slight shrug told me he had no idea.

Patrick and Hilda sat at a small table off to one side, eating. So far, other than Odin's statement about all the worlds being represented, I couldn't see any reason to have disturbed their day.

Time passed. Quite a bit as the platters emptied.

"We have come to consensus," Odin bellowed.

My eyes widened. We had? I didn't recall any discussion at all—not about anything relevant.

"We will begin with the outer borderworlds and repair the damage to the barrier that keeps them separate from all other worlds."

Talk about a long game approach. I nudged Bjorn. He shook his head very slightly, which was a warning for me to shut up. Meh. I've never been good with warnings or instructions.

I shot to my feet, unsure if I should raise my hand, or wait for Odin to acknowledge me, or just start talking. He didn't so much as look my way as he rattled off assignments for a couple of groups to assess what needed shoring up. The away teams—for want of a better tag—were heavy on dwarves and elves.

I was done being quiet. "Excuse me," I began. "Before you deploy dwarves anywhere, the last batch of evil we battled on Midgard included dwarves. There were also dead sprites, a dead worm-like monster, and huge bats."

I may as well have announced Odin's mother fucked donkeys. Every scrap of chatter died away. Every eye skewered me.

"Not possible." A dwarf drew himself up to his full height, which wasn't much more than a meter. "Ye should be flogged for spreading lies." He was garbed in dark brown leather pants and a leather vest. His chest was bare beneath the vest. White hair fluffed around his head, and his eyes glittered like cut sapphires.

Bjorn stood next to me and bowed to the dwarf. "Well met, Gramoli."

"Master sorcerer." Gramoli bowed stiffly back.

Bjorn circled the table until he stood next to the dwarf. "Please," he invited, "cast a truth net."

"Ye've never given me reason to doubt you," Gramoli muttered.

"Then you will hear me when I say Rowan speaks true. I saw dead dwarves with my own eyes. At least four. They were part of the enemy who attacked witches living in the Celts' old stronghold beneath Ben Nevis."

"Has darkness invaded Svartalfheim?" Odin cried.

Gramoli turned to face Odin and bowed so low, his white beard touched the ground. When he straightened he said, "Not that we ken, my liege."

Bjorn inclined his head toward Odin. "As you well know, much of the surface of Svartalfheim is uninhabited, sire. The dwarves dwell in caves."

"I see the problem," Odin muttered. He extended an arm, index finger extended at Gramoli's chest. "When ye return, ye will cease mining for however long it takes to do a thorough search for wickedness that may have invaded your world."

"Aye, sire. And if we find aught that doesna belong, we shall kill it."

The ravens must have approved because they broke into a stream of cawing. Odin batted them off his shoulders, and they flew around the room.

"We are done for today," Odin announced.

"No. We are not." I projected my voice, to make certain I didn't miss anyone.

He pushed heavily to his feet. "Ye're more trouble than that slutty mother of yours. What is it this time?"

I rolled my shoulders back and stood tall, facing him. Odin didn't scare me. Maybe he should, but he didn't. Ever since I'd outfoxed his Wild Hunt, I'd grown cocky. "While I agree with shutting off the gates at the far end so no more evil can enter Earth, uh Midgard, it will take a long time. Months, if not years. Meanwhile, Midgard may well crumple under the strain. You overfly it with your Riders."

I stopped to take a breath. "You've seen how bad things are. How mortals have barricaded themselves into rubble piles. They're starving to death, just like the witches were before we found food in Inverlochy Castle and began growing crops to take up the slack."

Odin bared his teeth at me. "Next, ye'll be asking me to provide handouts, set up a welfare system for the poor mortals who were nearly the death of Midgard even afore the Breaking."

I winced. What he said was true. Humans were a bunch of shortsighted fuckers who'd been intent on draining Earth down to fumes if there was a buck to be made.

"That world is gone," I said. "Long gone. We have to deal with what's left."

"Deal with it, how?" He made hurry-up motions with one huge hand. Damn he was big.

"First off, we must create a permanent seal for the Breaking site. Bjorn and I worked out a stopgap—"

"It's gone by now," Bjorn cut in. "Never was meant to

last." He strode back around the table until he stood next to me again.

I nodded. "Once we have a permanent fix that will shutter the Breaking site, we can deal with whatever has already beaten its way through."

I was on a roll, and I kept going. I was afraid if I stopped, Odin might order me from his halls. "The way I see it," I went on, "is a three-pronged approach. Your outer borderworlds barricade plus plugging the Breaking site and doing a search and destroy for remaining evil."

Dusting my hands together, I smiled at him to forestall the predictable: him calling me an upstart bitch and ignoring everything I'd lined out. He narrowed his eye at me. One of the ravens circled back, chittering double speed.

Odin's expression shifted, developed an appraising aspect. Magic prickled as the smell of the sea thickened around me. Too late to ward myself. What the fuck was Odin about? I wasn't especially worried. If he'd wanted to hurt me, he'd had plenty of opportunity, but Bjorn apparently didn't share my sanguine assessment.

He raised a hand. Power shot from it forming a noose around the flow of Odin's magic. "Leave her be. She is mine."

I wanted to drop my head in my hands. "For the love of all that's holy," I shouted. "Both of you, stop. Odin's not going to hurt me, and I don't require a knight protector."

"Smart wench," Odin offered as close to a smile as he ever came. "Pregnant wench. May I offer my congratulations."

Nidhogg lumbered close, and I felt magic probe me

again. Different this time. Dragon magic. Buckets of steam followed until I was blanketed in mist. Realization socked me in the guts. I carried his grandson. Batting mist aside, I took a couple of steps back.

"Do not even think about ordering me to sequester myself in a tower—" I began.

The Norse dragon bugled laughter. "Wouldna dream of it. Young dragons can fight by the time they're a few months old."

I reflexively splayed a hand over my concave belly. "Not my son," I hissed. "He's going to have a normal childhood, goddammit." Protectiveness enveloped me like an out-of-control fire. I would fight for my child, offer him everything I'd been deprived of. Even if it meant raising him on a borderworld with only him, me, and Bjorn.

Nope. That wouldn't work. He needed other children to play with. There weren't any. Not on Fire Mountain, nor anywhere else, either. I battled a deeply sinking feeling. Why have a baby at all if his existence was marked by strife from his birth?

I felt more than saw Zelli move close with Dewi right behind her. Being surrounded by dragons is claustrophobic as hell. Bjorn and I stood at the bottom of an abyss surrounded by scales and coated in steam.

"His upbringing will be normal—for a young dragon," Nidhogg said.

His words did not make me feel better, but I've never been one to shy away from conflict. "I get it that he has dragon blood from both sides, but he also has Norse and Celtic genetics," I pointed out.

Nidhogg's jaws lolled into a dragon grin. "Aye, child. All the above. He will carry unimaginable power."

"We must raise him on Fire Mountain," Dewi said, "to ensure he has everything he requires."

"No." Bjorn's voice cut into the argument I was about to float. "This is our child. Mine and Rowan's, and we shall do what we believe best for him."

I raked my hands through my hair. Fingers snagged on my mostly undone braids. Weariness racked me. The baby was barely more than a collection of cells and we were already haggling over his future.

Meanwhile, Patrick and Hilda had fought their way past dragon legs and flanked me. Both witches hugged me. "I'm happy for you," Hilda whispered into my ear.

Hel slithered through a gap between Zelli and Dewi. Tears shone in her eyes as she hugged first Bjorn and then me. I made a feeble attempt at diplomacy. "Thank all of you for your kind wishes. They're overwhelming. I'm certain we'll, erm, figure things out."

"Best to have the fine points tacked down ahead of time," Nidhogg said. At least he'd quit blowing steam.

"Absolutely." Hel leaned into him, proud grandmother-to-be that she was.

I thanked my lucky stars—and the not-so-lucky ones too —my own mother wasn't in a position to weigh in. Ceridwen would have had ideas of her own, but I felt certain she'd have sided with Dewi, both being Celts and all.

I'd been near the end of my tether before Dragon-baby showed up. I had to find a way out of Odin's halls before I gave up and teleported away, and the lot of them added rude to my other list of failings.

"*Get on.*" Zelli's words were followed by a jolt of dragon magic that left me astride her.

I didn't ask where we were going. I didn't care. Away from Valhalla would do it. "*What about the witches?*"

"*Nidhogg said he would return them.*"

The walls of Odin's meeting chamber developed the liquid aspect I've come to associate with teleporting. When the mists around me cleared, we were in front of Bjorn's cottage. I'd have liked nothing better than to let myself in and immerse myself in his lore collection—or fall on my face and sleep for a week. But people were lined up outside his door. I got to twenty and quit counting.

Midgard facing annihilation hadn't been a good enough reason for Odin to relieve Bjorn of his master sorcerer duties. I jumped down from Zelli and pasted a smile on my face. "Bjorn will be here soon. Meanwhile, I'm happy to offer my assistance."

Maybe I have a trustworthy face, but voices blasted me with a variety of problems. I was knee-deep working with a woman whose healing spells had gone awry when Bjorn showed up astride Quade.

"Thanks." He gave me a quick kiss before jumping down from the dragon and settling in to work. Neither of us would get to do anything else until we'd made a dent in the throng surrounding his cottage.

ABOUT THE AUTHOR

Ann Gimpel is a USA Today bestselling author. A lifelong aficionado of the unusual, she began writing speculative fiction a few years ago. Since then her short fiction has appeared in many webzines and anthologies. Her longer books run the gamut from urban fantasy to paranormal romance. Once upon a time, she nurtured clients. Now she nurtures dark, gritty fantasy stories that push hard against reality. When she's not writing, she's in the backcountry getting down and dirty with her camera. She's published over 70 books to date, with several more planned for 2019 and beyond. A husband, grown children, grandchildren, and wolf hybrids round out her family.

Keep up with her at www.anngimpel.com or http://anngimpel.blogspot.com

If you enjoyed what you read, get in line for special offers and pre-release special reads. Newsletter Signup!

Witches Rule

Dragon Heir (Summer and fall, 2019)

Dragon's Call

Dragon's Blood

Dragon's Storm

Dragon Lore

Highland Secrets

To Love a Highland Dragon

Dragon Maid

Dragon's Dare

Dragon Fury

Earth Reclaimed

Earth's Requiem

Earth's Blood

Earth's Hope

Elemental Witch

Timespell

Time's Curse

Time's Hostage

GenTech Rebellion

Winning Glory

Honor Bound

Claiming Charity

Loving Hope

Keeping Faith

Ice Dragon

Feral Ice

Cursed Ice

Primal Ice

Rubicon International

Garen

Lars

Soul Dance

Tarnished Beginnings

Tarnished Legacy

Tarnished Prophecy

Tarnished Journey

Soul Storm

Dark Prophecy

Dark Pursuit

Dark Promise

Underground Heat

Roman's Gold

Wolf Born

Blood Bond

Wolf Clan Shifters

Alice's Alphas

Megan's Mates

Sophie's Shifters

Wylde Magick

Gemstone

Lion's Lair

Unbalanced

STANDALONE BOOKS

Branded, That Old Black Magic Romance (paranormal romance)

Edge of Night (short story collection, paranormal and horror)

Grit is a 4-Letter Word (nonfiction)

Heart's Flame (post-apocalyptic romance)

Icy Passage (science fiction romance)

Marked by Fortune (post-apocalyptic coming of age story)

Melis's Gambit (historical paranormal romance)

Midnight Magic (paranormal romance)

Red Dawn (post-apocalyptic paranormal romance)

Shadow Play (historical paranormal romance)

Shadows in Time (Highland time travel romance)

Since We Fell (contemporary romance)

Warin's War (paranormal romance)

www.ingramcontent.com/pod-product-compliance
Lightning Source LLC
Chambersburg PA
CBHW071117180726
48291CB00007B/2065